LOCHDARNOCK

LOCHDARNOCK

The Kiss and The Curse

RI ADAM

The Book Guild Ltd

First published in Great Britain in 2018 by
The Book Guild Ltd
9 Priory Business Park
Wistow Road, Kibworth
Leicestershire, LE8 0RX
Freephone: 0800 999 2982
www.bookguild.co.uk
Email: info@bookguild.co.uk
Twitter: @bookguild

Typeset in Adobe Garamond Pro

Printed and bound in Great Britain by CPI Group (UK) Ltd, Croydon, CR0 4YY

ISBN 978 1912362 219

British Library Cataloguing in Publication Data.
A catalogue record for this book is available from the British Library.

For my Mother

BRIDGEND LIB & INFO SERVICE	
3 8030 60194 177 9	
Askews & Holts	6000560
	£8.99
	AGA

Acknowlegements

I would like to acknowledge the patience and indulgence of my daughter (Cassie Robinson) and my friends during the writing of this 'thing'.

To Beverley Bradburn, Yaffa Clarke, Patsy Cleary, Bev Hearson, Simon Crump, Caroline Ferris, Maggie Pittard, Clare Tuckett, June Sinclair for always being there and to Colette Zacca who never let me give up – dancers are like that aren't they?

1

I suppose it's all going to come out now. Am I relieved? I can't say just yet – but I knew as soon as I saw *the* woman walking into the house – as soon as I found out what she was – that the secrets of Lochdarnock (my spiritual retreat and true home, you might say) were bound to spill into the open at last.

I love this place. God knows that's the truth. The sheer beauty of the estate at this time of the year is startling.

Its river, The White Cart, quick-running and full – winds around the grounds, through frost-covered fields and interestingly shaped 'winter naked' trees – which seem to stand in dogged, dark majesty against the pallid afternoon skies which are common enough in these parts. Remnants of ancient woodland sit now as a determined metaphor for the folk who made this place what it once was, and is still.

Modern man has introduced to the landscape Highland cattle which attempt to graze the winter-hardened land but easily give up, preferring to take the soft option of food provided in the metallic mangers which are periodically dotted about the fencing that encloses the beasts. The small, hardy herd is kept outside, year round, adding to the picture postcard 'Scottishness' of the scene.

The animals' presence is clearly a marketing ploy which

works judging by the number of folk who drive slowly through the grounds with their cameras (usually sophisticated phone contraptions) ready to capture images to be sent back from whence the snapper comes.

Given the immediacy of new technologies, the interlopers share precious vacation shots almost instantaneously with friends and kin, no matter how far afield their home might be, making Lochdarnock accessible world-wide – a fact that I am uncomfortable with given the jealous regard I have for the place.

The house itself is a show-off affair, rebuilt in the eighteenth century and added to in the nineteenth and early twentieth. This monument to good-taste replaces the original building (a castle) situated far too near the river for safety's sake in the twelfth century and the later fifteenth-century building, also a castle, which was similarly unsuitably located and seems, according to the sources, to have fallen foul of an unpredicted bursting riverbank.

Whether it's my love of the estate or of the folk of Lochdarnock that has caused me to be protective in the way I have been for so long, I can no longer say. I just didn't and *don't* want the wrong people 'in on it'.

I am aware that I've been selfish keeping it, 'this story', to myself all these years. I've squirrelled away the source material, the historical evidence, that long I don't know *how* to share it.

Contrary to what you might think, I'm not a devious man by nature, so I can't imagine how to go about 'leaking the story' using the modern convention deployed by 'D' list celebrities and ambitious politicians alike. Maybe it's best to let the story emerge bit by bit – to let *her* find out the history through diligent attention to the archive as I did, after all it's obviously Jenny Munroe's story and history more than mine. How that came to be is as yet a mystery to her and there are bits of the puzzle I'm yet to put in proper place myself.

It's certain Jenny's here to gather as much as possible in the way of knowledge about Lochdarnock, and I know with this latest 'find' she'll be hunting down the story I have kept, the secret I have buried as best I could, now that she's got a sniff of it.

Unlike me, I think, Miss Munroe is a girl with the quarry firmly in her sights. She's the determined type – you can just tell. Her newly achieved title of Lochdarnock Estates' Promotions Director is impressive but not the prestigious job my daughter Heather would say 'floats' a girl like Jenny's boat.

Even if she hadn't already been employed to showcase the place, the resemblance she has with the Lochdarnocks is so uncanny a body couldn't help but wonder, wonder and pursue the truth of the matter of her family heritage – she just must have a genetic link with that crowd somewhere, I am sure. Aye, I know a lot about the Lochdarnock/Cassidy (Jenny's family) connection but even I am not aware of the full story, it seems – not yet anyway.

The portrait clearly came as a shock to the girl – girl! Given that Jenny Munroe is fifty plus I know it's wrong to keep calling her that – apart from the politically correct stuff that drives me to distraction, there appears to be little that is childlike about the lovely Ms Munroe. But a girl is what she seems to me at this advanced stage in my life, nonetheless.

The poor thing did her best to hide it but I saw her shaking after the unveiling – standing there in front of Lady Isabelle Lochdarnock's portrait, standing there in front of a picture of what could have been herself, a picture that she had been brought here to unveil as the first act in her plum new job.

I feel bad about that. The thinking was that all images of Lady Isabelle had been destroyed by the laird's second wife – Fiona Ewart – I was the only one who knew differently, having found several photos of Isabelle which had been secreted away by a concerned party an age ago, in amongst the books in the extensive library at the house.

Yes, the portrait had been identified as being of Isabelle years before but it had at some stage in the early part of the twentieth century, of course, been positioned above a well-used coal fire at the gatehouse to the hunting lodge up at Braeside – another Lochdarnock property in the Highlands.

The portrait had been collecting dirt and soot up there that long, it was discovered, or to be accurate, rediscovered more recently in a sorry, unidentifiable state.

But I knew the truth of the matter. I knew the image that Jenny Munroe was about to face having persuaded the conservators to let me take a peek at the restored picture the week before Jenny arrived at the house. Unlike the busy trustees who had failed to show the necessary inquisitiveness (as I like to see it) I knew every detail of the image and I failed to warn Jenny – was I totally wrong to hold my tongue? Ach, how could a body find the words to let the girl know what she was about to face?

There are, as I say, bits of the story I've yet to work out myself. All I can do, I think, is make sure Jenny Munroe has a starting point. She's a clever woman, better qualified in research than me by a mile, with the confidence and the drive to piece together the story easily, her story, as it now turns out.

Of course, the girl had already expressed a special interest in the famous 'Curse of the Lochdarnocks'. The subject is mentioned pretty frequently in the sources, but I sometimes think these things get built up out of nothing. May be I am just another member of the great sophisticated and educated public who generally pooh-pooh these kind of 'medieval' notions. Are we all scared of being enthralled by this sort of notion these days I wonder? Aye, we'd hate to be thought of as primitives, I suppose.

I know *you'll* think the idea of a 'curse' is nonsense but the evidence is mounting in favour of the myth being true or at least having a basis in truth. So my cynical view, which you no doubt share, might just be wrong – yet.

When I talked to Jenny after the unnerving unveiling she told me that she was keen to get to know the origin of the 'old wives' tale' (I think she was trying to divert attention – mine and her own – from the surprise the portrait's unveiling had brought.) So for now – for both Jenny and me, 'the curse' has to remain a side issue while we find out just where and how Miss Munroe got to be in the picture – quite literally, it seems

It's odd, too, how these matters mount up, these connections, coincidence upon coincidence. The day after she left for the lodge at Braeside (the hunting lodge that once belonged to the Lochdarnock family and is now run as an hotel by the estate) the obligatory American visitor barged in and collared me after one of the Christmas concerts we hold here every year at the Glasgow House. The American, a man, fifty odd I'd say, an assertive and determined man, big bugger but pleasant enough, strode in confident and long legged with a smile which revealed pearly white American teeth and a cheerful nature. When he gave his name I recognised it – not instantly, you understand, as his namesake, like my own grandfather, was a bit part player in the drama of Lochdarnock, a tale I've been slowly unravelling for the best part of sixty years now. So it would appear all is not done yet – with the 'plot thickening' by the day here at Lochdarnock House and elsewhere.

As I say, a Gil Delaney does get a cursory mention in the texts along with my own grandfather, and now here is – large as life, larger, the Yank, Gil Delaney IV.

Funny how the Americans have numbers like royalty, an affectation or an attempt to place themselves in some sort of historical order, I wonder? Maybe we'll never know. Sufficient to say that if I were to use the same kind of numbering system it would make me William Johnson III. Sounds good, eh?

The Delaney man claims he's here to look into the Ewart family and that knowing there to be a connection with the Lochdarnocks, this place was an intrigue to him, or that's how he put it. I don't think the fella has a clue what he's up to. A bored engineer needing some adventure is how he comes across. No doubt he'll show what he's made of in time, but I like him in spite of my every attempt not to.

I think I'll 'leak' the bit *I* got first and see where that takes either Gil Delaney IV or Jenny Munroe – since both their families are in there – in *this* story.

Is it the old grammar school teacher in me that's keen to turn this quest into some kind of competition? My son (also a William) and his sister, Heather, nicknamed me years ago 'The Master of the Merit-o-crats'. I'm not so sure the epithet is apt and I've to admit the accusation was made with both humour and a certain degree of criticism – young folk, eh! But, here I am releasing two blood hounds, giving them the scent, and champing at the bit to know where this trail will take them and which of the two will make it to the finishing line first.

This competitive trait I have is not a part of my nature I'm all that fond of, but everybody has a fault or two – wouldn't you say? Och, it's very probable they'll end up in totally different places, with entirely different stories and definitely a different story than the one that's been fermenting in my poor old, old-fashioned mind this last six decades.

Is this process giving me power at last? Is that what's really going on here? My wife would say this game I'm inventing is merely amusement for me at my late – last – stage of life. Hetty can be a bit patronising at times but it suits me to let her think I'm merely a worn out old duffer. The character I've adopted allows me to get away with what she would describe as 'murder'.

It might be helpful if I explain my sin – a sin, the Catholics would term 'a sin of omission'.

It was 1958 – not long after I came to the house for just the second time in my life, having visited as a boy in the 1930s. I remember it was in March, that's right, March 1958, that I found loose sheaves of paper in a book I was dusting. It was quiet in the library here at Lochdarnock House and I read the musty smelling pages in silence as the other volunteers milled about making a better job of cleaning the extensive library of books that is here in the house than I ever could…

I was thrilled and excited by what I read and most especially by its relevance to my own family…

2

THE TALE OF US – PART 1

More than ten years ago – Christ, is it that long?

It started – we – started with a death, and a death in the shipyard was never a pretty affair. I was young and hot-headed and in no mood to put up with sneering bosses shrugging their shoulders and walking away as if nothing had happened. No, I wanted them to pay for the poor man's death, I wanted to stop any other man suffering the way Willy Johnson suffered, freezing cold at his end, lungs filled to bursting with a mixture of blood and filthy air on the cruel, callous Clyde. I just couldn't stop brooding on how Willy's mind must have been tortured by the idea of his family starving and struggling on without him.

The thought of all that suffering for nothing choked me. (As it was, Violet Johnson did go on Parish Relief and the weans, the poor weans, empty-bellied and penniless were left without a father for either provision or comfort.)

God, aye – I admit it – I was out for a fight. I wanted to put Ewart and all the other evil, complacent bastards in their place. Me, wee Danny Cassidy – Christ, what youthful ideals I had then – that I still have at heart even now.

I probably drew attention to myself when I was handing out pamphlets (material to enlighten the men in their ignorance – the written word signifying the authority of knowledge, knowledge of which we had all been desperately starved). I was shouting at the gates, urging the men to come to the union meeting that night. (You had to be careful who you gave the pamphlets to – a lot of the men could barely read – men – very smart men – had just never had the teaching, never got the chance back then and it's really no better now – not yet.)

Kenneth Ewart was behind the attack on me later that day. It must have been him. I know you've your doubts but his father, Douglas, was at the Kelvin Halls with your father (Lord Lochdarnock) that day, preparing for the opening of the Glasgow Exhibition, if you remember. Me, I'll never forget 3rd May 1911 for a lot of reasons.

Yes, Kenneth Ewart made sure that he knew everything I was saying, everywhere I was going and the names of all the men I was talking to. I felt bad about that. I was not the only one who paid the price for trying to get justice for Willy Johnson.

I remember big Mick Brennan asking me at the time if all the shouting and bawling would amount to anything and me confidently replying:

"I have hope, Michael, I have hope!"

"That's because you're young, Dan." His reply was given with beleaguered, sad resignation, I remember.

I asked him if he was too 'auld' to put up a fight. He called me a "cheeky wee bastard". All the men laughed. Probably because they were old enough and wise enough to know that Mick's scepticism was justified. But me, I was eighteen years old and sure of myself and besides, I was a Cassidy, how could anything bad ever happen to me? My mammy had told me often enough that God and the angels were on my side. Not that I believed in all that business even then but that kind of inherited unquestioned belief sticks with you, sticks to you regardless of your youthful, semi-educated swagger and superior brand of common sense. Contrary to everything you ever witness, everything you experience – somehow you know that a 'Good Catholic Boy' like you is protected by the Divine. Aye, it's powerful stuff – you just can't

9

help feeling the invincibility of sacred sanction bestowed upon you. Madness or fearless courage? Are the two not just the same?

I called for a strike.

The motion was voted down at the meeting, three to one. The men had no stomach for the fight. It took most of the poor sods all their time and energy just to get through every working day. I suppose they could not countenance starving their weans in the vain hope of getting a meagre pay rise, improvements in working conditions in the Yard, or a paltry, insulting pay out from the Ewarts for poor Violet Johnson.

My union pal, Gil Delaney, and me – we were sick to the stomach we'd not carried the motion. We tried to leave the pub where the meeting was held early, but Mick Brennan insisted we stayed to take a drink with the boys – we'd to show there were no hard feelings that we'd lost the vote, I suppose.

I always hated beer, even then, but I supped my pint and looked on as the majority of men descended into numbing drunkenness. May be that was the only way they could obliterate the image of Willy's blue and bloodied body as it lay pierced through – spiked – his face a picture of pain and surprise – a picture that lives on in my mind even now. It's odd I know but that vision overshadows what I witnessed in the War and God and you know that stuff was bad enough.

I remember most of that day, 3rd May 1911 – vividly.

My mother, father and our Pat went to mass at night to say a prayer for Willy Johnson. I asked my ma' and our Patrick what the point was. Christ, Willy was a Prod – bitter Orange some said. They had no reply.

I suppose you do what you've always done in those circumstances. After all the kneeling and praying and beating of the breast, Ma' and Da' and our Patrick took the Johnson's plates of food and sat with the Johnson weans while his widow, poor Violet Johnson, did her weeping. That's the kind of people I come from – and I'm proud of it and wish to God that I had the courage to tell them over and over how lucky I've been to be a part of them.

My evening was different to theirs – I showed devotion to my *cause by rallying the troops. I thought I'd been smart arranging for the meeting to be held well away from the yard. Surely, I'd reasoned, Ewart's lackeys wouldn't be bothered to travel very far to do their spying? That was my mistake – you should never underestimate how low a Ewart is prepared to stoop or how determined he or she is to win.*

It was dark when I started the long walk home. Gil Delaney, who lived in the Gorbals like me, left the pub early, escaping the misery of watching good men spend their hard earned money trying to reach oblivion the fastest way they could. So it was that I headed for Shamrock Street alone. It wasn't that late but I remember the night being dark. It had been raining and the streets were puddled. Clouds still shut out the possibility of moonlight as I entered the alleyway, so the punches came out of nowhere. There were three men or may be four of them.

The first blows knocked me to my knees. I felt a foot impact on my chest as I slumped forward. And then they really laid into me. I don't know how long the beating, the kicking, lasted but I do remember one of them saying, "That's from the Ewarts, you stupid looking bastard."

I must have passed out. By the time I came round the cloud had dispersed a little and I was able to see quite a lot more by the moonlight. I picked myself up and stumbled on, holding my chest, not conscious of what direction I was walking. I was cold and disorientated. It was a while before I realised that I was near Lochdarnock House. In my stupor I'd headed for it, I suppose. May be it seemed to me the only safe option available.

There was a street light at the gate. I stood – no I slumped down on my hunkers – under it wondering if I had the strength to get to my sister, Mary, who worked as a maid up at the big House. I remember struggling to my feet and leaning on the gate gasping for a breath after a couple of minutes. It was then that Bob MacKenzie found me.

As you always say, Bob is a good man. I think he was shocked at the sight of me because he asked me if I had any business at Lochdarnock House, very formally – in that kind o' Butler voice he sometimes puts on. I remember he was ashen-faced. He looked worse than I did, or so I thought at the time.

I told Bob that my sister, Mary, worked in the house and that I needed to see her. Bob sat me down, somewhere near the gate, and he flew off to fetch our Mary. I closed my eyes for what seemed only a moment but must have been more. It was then that I heard footsteps again. It couldn't be MacKenzie back so soon, I knew that much. I suppose I was afraid to look up. When I did, it was you. Thank God it was you.

From where I sat curled up on the ground by now, you looked so tall. Do you remember helping me to my feet to take me under the lamplight again so you could see me more clearly? From the moment you appeared I felt safe. I hugged my chest as I rose. The broken ribs hurt like hell. You pushed back my hair and looked directly into my face. It was through swollen eyes that I saw you properly for the first time. You were tender and, atheist that I was, I thanked God for you, James Lochdarnock – and I still do.

MacKenzie arrived with Mary a couple of minutes later. I think they were both surprised to see you there.

Our Mary kept saying, "Oh, Danny. What have they done to you? What have they done?"

You sent her back to the house with MacKenzie pretty sharpish. You knew she'd get into bother with the housekeeper for not being there to clear up after the shindig all you posh folk had all been at in the house that night. And then you sat with me, bathing my wounds with the lint, carbolic and warm water she'd brought down from the house in a metal canister. You talked to me – asking me questions to keep me awake. I cannot remember half of what I said. I wish I could. It's strange and annoying to me that all the other events of the evening are so clear to me and yet the part that matters – us – is somehow obscured and I want to know every last word that passed between us, to store it up – forever fresh in my memory.

MacKenzie returned with the car – as you'd ordered.

I do remember that you said very formally and with authority, "MacKenzie will take you home, now. Do you understand?"

I must have nodded or something and you asked me where I lived as you placed me inside the Bentley. You wrapped a blanket around me. I remember my teeth had been chattering but I felt warm at last as you slid onto the back seat next to me. I'd expected you to leave me to MacKenzie but you sat right by me all the way back home. I was glad.

When we arrived in Shamrock Street you must have been shocked. The contrast with your life could not have been greater. You'd just been at that swanky party at your beautiful house, you were dressed to the nines in your dinner suit and now here you were in the Gorbals for the first time in your life. Talk about a fish out of water.

You held on to me as we approached the tenement. I could feel your firm grip under my arm.

We entered the close. I remember I heard you gasp as we passed the O'Riordans. You'd never seen people live like that before, I suppose.

God knows, we all felt terrible for the O'Riordans. The rest of us had precious little but the O'Riordans had nothing, literally nothing. The only roof over their heads that could be afforded was an under-stair recess on the ground floor of our tenement building – many people had and still to this day have no better choice than to 'live on the stairs'. You saw only their feet (you told me later) two adults and five children – feet sticking out under a tattered curtain which allowed them scant privacy and no protection against the elements. Wind howled through the entrances of the tenements, front and rear on the ground floor. The O'Riordans were covered in sacks and slept in their clothes. Did you know that? Is that what you saw or did you just imagine, did you just put the picture together for yourself?

Glasgow was the first British city to be hit by the Spanish Flu epidemic. In May 1918, all the O'Riordans ended up in a pauper's grave, with only a few neighbours to mourn their passing. More heartbreak.

I must have been unsteady on my feet because it took both you and MacKenzie to get me up the stone stairway safely to the front door of our tenement apartment.

When we reached my door, Ma' came flying out, crying. She'd

13

known something was wrong. I had never been one to stay out so late. My da just sat there looking shocked and you were so kind to them. Do you remember what you said? I do.

"We've brought your son home to you, Mrs Cassidy. He's had the most terrible beating but he will be well quite soon now he's with his family."

You said to me much later that you'd been relieved as you walked into our tenement flat –

"I was so glad that not all of 'you' live like the O'Riordans, relieved that your place though very basic was at least clean and smelled of coal and candles and soap."

That was my ma's doing. She always kept a good, neat, clean house. Me and my brothers and sisters were the lucky ones. The Cassidys – hardworking, good-living, sober Irish Catholics who'd made it.

Danny Cassidy

3

You can see why I couldn't let this out, not in the '50s when I first found the letter. God knows *it* was still illegal then. Any roads, I'd met James Lochdarnock's father (Lord Alistair) when I was a boy, visiting the house with my father who was a gardener here before and after the Second War. I suppose I felt bound by some kind of unwritten code – a strange kind of loyalty, given my politics – to keep the matter to myself in order to protect the name of Lochdarnock. That's how much the old man, Lord Alistair, had impressed me.

I told the wife, Hetty, not so long ago about the letter and she said: 'You're daft keeping this to yerself for so long, we coulda made a few bob in the tabloids.'

That's Hetty for you. Not so much a practical woman as an arch materialist, whose fault it is that I'd become involved at the house after it was left to the city by Lord Alistair Lochdarnock, in the first place. It was 1955 when he let the place go finally, another victim of taxes and disrepair.

"I'll need you out from under my feet," Hetty'd said. "And you can take William and Heather with you to whatever it is that you're doing."

The Second War was not that long over and women were

used, by then, to what is now called 'their own space'. Hetty had always been ahead of her time, anyhow. She'd warned me not to go drinking with my National Service pals, hence her insistence on me having the weans with me.

I've seen a few of the 'Brillcream Boys' off to the 'daemon drink' right enough.

It took me a couple of years of trying various things – archaeology, photography and the like, until I found a hobby which occupied and satisfied me enough. So it was the house, from one bright Saturday morning in 1958 until now, that's occupied the majority of my free time and my free thoughts.

While Hetty and her friends drank tea and gossiped and drooled over the latest hairdos and fashions, child free and smoking like hussies on a Saturday, I was pursuing my own particular passion in the cold comfort of Lochdarnock House.

Me and Hetty are off up to the lodge at Braeside for the New Year. Ach, it was her idea as she doesn't fancy cooking or going to Heather's for the holiday. She's annoyed that William's wife has failed to invite us down to London again.

"That woman has destroyed our family," she complained bitterly after another unsatisfactory call to them the other day.

"Whit's the matter wi' you? Ye hate London," I snarled, knowing that wasn't the point she was making.

I am secretly glad that they have a room at the newly done up Lodge left for New Year. I want to see what happens with the historical fragments I'm about to leave lying about for Jenny Munroe and I'll try to steer Gil Delaney IV (the American, you'll remember) in the right direction, or more specifically I'm about to steer them both in the direction of the story I've uncovered, and all.

It was amazing how quick he (Gil Delaney IV) was to take my suggestion that he should spend a few days up at Braeside – a good sales job on my part – I hear he got the last room they had available over the New Year.

4

Now I'm up here at Braeside, the Lochdarnock hunting, shooting and fishing estate, I'm less impressed by 'the country residence' than I thought I'd be but that's probably because of the amount of snow which is lying so thickly around and the mist that covers the place from ground to sky.

Aye, you're right – this weather should make the place atmospheric but in my old age it just makes the conditions here that much more treacherous and, therefore, a worry to me.

I was thinking the lodge would be done out in all things 'taxidermy and tartan' but the plaid has got the push in favour of warm autumn colours and fancy 'boutique hotel' style furnishings *and* there is not a dead animal in sight. 'Whit a shame!'

Gil Delaney IV was in the bar when Hetty and I arrived.

He invited me for a drink which I was glad of after the taxi ride up here. The roads are still quite bad in the frozen North at times.

Hetty took herself off for a wee sleep, claiming her nerves were 'jangled' after the taxi finally clattered to a halt in the car park of Braeside Lodge, the journey being as much a problem with the clapped out car the taxi firm had sent, if truth be told, as the bumpy roads which led up to the hill top lodge.

"I'll leave you two to natter," she told the Delaney 'boy' in that girly sing-song way she reserves for strangers – well, male strangers at any rate.

"You have a charming wife," he said as she left.

I knew the American was lying because the Yanks don't do irony, so I'm told, and charm is not an adjective I would use in the description of my Hetty.

I did the usual – asking him how he'd enjoyed Glasgow and he gave the expected responses about the quality of food, weather and hotel accommodation. To be honest I wasn't really listening. Instead I was working out a way of him finding the first part of the puzzle which I was keeping safe in my trouser pocket.

Yes, I know! An old history teacher like me should have greater respect for original source material but a briefcase would have aroused suspicion from Hetty, who would have just started going on about tabloids and money and the like if she found out my true purpose in being here.

Quite soon after Gil and I had settled in our seats I spied Jenny Munroe with a young man coming through the door at the lodge. The two seemed puffed out. I found out later that they'd walked up from the gatehouse where *they* were staying gratis (a perk of her job!). They must have had some hike up the hill and when you consider the weather and the state of the ground, I (for one) did not envy them their efforts.

The young man is her son, a lanky big boy of about twenty or so called Jaz (short for James, I imagine).

"Miss Munroe," I called out – she and the boy came over and took seats with me and Gil.

"Let me introduce you to Gil, Gil Delaney IV of New York – was it Manhattan, you said?"

"Manhattan it is," Gil responded dutifully, shaking both Jenny and Jaz' hands.

Jenny Munroe is very formal and English and replied that she was pleased to meet him. The boy's more upbeat and very casual, a bit over the top in fact.

"Jaz Marteneau. I'm her son," he said loudly pointing at Jenny.

Come to think of it, he is as much a replica of Jenny (in the looks department) as she is of Lady Isabelle Lochdarnock – all tall, blonde, slim, and leggy with what I have come to recognise as Lochdarnock blue-eyes – a continuous line from Lady Isabelle and her family the Farquarson's before her. The record shows that Isabelle and Alistair Lochdarnock were second cousins, twice removed which explains *their* family resemblance – like I said before connections on connections.

The conversation seemed very stilted and would have died out without the efforts of the boy who seemed determined that Gil and his mother got to know one another better.

Jaz confessed to me the next day that he was looking for a man for his mother and another for himself. People are much looser about these things than they used to be and it must be a good thing in spite of Hetty's objections on the moral grounds she espouses – when it suits her. Her views are brought about by a rigid Presbyterian upbringing which only stands the test on subjects, I've noticed, of her choosing.

Having got myself an invite to the gatehouse where Jenny and her boy were staying, later that day for a drink, I left the trio to their chat and Jaz to his matchmaking. I've to admit I'm warming to the boy already. He's a character.

5

Getting myself and the documents through the door of the old gatehouse was no trouble.

Of course, Hetty moaned on for forty minutes non-stop on the way down the steep and perilous path we had to walk from the lodge to the gatehouse about the 'slippy' conditions we faced having to get there. Mind you, it *was* a bit of a challenging walk for doddery old folk like us, right enough.

The gatehouse, originally the home of the 'gamekeeper', was a mess. Some bright-spark had taken a lot of the archive from the lodge when that place was being refurbished and dumped it in the gatehouse's tiny living room which was in clear need of an update. As yet the archive material hadn't been dealt with and lay about in piles all over the place. I was dying to get my hands on it, of course.

Gil arrived half an hour before Hetty and me. Apparently, he'd been out for a walk earlier and had planned his route carefully so he ended up at the gatehouse at the right time. As it turned out, he had made quick work of what was for him, at least, a wee trek and ended up walking around the grounds near the gatehouse to avoid being too early. Speed merchant! That's what comes of having those long legs, I suppose.

"I was earlier than I thought. Couldn't take the cold and that's saying something for a guy used to New York winters." Gil gasped, explaining his punctual appearance. "It's unusual for me to be early for anything."

"Generally socially late?" Jenny asked.

"No. It turns out I'm just a common or garden guy who can't get his act together!" the Yank replied. We all laughed.

The five of us had tea in the kitchen. Squeals accompanied Jaz's tales about the mouse-droppings he and Jenny had found in the cupboards down here when they arrived yesterday. I saw Hetty flinch and Jenny was not much better. Gil and I exchanged a kind of macho look which on my part at least belies a real fear of the vile rodents.

I decided to take my chance and plant the Lochdarnock papers I'd found in the archive at the Glasgow House, early on during the afternoon.

Hetty was by now in full flow, entertaining the troops and inadvertently keeping them out of my hair. She seemed to be getting on well with Jaz while Gil and Jenny sat back and listened (studiously avoiding eye contact with one another, Hetty told me later). That Hetty woman is a wonder. She blethers away whilst taking in every nuance of behaviour as well as every word people around her are saying.

When I saw them all quite settled to their chat I got to work.

I made the usual non-fuss about getting to the toilet and 'accidentally' got lost on the way back. It's a privilege of age that polite people don't comment on evidence of dementia so I got away with it, telling the company when I finally returned, "I just wandered into the wrong room." (If they'd quizzed me about the length of time I was lost, I would have had a hard job explaining myself. It takes a while to poke various papers into files and books and make their existence in that particular place look kosher, I'd found to my surprise.

"What would you do with him?" Hetty's eyes fluttered and

her lips smiled as she made the comment but I knew she was really thinking, "Daft old sod – embarrassing me like that!"

I changed the subject, brazen now having achieved my primary objective.

"That must be where the Guthrie was hanging," I said, pointing shakily at the distinct pale mark on the wall above the fireplace where a picture clearly once hung.

"I'm told it was quite a cleaning job for the conservators to get Guthrie's picture of Lady Isabelle spruced up."

I know I was playing 'old man dottled' but I had to get the thoughts and the conversation flowing in the right direction and bringing up the 1907 portrait of Lady Isabelle Lochdarnock was crucial if my plans were to pan out.

"I was just telling Jenny," Gil began, "that she bears an uncanny likeness to Isabelle Lochdarnock."

"That struck you too?" I asked as innocently as I could. I'd done a bit of amateur dramatics years back and I was relishing my latest role, working on the principle that less-is-more in the acting business, of course.

Jenny seemed to stiffen. The conversation was clearly not going in the right direction for her.

"I do see it a little but it's not as extraordinary as you two are making out," she offered, nervously.

Gil produced his mobile phone and flashed the illicit image of the Guthrie portrait of Isabelle he had captured at the house in Jenny's direction.

"Not so extraordinary. My god, you *are* the woman," Gil proclaimed.

Jaz grabbed the phone, looked intently at the image, and piped up in a deep and husky voice,

"Mummy, Gil here is quite right. I sniff a story in the air."

6

I think the plan is working. Jenny Munroe came to the Hogmanay Ceilidh looking awful pale. The woman could barely stand upright. Strange, as she doesn't look like a drinker. She claimed an ear infection. The American was very attentive to her and they spent a wee while in a huddle away from the fire that was on-the-go in the main residents' sitting room at the lodge, as she claimed to be feeling hot. I was a bit annoyed that Hetty insisted on sitting on top of the blazing log inferno situated in the opposite corner of the room occupied by my two 'soon-to-be bloodhounds'.

Hetty was sipping a sherry of all things. It's a drink she claims to hate but that didn't stop her at her attempt at 1970s style sophistication. She and young Jaz, who was similarly 'frozen to death' and needed to enjoy the heat of the faux log fire, were quite the pair, exchanging anecdotes and laughing away like a couple of inebriated school girls whilst clinging tightly to their 'schooners' of the ruby coloured fluid.

I used the first excuse I could find to get over to the main action – to see if my elected detectives had in fact taken the scent.

I was gratified to find they had.

"I was just saying to Jenny that she should run a find she made today, by you since you're the expert on all things Lochdarnock." Gil Delaney confided.

"Oh?" I replied continuing to underplay my part, with an air of casual confidence.

"Mr Delaney is more excited than I am but I found a diary extract which may be of interest to you. I remember you mentioned that you had a grandfather who died in Ewart's Yard before the First World War. There's a report of his death, well an account surrounding it, in an extract I came across from Lord Alistair Lochdarnock's diary." Jenny said in a matter-of-fact manner.

'Damn,' I thought. 'They've found the wrong bit first.'

I was disappointed to say the least that they hadn't yet found the first part of the 'Story of Us', but that's the way it goes with research at times I suppose. Nothing in life or research for that matter is all that predictable.

"Is that right?" I couldn't help myself continuing. "Have you found any other interesting references to the Ewarts or other?"

Gil Delaney IV piped up confidently, "Not yet but I'm promised access to the archive tomorrow. Jenny, show the guy the extract you found."

You could tell the lovely Jenny was not a bit pleased to be ordered about by the American but she produced the diary extract as ordered plus pages from a manuscript I'd never seen before. Handing them to me she muttered,

"I'm sure all this can wait until the morning. You and your wife are here to have a bit of New Year's fun." Jenny glared at Delaney, who had the cheek to smile at the clear rebuke, which Ms Munroe had delivered in the frostiest of tones.

I grabbed the sheets of paper from her greedily, having not expected any further bits of the puzzle I'd been working on so long to turn up. I read the unrecognised sheet first.

7

EXTRACT FROM A GOOD PLACE
BY MARGARET MUNROE, 1997

Chapter 1 – Patrick and Elizabeth – 3rd May 1911

Patrick Cassidy at last caught sight of Mary walking arm in arm through the rain toward the Kelvin Halls with another young woman he hadn't seen before, a pretty girl with coal-black eyes like his own and raven hair like his own now saturated by rain.

"Patrick!" Mary shouted above the cacophony of noise as he touched her arm at last and spun her round to face him. She hugged her brother and pushed him back a little, smiling at her friend,

"My brother, Patrick," Mary said proudly, hugging the boy whilst introducing him to her friend. She noticed the beaming smile that passed between Patrick and Elizabeth.

'Oh, aye!' Mary thought.

"We'd better get away fae the rain, we'll get the cold if we ston' aboot in this!" Mary continued, registering the looks that were passing between the young pair as she dragged them through the crowds and headed towards an awning under an advertising slogan which announced:

THE GLASGOW EXHIBITION OF ART
AND INDUSTRY – 1911

***

When I finished reading the piece, Jenny leaned towards me explaining, "My mother wrote a novel about her family, the Cassidys. The Mary in this extract worked as a maid at Lochdarnock House at the time of your Grandfather's death. The 3rd of May 1911 seems to be especially significant in what we've found so far. Oh, and Mary may well have got the Elizabeth mentioned in the extract, work there too, perhaps on a casual basis?"

I simply shrugged. It was a possibility, of course. Her next comment got my full attention, however.

"Elizabeth and Patrick had my grandmother – Alice – within the next few years. I look very much like Nanna Alice," Jenny explained.

I thought that scenario a distinct possibility and felt for poor Patrick being cuckolded that way by a Lochdarnock (perhaps that crowd were not all they were cracked up to be).

So Nanna Alice was the lovechild of Elizabeth Cassidy and a Lochdarnock – that *was* interesting to me – but which one, which Lochdarnock? I could not help asking myself, which one of the many possibilities there existed in the Lochdarnock family could be the father of Alice Cassidy.

"Is there more of this manuscript of your mother's?" I asked for want of something better to say.

To make myself look good, I made a play of donning my specs. Always gives a boy a hint of the intellect! Or so I am led to believe.

Jenny told me she would pass the rest to me the following day.

Delaney piped up, "Mary, Patrick's sister, was childless but Margaret's manuscript begs an interesting question."

"I don't think it means anything. You have to understand, Gil, that my mother was desperately aspirational and wanted to take up the 'Posh auntie's offer,' Jenny's voice strained.

"I'm sorry, Jenny, but I'm a wee bit out on a limb not knowing the story, your story."

I was conscious as I uttered the words not to sound too excited but I smelled an interesting lead and was determined to miss out on nothing which might make more plain the Lochdarnock/Cassidy story – the evidence of which was sitting in front of me in the form of J. Munroe.

"Posh great aunt Mary – my god, in my family, servants were seen as posh – asked Alice Maguire née Cassidy, if she could take my mother south with her. Mary had left Lochdarnock House just after the Second War to take up a job as housekeeper to a doctor in Brighton we think. Anyway, Nanna Alice was horrified by the proposition and totally refused to let my mother, Margaret, go.

Somewhere along the line, Mary got lost and nobody can find what happened to her."

"They looked for Mary Cassidy, did they?" I asked, also curious now.

"My mother did. Poor Mummy had become very excited about going off to live the good life in England when she was a youngster. I don't think she resented Alice for keeping her with the family in Scotland but a little part of her wondered what life would have been if she'd gone south with the 'posh Aunt' to live a totally different life."

Jenny paused before adding wistfully, "It must be lovely to be wanted."

"It's not uncommon for an aunt who's getting ahead to want to bring one of her own up in the world, so what's significant in this story?"

My enquiry was a genuine one, I was not about to leap to conclusions as to the parentage of Alice and hold either one Cassidy or one Lochdarnock *responsible* for Alice's existence without adequate evidence.

"Why my mother?" Jenny replied, quickly. "There were plenty of other females in the family of that age, at that time. Why did Margaret, who was twelve or thirteen at the time, get picked out for special attention? Did Lord Lochdarnock have a hand in having one of 'his own' taken care of, maybe? Oh, listen to me. I'm getting as bad as Gil. The three of us are inventing a story here to fit with my resemblance to Isabelle. It's probably just rubbish and a complete coincidence that I look similar to Lady L anyway," Jenny said wearily now.

"Ewarts, Lochdarnocks, and Cassidys all in the story. Come on, Jenny." Gil looked at me and added. "Look, she found this journal entry for the same day in the papers at the gatehouse."

The big Yank was keen as mustard to get on and come to conclusions. I think, like Ms Munroe, in fact I am bloody sure – life and research are never that simple.

Having read the extract a million times by now I had to feign a degree of interest I found hard to muster.

8

Today was, it seems, the predictable grand success that myself and fellow organisers had planned and had so dearly wished to come about. And the crowds hurly-burlying about in the rain, regardless of their own comforts, seemed to truly appreciate the attentions and labours lavished on the event.

If only the day had not been marred by the news from Ewart's yard! I find Douglas Ewart difficult enough at the best of times but today he descended in my eyes to a new low. He is the sort of fellow one would wish to discourage, not in his enterprise, but in his blatant pursuit of capital regardless of human cost, regardless of any sacrifice his men might make in order to achieve his ends which as far as I can see are entirely fiscal.

Perhaps I would not be so horribly sickened by this event had not Isabelle arrived at the Kelvin Halls at the moment of the announcement of the poor unnamed man's death. My wife is not able to cope with news of this sort, I believe she is – as many women seem to be – capable of imagining such a scene as was suggested in its full horror, so acute is her sensitivity. Isabelle had to be escorted directly home by James who was furious and intent on challenging Ewart directly about what is

29

seen by young men of a particular political persuasion as murderous and contemptible acts of greed or negligence.

I confess that James' politics are anathema to me, as much as the beliefs expressed by Ewart and his like.

I was forced to intervene in their exchange and require James to take his mother directly home as both he and Ewart seemed intent on engaging in a verbal sparring match that I knew could lead nowhere and would only upset my wife's delicate condition further.

Difficult times!

The dinner party at Lochdarnock House that evening was similarly marred by James and Sir Douglas Ewart (who became quite drunk and unnervingly venomous by the end of the triumphant, yet trying, first day of the exhibition). I truly believe things would have come to blows between Sir Douglas and my son, had not Isabelle intervened so delicately and expertly. She has a particular way of soothing situations and James' temper especially.

Angus his brother, however, is a different sort with little outward evidence of fury but indulgent in deeds so senseless that I sometimes despair. He and Sir Douglas' son, Kenneth, appear to be worryingly close. If I have reservations about Douglas Ewart, then even stronger are my doubts about his son – a young man bent on the pursuit of pleasures as well as money at the cost of any fellow at any station.

Lady Helen Ewart is a quiet woman by contrast, but I think remarkably strong. The Ewart's daughter, Fiona, seems not to fit with the rest and is a delightful young woman, gentle and sweet – with the shyest, prettiest smile. I pitied her.

When the reels started later in the evening, Fiona danced gracefully with me, I was glad of a partner tonight as poor Isabelle is no longer able to perform her duties as hostess to the full, so debilitating is her condition.

James disappeared early, claiming he needed to walk in the fresh air and Angus simply drank with Kenneth Ewart until they were both quite horribly inebriated. At some point my second son disappeared at a similar time too. Perhaps one of the servants put Angus to bed? What am I to do with Angus? What shall I do with either of my sons?

I was lucky to be spared the embarrassment of commenting on Alistair's diary extract by an interruption of proceedings by the maitre d' who called us into dinner, thank God. I've to admit I was a bit disappointed that Danny Cassidy's *The Tale of Us – Part I* hadn't been the first rabbit to be pulled out of the hat but there was time, and then Delaney too would have a connection to the story and the fun could really begin. Besides, the nosy old woman who resides in every man regardless of his protestations of innocence wanted to know who the female might be who had obviously got herself 'in the family way' with a Lochdarnock.

9

Hetty had promised I would have a sore head in the morning after all the drink I had on New Year's Eve. I've to admit that two halves of heavy and a glass of Dom Perignon are a bit much for an old codger like me these days.

Fortunately, I feel amazingly fit and well on New Year's Day – unlike Hetty who, encouraged by the boy Jaz, went into overdrive last night, indulging in copious amounts of the Amontillado and dance-floor tom-foolery to boot (11 a.m. and the woman still hasn't surfaced – could you bear it?) Jaz and Hetty's attempt at 'The Gay Gordons' will live in my memory a while, I can tell you! I even saw the glimmer of a smile on Jenny's face as she watched her son hurl Hetty (who's not as petite as she'd like to be) about the dance floor, inexpertly to say the least.

The big Delaney fella too made an attempt with Jenny to trip the light fantastic. I'd expected her to be fleet of foot but I think the ear infection she complains of must be affecting Jenny more than she'll admit. Consequently, her balance and ability to manoeuvre on the dance floor were a disappointment. I'd expected the leggy and graceful girl to acquit herself better, I've to say.

The American was confident in his struttings, having clearly watched Patrick Swayze rather than Kelly or Astair as a youngster, but even so he didn't quite hit the right note with his dancing. A kinder critic than me would describe Gil's style as 'International Abandon.' The truth being that it was simply a bad effort on his part. I sat quietly wishing I could take the tall woman in my arms and lead her through the dance with elegance as well as energy. But there you are. Old age makes 'stookies' of us all and a blank dance card is all that can be expected at my time of life – New Year or not.

My slide down the hill to the gatehouse was made tentatively this morning – a crisp and clear one. I wasn't sure that Jenny Munroe would be up even though she'd made this early appointment, well early for New Year's Day up here. My arrival at the gatehouse coincided with Jaz's first attempt to cure his hangover, which looked to be a bad one.

Jenny handed him the tablets and water ordering, "Back to bed, you idiot!"

But the boy got a smile which is more than my William could have expected from his mother in similar circumstances at that age.

Jenny, who was dressed in black trousers and a black T shirt, had her hair pulled back and glasses on and was clearly champing at the bit to get down to business, despite her delicate health.

"I've just found another piece of interesting information," she announced.

"More of Sir Alistair's journal?" I enquired, acting the innocent and sipping the tea she'd just put in front of me.

"Actually, no. This stuff is much more explosive."

"May be we should wait 'til the American gets here?" I suggested, feeling a tingle of excitement now and an added determination that the two should continue on their quest at the same steady rate together, or maybe I was turning into Jaz or Hetty and expecting a romance to blossom – perish the thought. Selfish, I know, but I want nothing to get in the way of my two researchers' progress.

With such questions rattling in my mind, there was a chap on the door. The leggy American strode in looking not a bit the worse for wear. I don't think he'd had that much booze at all the night before, he couldn't have had a fair amount and maintained his positive glow and high energy, which I was (I've to admit) feeling a little tired of by now. I commented on his apparent sobriety at Hogmanay.

"Son of an alcoholic, I limit myself," he smiled.

"You too?" Jenny responded, setting down his tea in a chunky mug, in front of him. It seemed that this pair had more in common than either of them expected.

"Jenny's found an interesting, letter, was it?" I said, playing along with the pair's matter-of-fact approach.

"It's a kind of novel-come-love letter I think, but I'd have to see the rest of it to decide," Jenny commented.

"Oh, you've only found a bit?" I asked, pushing my luck and sucking on the ginger-nut biscuit I'd taken from the plate she'd offered.

"A fragment of something much larger, it must be, yes!" said Jenny, looking pensive. "You two need to read it. I've taken a copy for each of you."

Jenny handed us pristine copies of the original – *The Story of Us – Part 1*. Very organised is Miss Munroe. I mimed reading the document while listening to Gil's sighs and "Wows" and "God!", and "Jesus, Gil the first!" comments, in a feigned, shocked silence.

We both finished at the same time, me in my mock reading and Gil in his first enthralled look at Danny Cassidy's report of his first meeting with his amour, James Lochdarnock.

"Surprising!" I said in a low voice.

"A love affair," said Jenny, standing over me looking at the papers.

"Not one your grandmother might have sprung from, Jenny," Gil uttered with a serious look on his face.

"No. But I suppose I have to follow this clue having established the Cassidy/Lochdarnock connection in more than one way and see where else it might lead," said Jenny, "Who knows – James Lochdarnock may have had a general liking for all things 'Cassidy'. I'm determined not to fall into speculating on the matter. I want to see hard evidence, if any exists."

"Quite wise of you, Jenny," I muttered, feeling a thrill of excitement as my plan seemed to be progressing nicely now.

Gil Delaney got up and started to move furniture around.

"You don't mind? I just think we'll work better if we set the place up for research." Gil was in a land of his own now muttering about detectives and crime-boards and the like.

The boy had fair got the bit between his teeth. Whether he was just trying to impress the lovely Ms Munroe or is genuinely fascinated by the material, I had yet to decide.

"Do you think we can pick up a decent sized whiteboard?" he asked with a serious look on his face.

"You'd need to order one from Glasgow or Edinburgh. I doubt they'd have such a stash of stuff in Inverness," I replied, admiring his foresight and the methodical 'engineer-like' approach he was planning to take.

"I can set up a spreadsheet. You don't mind do you, Jen," Gil said, bustling about the place.

"Jenny!" she replied tight-lipped. "I suppose that's one way of pursuing matters."

"Have you noticed how snotty the English can be?" laughed Gil.

I was reluctant to answer having already been assured by Jenny that she was born here in Scotland and besides I'm not as daft as to get involved in 'domestics' as they call them, I've had enough of my own of those to deal with over the years and learned that least said, etc…

I was glad when young Jaz came into the room, requesting that we, "Keep it down".

Excitement had got the better of the American who was rearranging papers now as well as furniture and lugging boxes in from the dilapidated gatehouse living room and depositing them in our wee room which seems to have become a kitchen/diner in this modern age, a room which does for all living requirements 'and then some', as Jaz and the like might say.

"Sorry," replied Gil perfunctorily without an ounce of remorse on show. "You want tea?"

"Coffee," demanded Jaz, monosyllabically.

His mother was quick to intervene.

"He can get it himself," she said coldly. Jaz's lip curled.

"OK," was Jenny's impatient response.

Mothers the world over threaten to do the right thing and then back down in the face of a 'petted lip'. Jenny handed the boy his coffee and tried to shoo him out of the room. He refused to leave and sat looking miserable while we three organised ourselves.

Gil ran through the morning's proceedings. Jaz was sitting up in response to the revelations about Danny and James.

"Well, that's where it comes from. It really is in the genes after all." He smiled.

"We don't know that yet," Jenny spat out. "Let's stay…"

"Professional," Gil said finishing her sentence for her.

"Quite," replied Jenny.

I had been quiet for a while and was sick of the endless tea which was being streamed into my cup by the lovely Jenny.

"No more tea for me," I said looking at one of the boxes.

I recognised a file and knowing that I'd put another of my wee time bombs in it, made a show of digging in deep. I didn't want to find the paperwork too soon. I had to make this look good, so I delved away taking little notice of the conversation that continued between the three. When I eventually picked out the paper I made a show of reading it carefully before drawing the attention of the trio to my 'find'.

10

THE TALE OF US – PART 2

Finlay Anderson was a sadist. A clear foot taller than me, Sergeant Anderson was an experienced soldier and very muscled. As he marched me into your office at Maryhill that day, I tried to hide the terror that was rising in my stomach.

Anderson had taken a dislike to me along with all the other Catholic boys, though I've to admit he seemed to have a special interest in causing me as much discomfort as he could possibly get away with. Several of the boys had already ended up in front of an officer for punishment to be sanctioned and they had earned scars to show for their misdemeanours. It was my turn today. I suppose I'd been careful up to that point not to give the man any excuse. On that cold November day I was braced and ready for whatever an officer was naively to believe was my punishment, knowing that my body would bear the brunt of an onslaught disproportionate to any crime I'd committed, at the hands of the sadistic sergeant. In this case, Anderson was accusing me of insurrection. I was organising the men to ask for better rations. Foolish of me, I'm aware of that now, but you know me and my hatred of injustice!

Of course, I'd known you were at the camp. I'd seen you a few days before. You joined us late, having been on your officer training course and you knew none of the men who'd already been brutalised over several weeks now in the name of basic training there at the Highland Light Infantry's training camp at Maryhill.

You were sitting at your desk when Anderson marched me into the cramped office. You looked up but showed no surprise. You told me later that you'd recognised me immediately and were more than pleased to see me. My heart was beating like an out of control engine from more than just fear. You dismissed Anderson, almost immediately he'd explained my sins. My thought was, 'Christ, that big bastard's gonnae kill me now.' Of course, you were careful to make his dismissal polite and matter-of-fact but nonetheless…

You looked down at the charge sheet and told me to take a seat. I wasn't expecting that. When you looked up you smiled at me. I'd obviously been reading too many of my sister's books because what I did expect you to say was, "So we meet again!"

In the event, you weren't so predictable. Your words were to the effect that you had no choice but to mete out a punishment given the accusations being made by Anderson. I remember looking at you with a deliberate glare of contempt and you said,

"One war at a time, Danny!" That was all. It took me a moment to answer you.

"I'm no' so bloody sure the Germans are the worst enemy here."

You smiled again. "To be quite frank, I think you may be quite right but we need to get this war over with first before we embark on the more important battles."

Do you remember handing me the books? You slid three of them across the desk to me. I'd already read the Marx, of course, but I took the Hutcheson and the Hulme with me and devoured them over the next few days at any opportunity I got.

Before calling Anderson back into the room, you smiled at me.

"When you have done with these come back to see me again. I have several other tomes that may interest you." Then you looked kind of embarrassed probably because I was silent. I didn't even

thank you. You called Anderson in and said something about latrine duties.

I thought, 'In the shit again, Danny boy,' and I must have smiled to myself because that smile was the excuse Anderson gave for kicking hell out of me for an age later that day.

11

"Ok," Jenny drawled.

It took the American and Jaz a couple of minutes to catch up as they were reading over her shoulder. Jenny nodded her head as the two men continued reading, enthralled by what they – we – had found.

"That must be when their affair started," Jaz said, clapping his hands. "We have to find the rest. There just have to be some really juicy bits somewhere."

"If it's gay porn you're after," Jenny piped up, "there *are* online sites, you know."

"This is a romance, people. I doubt it will get too lurid." said Gil, looking at me.

I tried to remain with a neutral expression but the thought 'If only you knew…' kept running through my mind.

I've spent the rest of today watching the three of them searching hungrily through the archive and I've seen the way they get on. It is interesting to watch the trio, to say the least.

Jenny looked tired after a couple of hours and took to her bed, leaving the two 'boys' – as she insists on calling them – to it. She was putting herself in charge, I suppose. Jenny Munroe knows her business best, I think, and coped casually and easily with getting the 'two' boys trotting ahead with the work in her absence.

I busied myself by providing cheese pieces for their lunch. Jaz opened a bottle of wine to go with the 'make do and mend' affair that passed for lunch, claiming, "Just cheering things up a bit." Youngsters' capacity to recover from the punishment of their sins is stupefying and gratifying all at once. Ach, we were probably all like that in the day.

About two o'clock Gil asked if I wanted to join him and Jaz for a walk. The prospect of keeping up with their long legs was daunting so I politely declined.

Instead I waited for Jenny to come down, gave her the now curled up sandwich which was left over and suggested wine – which she declined. She was pale, very pale but seemed to have enough energy to trawl on, in a more languid fashion than I'd seen her behave before.

The huge sheet of white paper that Gil had plastered to the wall, actually sixteen sheets of A4 stapled together, had been written on in an attempt to map out information so far gleaned from the archives and the bits and pieces I'd supplemented.

I noticed the difference in Gil and Ms Munroe's handwriting styles, the American's being looser and Jenny's hand controlled and precise – a reflection of their personalities perhaps?

The boy, Jaz, hadn't attempted to add to the graphics. He told me later that he didn't dare as it was their 'thing'. I told him that I could 'relate' to that – amazing the language you pick up watching daytime TV, don't you think?

The American took me back up to the lodge before it got dark, the conditions hadn't improved a bit during the day, and I've to admit I was regretting sharing in the lunchtime wine drinking now – even though I only partook of minimal amounts of the ruby coloured liquid Jaz had offered.

Hetty was recovered now and talked nineteen to the dozen about the previous night, enquiring about the American and the woman, once we were alone.

"I've a notion there's something going on there!" she said, nodding her head as sagely as she could.

I feigned ignorance. "Ye know nothing, woman," I barked at her, thinking 'Ah, ye auld witch, ye *would* have got a sniff of it.' I was feeling jealous that Hetty was nudging her way into something that was mine, and mine alone.

12

The boy, Jaz, left this morning for France. His mother tells me he's headed off to improve his 'language skills' before taking up an internship at a theatre in Quebec. I kind of remembered him explaining what the particular theatre was all about – he used the term 'avant-garde' quite a bit which made my mind close over – daft I know and prejudiced but then I do have the excuse of age on my side. The prospect of a lot of young folk up to all sorts of nonsense in the name of 'Art' was not a comfortable one for an auld traditionalist like me.

"He's let his French slide since A-levels. Of course, it's my fault for not encouraging him to continue," Jenny confessed.

"Has he good French?" I asked.

"His father was French. Not that Jaz knew him. But, yes. We've spent a lot of time over there. Mainly in Paris but a little of our time was spent in Normandy."

"You still see his da?" I asked, pushing my luck.

She looked a wee bit surprised but answered me anyway.

"Phillipe died before Jaz was born."

I was the one to feel surprised and I felt startled by the news Jenny Munroe had just given. How history repeats itself!

I wanted to ask how poor Phillipe had met his end –

romanticising about a motorbike accident, but she had that drawn down look shy folk like her get when matters become personal and I knew not to push my luck.

"I'm sorry for that," I replied.

Neither Jenny nor I had noticed the Big American fella standing there listening to us converse. There seemed to be a sympathetic look on his face as he gazed at Jenny. I hadn't seen him show much tenderness to her before now but I suspect that was because Jenny is a woman who doesn't invite comforting. Hetty could give lessons in playing the distraught female, maybe I'll get her to teach Ms Munroe the technique. Having said that, I like Jenny's kind of standoffish behaviour, it has a Scottishness in its Englishness, if that makes sense.

Gil didn't comment on what he overheard but simply asked, "Jaz gone?"

Jenny nodded in reply.

"The taxi was a wee bit late. We're waiting up here at the lodge to see if Jaz gets to Inverness for the plane on time," I replied.

Jenny added by way of explanation, "Signal's better up here."

Gil joined us for coffee. The three of us were quiet this morning, taking in the look of the lounge and the demeanour of one another. I was the one who broke the embarrassed silence, having been through a number of things to say in my mind, it didn't seem appropriate to talk about the research so I simply wittered on, "It's at times like this I'd like a cigarette."

"When did you give up?" Gil asked.

"Years ago."

"I gave up at thirty. It seemed the adult thing to do given Richard Doll and his followers. You, Jenny?" Gil added.

Jenny looked up, surprised. "I never started."

There was no smugness to the reply. She was still probably thinking of her son, thinking of family dead and gone, thinking about what she knew and wondering about what she was yet to ascertain for all I know.

The text message came not a minute too soon and, watching Jenny read it, Gil and I got to our feet double quick. The man was champing at the bit to get on with the research now and I was keen to avoid Hetty who was not best pleased that I was off to the gatehouse without her – again!

"I thought coming here was about spending time together." She'd moaned on, making the most of my apparent 'badness' to her.

I thought of her Saturday sessions with her friends while William, Heather and I wandered off in the freezing cold to help out at Lochdarnock House, which was colder inside (in those days) than on the outside. I felt no guilt about leaving the biddy up at the comfy lodge. Anyhow, half the other guests would know her life story by lunchtime and she would know *all* of theirs much sooner.

Hetty's a way of getting people to loosen up, a kind of gentle nosiness which masquerades as a deep interest in her fellow humans. I shouldn't complain. It keeps her amused and, therefore, out of my hair – not that I've much left of that stuff these days – baldness beckons and it will be a race to see whether the hair or the life gives out first.

Gil was attentive to me on the way down the slope to the gatehouse making sure I remained upright, in spite of the dire conditions, but it was actually Jenny who keeled over in the snow. She made not a bit of fuss about falling – stoic that one – and got up trying to appear fine. I've to report that Jenny confessed later that she was bruised and shaken by the accident.

We three took the descent very gingerly after that with the big Yank holding on fast to the two of us – both Jenny and me. The prim Ms Munroe was desperately embarrassed and a wee bit annoyed about all the fuss Gil was making – I could see that.

"I'll be absolutely fine. There really is no need to fuss," she seethed quietly.

"I'm not fussing, as you say, I'm kinda mindful that any one of us could have an accident in these kind of conditions, Jenny."

I've to admit I had no choice but to agree with him and I, for one, was glad he was there to make sure I didn't fall on my rather ancient and now bony backside.

"Och, in this terrain the best of them can come a cropper," I piped up in the American's defence. "Look at what happened to Robin Cook." I shook my head. "The man was an experienced walker and then pphut… "

"I thought he was on the Munros," Jenny replied. I could tell she was being short and snotty with me but I chose not to be similarly annoyed.

"Aye, but he could have fallen anywhere," I replied.

The Yank looked non-plussed. He probably doesn't know one British politician (alive or dead) from another.

We continued our slow and steady trudge. I spied a lot of wild life along the way or at least signs of creatures. The imprints of paws and claws on the fresh snow were clear and I wished I'd spent more time studying this kind of stuff long ago and not left glaring gaps in my knowledge which I now regret.

It's funny how you make your mind up about interests at a young age and barely diversify during a life time. I suppose what happens is that you become loyal to whatever your initial interest might be and then by the time you realise you're a 'one trick pony' it's almost too late. I made a mental note that morning to address this problem of mine and to 'diversify' my interests, to 'satisfy my natural curiosity for all things' historical and other.

"That's it," I decided, "I'll take a course on 'Trailing Nature'." Then I thought again. Was my interest in history not just the same as those naturalists who are looking for imprints in the snow, fleeting deposits of evidence that transmute and change with the temperature? Am I in some kind of strange way not just doing the same thing – tracking the presence of what has once landed there on the Earth and judging the mark then made by the current conditions in which I find it. Am I not just looking for the signs and the prints of those of the past and the trace they leave in the present?

This kind of thinking probably bores the normal person to death but it fascinates me. How is history created? How do we glean from the imprints that are left in the snow or on the sand or mud just what has been there and what events actually occurred in that place?

Hetty thinks I talk a lot of nonsense about this kind of stuff. Presumably she'd rather I was bothered about the spin cycle on washing machines or the cost of the latest fashion fad for the over-eighties. God help me, I was never interested in clothes, and as for machines! Hetty says that's the reason I'm not the 'normal' man. My lack of technical knowledge and practical ability proving my inferiority as a masculine type. Now there *is* a mercy.

The first hour at the gatehouse was a complete disappointment. I was the one who took to making tea – cup after cup. In spite of my encouragement Gil and Jenny found nothing, so I had to do the 'finding' again! I can't pull that stroke too often. That pair are bright as buttons and are bound to pick up on my success in locating interesting stuff, in light of their failure.

I presented them with an extract in the hope that they would have a flavour of what family life was like for the post-Edwardian Lochdarnocks and what connection there might be at this time with a Ewart, aye, that crowd are right in there too.

13

I hate to complain about Angus, yet again, but I am afraid I have been rather too lax and lenient with my younger son over the years.

Once again last night he was out and about in town with Kenneth Ewart. I am afraid this particular young Ewart man seems to have a worrying influence on my youngest boy.

I gather they were attending the 'show' at the Panopticon Theatre. Of course, I understand the young people's fascination with the sort of entertainment provided at such a venue but it is the insistence of the pair, Angus and young Ewart, on becoming very drunk and misbehaving publicly which I find somewhat disturbing to say the least.

I had to send Wemyss (my solicitor) to have Angus extracted from police custody. I have, of course, impressed upon Angus the need to behave appropriately given his station in life. I fear that my boy does not listen to me.

Perhaps I was wrong to ask James to speak with his younger brother as this seems only to have made the situation worse.

James claims that he merely mentioned to Angus that Kenneth Ewart was a 'bad sort' and that taking care in choosing friends was of paramount importance.

I imagine both James and I come across as being somewhat stuffy given the serious natures we both present to the world – or this is Isabelle's assessment of the two of us – James and me. Both James and I are convinced that we differ in many respects.

James reports that Angus finds the whole issue surrounding his incarceration 'amusing'. I, too, was horrified to hear of the boy's response to the officers who held him at the city cells overnight.

James tells me the story of how Angus, instead of being mild and grateful to the officers, merely laughed off his predicament.

When an officer responded to Angus' frantic morn-time knockings on the cell door and asked my son, "What is it you want?"

Angus replied, "A pot of Earl Grey and a copy of The Times, *my dear man."*

This was, apparently, a cause of great mirth to both Angus and Kenneth Ewart who seem to intend 'dining out' on the story, I gather the other cell inmates were similarly amused and I fear I also detected a glimmer of a smile of James' serious lips.

Both Kenneth Ewart and Angus seem unable to imagine the embarrassment and inconvenience they are causing to family and staff who are compelled to rescue them from the results of their wild antics. James assures me that Angus does not descend to the debauched limits indulged in by Kenneth Ewart. I do hope not…

I shall not, of course, make Isabelle aware of this latest misdemeanour on Angus' part.

I have begged him, for his mother's sake, to acquit himself better. Fortunately, Wemyss was able to speak with the magistrate on Angus' behalf and a lecture from the court official was as much punishment as was meted out to Angus and by association to his 'friend' Ewart also, who had languished in the cramped and uncomfortable cell overnight alongside Angus. I do hope each of the two learn something from the unpleasant experience.

Was I right to intervene on my son's behalf? James believes that I should have allowed the courts to deal with Angus as they would with any drunken vagrant and my eldest son sees no reason why special treatment should be given just because Angus bears the name Lochdarnock. No amount of explaining to James that I did not want Angus' life to be blighted because of a drunken evening would placate James, who is quite right to say that we are no more entitled to the 'understanding' of the law than any other citizens. Perhaps James was as put out that Kenneth Ewart benefitted as much from my intervention as Angus. How could he not?

Perhaps James will come to understand my position and attitude when he is a father himself one day?

14

I noticed that Gil Delaney IV was laughing as he finished reading this piece.

"What's funny?" I asked.

"You don't find it funny? 'A pot of Earl Grey and a copy of *The Times*, my man!' This guy is great," Gil replied.

Jenny was laughing too. "No, Bill's right. Put in context for the Lochdarnock's this was a big deal, a real social embarrassment. Angus was behaving very badly."

"But you like Angus, right?" Gil asked.

"I find him 'naughty' and I must say I *am* fond of naughty boys. I suppose it's what comes of having given birth to a bad boy myself," Jenny confessed with a beaming smile.

"But you do get James Lochdarnock's criticism? Should Angus Lochdarnock and Kenneth Ewart have had special treatment when an ordinary man would have done hard labour at the time for that kind of misdemeanour?"

I slid the idea into the conversation just to bring the two of them back to the reality and seriousness of the situation at that particular historical period of time.

"Of course, it was wrong that Angus got off the hook when others would have been punished so severely, of course," said Jenny looking sheepish now.

"I kinda like Angus' Cavalier attitude. You know – one brother a Cavalier – all flowing locks and Errol Flynn style and the other a Puritan, of sorts." Gil grinned.

"So you think Angus was a dashing sort?" I asked.

"I imagine they were both rather dashing. Do we know what they looked like?" asked Jenny.

I had seen photographs of both boys, who were in fact, almost identical in look despite the two years that separated their births. Equally good looking, but not equally smart is all that I have gleaned from my research about the two young Lochdarnock men of that era.

James Lochdarnock was a keen intellectual who did well at school and university. Angus, well, Angus wasn't gifted mind-wise but seems to have been as athletic and able as his brother physically and, obviously, just as good looking as all the Lochdarnocks appear to have been – and quite plainly still remain if Jenny Munroe and Jaz Marteneau are anything to go by.

I went upstairs and took a couple of photos out of a drawer. I'd seen them here at the gatehouse when I was rummaging round earlier and thought that my fellow researchers might be interested in having sight of these two very similar but ultimately different Lochdarnock boys – James and Angus.

"They look like you," Gil commented, staring intently at Jenny when I provided them with the photos.

"I think it's me who looks like them," Jenny, ever the pedant, replied.

"Shame they never got to be friends," Gil replied.

"How do we know they didn't have some kind of reconciliation?" Jenny brusquely and quite rightly asked.

I, of course, said nothing and put the kettle on – again. It was after that cup of tea that Gil announced that he needed a walk to clear his head. Jenny declined the offer of an amble round the gatehouse but as it appeared I'd have the big Yank to support me (and only me) along the way, I braved it and I ventured out with him – both Gil and I duly wrapped up against the elements – him looking like an intrepid explorer and me an aged round old, dawdling, duck of a man.

I was, by now, keen to get on with my new hobby and look at the signs of nature in this snow and frost-covered land. I only wished I'd had a reference book to help me in my new pursuit.

As it turned out Gil Delaney IV had been, as the American's say, holding out on me and was a bit of a 'keen nature watcher', as he put it.

I could have sworn I saw a Golden Eagle but the American told me I was looking at a White-Tailed Eagle – a rare specimen allegedly. Whatever the creature was, I was fascinated by its flight. The bird was a graceful silhouette in the grey sky it soared against – time up here in the open seems to happen in slow motion and I watched the bird now – enthralled as it elegantly glided through the sky above me.

It's amazing what you see when you just look, as well. Gil pointed out scurrying creatures in the undergrowth that I hadn't ever noticed and I'm determined next time I'm out with him to take a note book and write down what I've seen and his interpretation of my findings.

Of course, our best find was the long look we managed to get at a red deer which stood brazen and staring defiantly in our gaze. Admittedly we were quite a distance from it but I could make out its form and that kind of snotty look those creatures can have as they eye you up.

"Remind you of somebody?" Gil asked.

I was puzzled and shook my head.

"The lovely Jenny – in one of her moods," the Yank laughed.

"I wouldn't let her hear you saying things like that," I rebuked him.

"I know, but she does have a certain kind of look. Maybe one she reserves just for me?" Gil retorted sadly.

I wanted to contradict him as I'd seen Jenny's majestic look doled out to several people in my presence. I decided to plough on and ignore the American who was getting a wee bit maudlin for my liking.

We were a few hundred yards away from the lodge. The angle we approached it made me look at the building anew.

The place was Victorian, I knew. The lodge's round turret (a very Scottish affectation) stood higher than the rest of the solid building, making the whole façade look properly placed. I wondered what the hotel people who were running the lodge put up there in that high round room.

"Do you think they use the turret for storage?" I asked.

"They probably don't need to store ammunition up there, these days – right?" the Yank replied.

"Oh, that building went up long after the period you're talking about. It was built for Victorian weekend hunters and party-goers."

Gil looked disappointed.

"I was hoping the place was older than that," Gil replied.

"No, 1860s. Definitely. The lodge was built well after all the fighting and brawling up in these parts was over. This place was put up some considerable time after the Union of Crowns even."

Gil looked non-plussed again. He was clearly not au fait with Scottish history.

"You're gonna have to fill me in on all things history wise. I doubt I know the very basic stuff. Of course, I've heard tell of the Jacobites and the Union of Crowns and stuff but that's my limit and even my knowledge of that is kinda sketchy," Gil admitted.

I must say I'm looking forward to 'filling in' the missing bits of Scots' history for the Yank but I have to admit, I was getting very cold. My thoughts went to Jenny Munroe and I imagined we'd probably left the lovely girl alone long enough for one day.

When we got back it was obvious Jenny had found something of interest. She looked excited but had clearly had a tear or two about something.

"I found this when you two were galavanting," she said handing each of us a copy of something hot off her photocopier.

She offered hot chocolate which we were both glad to have before reading the latest revelation about the Lochdarnocks.

15

It is several days now since the terrible news arrived. The house is silent and the servants creep around, afraid I think to become visible. Isabelle is confined to her bed and weeps constantly, poor dear heart-broken woman. For my part, I seem unable to talk with anyone. Words, which have always been difficult for me, die even more readily than before on my tongue before they are uttered.

We have, of course, informed James. His letter in reply betrays nothing. How can it?

He writes simply: 'I am limited by the rationing of paper in my response, suffice it to say (is it sufficient? How can it be?) I am torn by the news of this tragedy – the loss of dear Angus – and must make the greatest of effort for the sake of my men to bear the dreadful news as stoically as I might. I have made arrangements to visit the house before my regiment leaves for the Continent.'

James, the poor dear boy, has not even the security of home to sustain him and comfort him in the loss of his younger brother. James' regiment is off to France next week and I know this is a prospect which Isabelle finds hard to endure. It is a comfort to know that we shall see

James in the days to follow and before his embarkation – I can only pray that God will spare our eldest son, at least.

In the circumstances, I am more determined than before to clear the name of Angus, who was so wrongly accused of taking that girl's life in London.

The Gillie at Braeside assures me that Angus was at the lodge on the weekend of the poor young woman's death in London and that my youngest son could not possibly have been involved in that hideous crime.

I put the Gillie, who gave evidence of Angus innocence – his presence at the lodge, under questioning for a time. The man resolutely told me that Angus was alone during his time at Braeside but when I introduced the possibility of passing money to the man if he were to tell 'the truth' to me the Gillie's story altered subtly.

He now claims that a young woman of undetermined origin accompanied my son to the lodge that weekend. He did not know her name or from where she came, the only clue I was given was that the young woman wore a 'very smart' red dress and had dark hair. More about this woman, the Gillie was unable to say. The Gillie claims that Angus extracted a promise from him that the young woman should not be mentioned, no matter what transpired.

I will pursue the matter in my attempt to clear my poor dead son's good name.

Perhaps such a finding might help poor Isabelle endure her grief at the death of Angus, better?

As I say, I can only pray for James' safe return as I truly believe that the loss of both boys would kill Isabelle – will end the will of each of us to go on but as James so rightly comments, we must bear our fate as best we might.

MacKenzie and Jillings have quite given up serving me.

Instead poor dear little Mary comes. She tells me she has one brother readying to sail for France also. Mercifully, her other siblings are either too young or are engaged in reserved occupations and so must serve their country in the relative quietude of home – waiting as we all wait (heart-stung) for news of the men who battle abroad.

It is strange, I know, but I take comfort in comforting little Mary and assuring her that her brother, Daniel, will return to her as James must return to us – unharmed. I make such vain promises knowing that I can do nothing to ensure their outcome and Mary smiles wanly and shakes her head saying, "I'm sure you're quite right, sir."

My only wish is that I am indeed correct in my assumptions – vain hopes – for I am unsure just how much tragedy the human heart can endure.

I feel a terrible sting as I go off to Edinburgh next week.

My hope is that in meeting with 'F' I can quell a little of the burden of grief I feel and in doing so become more able to comfort my poor distraught Isabelle who seems quite distant now, silent and barely a part of this world.

I have asked that Mary, who is proving to be a comfort to me, might be assigned duties in order to help my wife.

Mrs MacDonald has assured me that the girl is a good choice for such duties. I feel I can do little else for my wife but surround her by those who are well-disposed to her recovery. In truth, I hold out little hope that my wife's despair will lift.

16

Gil read this and I saw a little sadness in his eyes.

"Poor old Angus – no 'young' Angus," Gil managed.

I knew they'd be even more interested when they read the next bits *I'd* hidden but I didn't want to push things. One 'find' a day was pretty good going after all.

"Mary there again," Jenny said quietly.

"She keeps turning up, everywhere," Gil replied. "Like a bad penny. No, I'm wrong. May be she's a *good* luck charm?" the American commented, reading the extract again.

They still hadn't managed to put two and two together. Why should they? Getting as far as *I* have has taken me decades.

We trawled through a load of rubbish before dark started to descend and the American and I left Jenny alone down at the gatehouse.

He was quiet on the way back to the lodge.

"Do you think she'll be OK on her own down there?" I asked attempting to stir things up a little – though God alone knows why.

"Yeah," he replied confidently, but then I saw Gil's head drop. "May be I'll go back. I could stay the night in the spare-room," he said as any gentleman might.

"Aye, woman kid themselves on but you heard the fuss she made about a few wee mice the first day we were up here." I wittered, using any excuse to help in the 'development of this romance' as Hetty would have put it. All the time, I kept thinking 'Whit am I turning into here?'

It was a long walk but the American and I got to the lodge and said good night, shaking hands for some unfathomable reason. I was tired and jaded, frustrated by their slow progress with the research and I've to admit it the long walk I'd had that afternoon had fairly worn me out.

The American went to get his 'bag together' and I saw him walk back down to the gatehouse, striding out happily, a man on a mission – a man with a head full of daft romantic notions, to boot, no doubt. Hetty saw the smirk on my face as I watched him go. I could see him out of the lodge's high windows in our room. Of course, the nosy biddy asked, "What's going on?" high-pitched and eager.

I told Hetty that the American thought Jenny might be a wee bit 'feart' on her own.

I was slow to reply that the American could have a point and that the English woman might be putting on a brave face, down there alone at the gatehouse and then I got tetchy and asked Hetty what business it might be of hers what happened between the two of them anyway. By this time, of course, Hetty had the 'sucking a lemon' look on her face – at once disapproving of any impending jiggery-pokery and delighting, at the same time, in the thought of a 'romance'.

"I just hope he behaves his-self," she replied.

Hetty was packing this morning, getting ready to leave the following day as scheduled. I told her Jenny and Gil wanted me to stay on a few more days to help them out with their research and that going to her sister, Moira, for a 'wee while' would do her good.

"We've been cooped up together the whole holiday," I added.

May be I was a wee bit obvious but I continued, anyhow. "You need a wee break from me," I said.

I should have known by the look on her face she was on to me, "A likely story. Just what are you up to Bill Johnson?"

Hetty was on form this morning and she seemed determined to make me pay for deserting her the day before and for suggesting that I was deserting her again – 'At this time of the year' as she put it.

"It's for the house," I insisted, reverting to the grumpy demeanour I'd taught Hetty to expect from me over the years.

"Well, I'll need a taxi to the train. You better hope it's not a bone shaker like the one on the way up," she warned me, huffy now.

"Aye, I'll insist they get Steve MacQueen to drive you doon the toon," I replied under my breath.

I think she swore at me. I can't be sure as I'd put off my hearing aid as I usually did when I was alone with her and deployed 'selective deafness' as my mental default to boot.

17

By the time I'd got rid of Hetty and staggered down to the gatehouse, Jenny and Gil were dressed and making breakfast together. They looked cosy. He kept smiling at her and I'm sure I saw her blush.

What had happened the night before? I wondered. I was convinced something did, but I'm probably just putting two and two together and making twenty-two. God help me, I may be *turning into* Hetty – perish the thought.

At lunch we talked about our lack of success at finding anything concrete which would take our research further.

"That's mostly the way research goes. Ninety per cent perspiration, etc," Jenny said.

"Och, we're bound to come up with something in the next couple of days," I replied biting into a mouthful of pasta that Jenny had cooked.

The dish was good. I'm not fond of the stuff as a rule but she'd done something to the food to make it not only edible but have a wee bit of taste as well.

"We've been incredibly lucky so far. In my experience it can take months to get to where we are now," Jenny added.

"Months?" asked Gil.

"You don't build a bridge in a day, do you?" Jenny replied as she looked at her plate, stabbing her fork into the food and taking a generous mouthful – some of which tumbled from her lips.

The three of us laughed. I think that was the first time I'd seen her give anything more than a faint smile. Laughter suits Jenny Munroe.

We finished dinner but continued to sit on the uncomfortable kitchen chairs while we drank coffee that Gil had got hold of from the restaurant at the lodge, well the coffee beans anyway. He'd had the kitchen people grind up the coffee beans. I've to admit it was a decent cup of the brown liquid which I usually detest. Jenny was hesitant to take it instead of having her usual herbal.

"You're very careful about your diet, Jen," Gil said, risking another rebuke for calling her by the shortened name version.

Jenny gave her explanation hesitantly. Gil seemed 'all ears' and I've to admit I was interested in her response.

"Allergies. I'm a martyr to them," Jenny smiled again. It was all getting a bit cosy for my liking so I excused myself – what with 'looks' passing between the two of them and the odd wee smile to boot they were sharing, it was no wonder a body felt shy.

I was determined to stir things up this morning on the Lochdarnock story front – ach well, before you know it, it'll be back to Hetty-land.

I made a show of romping around upstairs and I stopped on the way back to our now cosy wee research nest. Once again on my now familiar rounds, I placed a file on the top of the pile just so we could proceed at a brisker pace. I was aware that my time up here was limited, as was the time of the Yank and Ms Munroe.

These two modern people were not in the slightest bit shocked by *Story of Us – Part I*. I hadn't expected them to be – but all the same, their lack of enthusiasm was getting on my nerves.

I wonder if their placid behaviour in relation to the Lochdarnock story had anything to do with them eyeing one-another up. I decided in retrospect that I really should not have encouraged their romance, in the first place. Have you noticed how sex or the potential for sex, gets in the way of progress? The minds of these two were, I felt, not adequately focused on the job at hand, so my decision to 'let out' the next bit of the Lochdarnock story was based on a clear continuity as well as mild irritation.

The two 'researchers' had seemed genuinely enthused by this sudden sad loss suffered by the Lochdarnocks at the demise of poor Angus, in spite of themselves and their wee 'love' interest in one another.

There was still so much missing from the Lochdarnock puzzle and I knew how they felt – both of them eager to get to the bottom of the matter, struggling against their own carnal feelings.

I knew that it had taken me years to put the jigsaw together and that these two didn't have the luxury of waiting for years uninterrupted. And my ineptitude in allowing them to fall for one another was going to bug me.

Added to that, Gil was to travel to Edinburgh in a few days and Jenny had to be back at her job in Glasgow. OK, they could both come back up to Braeside at any time in the near future but there seemed a real urgency about the American and if he'd taken up with the lady – well! Would all that lovey-dovey stuff work in my own interests?

Considering the amount of work I'd put in up until now, I decided I was glad to have planted the next instalment to move the pair on a-pace by recapturing their interest in the drama and tragedy of the tale.

18

THE TALE OF US – PART 3

I watched you the day you were given news of your brother's death. There was extra effort in the way you walked. For an officer you had always slouched about but that day you stood with your head held high and your shoulders back.

That was how I knew there was something wrong.

I made a pretence of bringing back books to you. Just to be close – just to know what it was that was making you act so differently.

I couldn't get to you in Maryhill – the day you found out the terrible news. As usual Anderson was watching me like a hawk but the big 'B' was supposedly re-organising things at the camp, ready for our embarkation to the continent. He was throwing his weight about, as usual.

When I eventually got to you five days after I heard the news you'd had from another officer as it happens, we were in our camp in France. The place was heaving with people and wagons and guns. Tension amongst the men, us seeing all the casualties coming in from the front, was increasing by the minute.

We knew that this war, the war we'd all chosen to come and fight for valour and glory – Christ help us – was going to be anything but those hoped for dreams.

Men with heads shattered by blasts, arms missing, stomach innards hanging out were screaming and moaning, many of them for their mothers and most of them for God.

I have to admit I was frightened but how must it have been for you – knowing that your brother had taken his last breath, I still cannot imagine?

I remember you telling me after the war, when I came back finally, that you had gone to a lot of trouble to find out the details of how Angus died. You said you'd thought it would have been a banal kind of passing like most of the deaths in that horror story, but that you had found that Angus had really been as brave as the commendations had mentioned and that your parents had been right to treasure his bravery medal and position it in the most esteemed place they could find in the house.

Your brother who had always been such a problem to your family in life, in death had actually been a genuine hero, saving lives and in the process making you feel closer to him than you ever had. I think that was because at last you recognised something of yourself in your brother and that it had been proven to you completely that 'the apple never falls too far from the tree' after all. It had probably always been there, James, Angus' basic decency. Poor man – boy – had just been living in your shadow for so long there was no way he could properly show what kind of man he actually was until the war gave him the chance. It was like that for a lot of men. That's why you carry so much pain, I think. It's kind of good to know that it is not just Catholics like me who wrestle with guilt – but you shouldn't you know, that last letter your mother had from Angus showed that he recognised you as the man you truly are.

I remember entering the officers' rooms and being pushed back by a sergeant – not Anderson, thank God, as I would have come away from the incident with fewer teeth, I am sure.

I stood my ground with the sergeant and told him I had to deliver the last two books you'd lent me to you personally. I was marched in and you looked up at me. Your eyes were red and swollen. I put the books in front of you and you dismissed the Sergeant who seemed more than willing to walk away. I suppose the man recognised your grief and had an understandable urge to flee it.

"Sit down," you said. Your voice was strange.

"I'm sorry," I said.

You nodded – and then nodded again before the tears overcame you.

I have to confess, I didn't know what to do. I remember I said I was sorry again (no imagination at times, me) and then you started talking and I couldn't stop you. I felt like a priest so I talked like I thought a priest would talk. You wiped your eyes as someone knocked on the door and you handed me some other books to make things look good and I left not knowing whether my words had made a difference. I thought about you all that day and the next and I wished I could take some of that pain you were suffering and that's when I knew for sure!

19

"What do you think?" Gil asked Jenny, who was matter-of-fact in her response.

"Yes, it confirms what we know. James Lochdarnock and Danny Cassidy had an affair."

"The old Scots in my family reserve a particular expression for that kind of response and the person who makes it," Gil said smiling indulgently.

I, of course, played the innocent, knowing what was coming. I had been as surprised by Jenny's response as the big Yank. She wasn't exactly cold but there was something clinical in her reserved reply.

"Girl's got a swinging brick!" Gil uttered in feigned shock.

"What?" Jenny asked.

Gil was looking at me, perhaps for support.

If the girl had had a brick – swinging or otherwise – it would have interfaced with Gil Delaney's skull. The look on her face could only be read as intent to 'gub' the Yank! She said nothing about understanding his point completely and at last the Yank got the message that he should shut up.

He seemed to be taking pleasure in teasing her. I would never have risked it. The Yank cannot smell danger even when it's under his nose and he clearly does not know women.

"So *this* is the 'white volcano' look Jaz talked about, uh?" Gil asked smiling.

I thought him brave but stupid.

Thankfully, Jenny turned on her heel and left the room quite dramatically for her. I wondered if I should go after her but decided to sit mute now, watching Gil's response.

He said nothing. After a minute he hung his head and asked me, "A step too far? I'll go see her." The lanky Yank got up, leaving me alone.

They were gone a good while. I adjusted my hearing aid in the hope of catching something of their exchange.

Frighteningly, I was indeed turning into a male version of Hetty and corrected myself so I pulled away from making that mistake and used their absence as an excuse to put on top of the pile the few fragments that would lead them ahead – placing these bits neatly together.

I know that I should be ashamed and embarrassed to admit it but I caught a glimpse of Jenny's diary the next day!

It revealed nothing – nonetheless if Hetty knew about my antics there would be hell to pay, after all the years of me berating her for being a nosy auld biddy, I can just hear her reaction to my actions now: "Looking in the old diaries of dead people is one thing but this Bill Johnston!"

And she'd be right, of course. I just don't seem able to help myself. Is there something about tying up loose ends going on for me or is Hetty's assessment right, am I really just a 'nosy, dottled auld man'?

I was reading an article recently about how we're all autistic. It's very fashionable to claim you are 'on the spectrum' these days, apparently. But may be mankind has always been prone to categorising and organising things into some kind of coherent whole. Is that not why the Celts are storytellers in the first place? I think it is. We've an overwhelming desire to have that beginning, middle and end to things.

I wonder if other cultures are the same. I'm not sure, from what I've read, that they are. By all accounts, the Hindus can leave things 'floating about', like the Buddhists, for millennia but us, oh no – we like it tidy, each story tied up in a nice wee bundle with a tendency to the predictable. No ragged edges in our soap operas. Resolution is our catharsis, what we crave, even if everybody's dead on the stage at the end at least we know it *is* the end and that there will be a new tale in the offing.

The current question being, of course, where all the latest finds in the Lochdarnock archive would take our story.

20

Time was up.

I didn't have the heart to get them unearthing more of the Lochdarnock story before we all had to head back to town, Jenny and me to Glasgow and Gil to his stay in Edinburgh.

The poor man was about to tackle the family records' office there in the Capital. I didn't envy him – soul destroying stuff, research-wise – but may be that's just me who thinks in that way. I've never found out the really meaty business at the research centres in Edinburgh and as you know, being old and death standing outside my door, I'm impatient these days for solid progress.

I was regretting not giving Gil Delaney IV my writings on Kenneth Ewart.

Yes, I know quite a lot about that boy too. But the vile Kenneth's link with Lochdarnock was tenuous and I put the material I had on the Ewarts and Kenneth in particular, behind me many years ago. Much of what I knew about Kenneth Ewart I'd forgotten and something in me did not want to think too much about that man, if I could help it.

We all took the same taxi back to the station.

Jenny and I had a long wait for our train as a result of

accompanying the American whose Edinburgh train arrived some forty minutes earlier than our Glasgow train.

Gil left us both on the platform with a shake of the hand for me and an embarrassed peck on the cheek for Jenny, an action which was received with surprise more than joy. I was wishing the two of them would just get on with it, having revised my view about how close they'd got 'that night'– I know he's interested, that's clear but then who knows if the lovely Jenny is in the slightest bit interested in him – she shows nothing. The girl is either a very good actress or not at all in the mood to become involved with the Yank, she's that 'cool'. Gil, well – he's an open book – another Bridget Riley – och, I haven't mentioned her yet, have I? You'll need to wait and see where that girl fits into the story too.

Aye, back to Gil Delaney IV! What can I say? Poor sod – is a man standing about with his heart on his sleeve, just waiting for it to be stabbed.

I had, as I say, peppered the remainder of files with juicy bits of documentation. I imagined now it would be something for Jenny to uncover when she was up at the lodge again – next month, she says – or that was certainly my best hope.

The matter turned out better than that. Jenny Munroe had had the Yank and the cabbie cart three boxes down from the gatehouse to the station. It was a wee bit of a fuss getting the boxes on and off the train at either end, especially as the American had disappeared before the arrival of the Glasgow train but the guard was helpful and the struggle we had will be worth it, no doubt. The truth of the matter is, I can't wait to get to the house after next weekend to see what progress the Munroe girl is making.

Jenny and I parted at Central Station. I took the train home to Hetty – a short journey from Central Station – and Jenny hopped in a cab to Lochdarnock House, the cab piled high with boxes and luggage, of course.

I definitely *wanted* to see her again before she went back up to Braeside but I guessed that I wouldn't be that lucky, having to justify my presence at the house by actually doing what I was supposed to do there in terms of voluntary work.

Jenny Munroe had taken my e.mail address on the train, out of politeness more than anything else I'll be bound, saying she would contact me if anything of interest came up. I was doubtful I'd hear from her. I felt a real pang of loss when she took off in the blue motor (the overladen shabby cab) which charged on to Lochdarnock House, Ms Munroe and precious archive aboard. The American, I guess, will be more forthcoming – wanting to share his triumphs with even an old man like me.

I was surprised to find that I was pleased to see Hetty when I got home. The biddy was in a good mood when I arrived. She'd made steak-pie for tea. Hetty's an accomplished baker of pies. I'm told the success of the pastry comes by way of her cold hands – to go with the woman's heart, obviously.

I am told that it was 3 a.m. – the day following her return to Lochdarnock House – when Jenny found the next instalment I'd secreted in the boxed files she had by now piled up in a corner of her office at the house. She hadn't been able to sleep, so she reports, again. Jenny tells me she had considered calling Gil and me – thinking we, too, might still be awake at that ungodly hour.

Thankfully, the girl decided against making contact at that time – the New Year up at the lodge had taken it out of me and I was catching up on rest and according to Hetty snoring like the proverbial pig all that night.

On the other hand, I'd to wait a full week before I heard from the Yank. I was not expecting much from him by way of information old or new. I was to be pleasantly surprised.

Indeed, it was the Yank who caught my interest rather than the lady when he told the story of his progress – aye, there was a surprising revelation waiting for me that I could never have anticipated and, I can tell you, it put all the efforts and progress I had made on all things Lochdarnock into the pale.

In the meanwhile, the Delaney boy and I got the material by email as promised in the morning following Jenny Munroe's fitful night of sleep.

Of course, what she had found was 'hot' interesting stuff, they would say but obviously nothing I hadn't seen before.

21

Coming back to Glasgow the first time on leave was hard. I knew my mother would be appalled by the state I was in, it was partly your fault – it had been months since you'd been shipped out. I had no idea where they'd taken you. I'd missed you and my face showed this in its exhausted and fallen expression. The first thing my ma' noticed, however, was my hair.

"Yer goin' grey." She was nearly weeping over a few grey hairs – Christ! Having been through filth and dirt fighting in France, a few stray greys hardly mattered to me.

The tenements of Shamrock Street (and I don't doubt those across the whole city) were quiet. Too many boys and men had been shipped out to death and disease across Europe. It was the women who paid the price at home – things were terrible in Shamrock Street and many other roads like it, I'm sure. The deprivations being devastating before the war were undoubtedly made so much less bearable during the conflict.

My mother was lucky. Pat, Martin and my da had reserved jobs and were home safe, if not entirely sound. They were not men to complain about much but mentions of hunger were frequent. For

Annie, she had only me 'abroad' to worry about so I suppose she put all her angst into me and my 'heid of white-peppered hair'.

I don't think the family had seen me so silent since that time in 1912 when I'd tried to get away but was dragged back up from England by our Martin. You'll remember I told you that tale.

What was it you called my mother – 'manipulative'. Aye, that was Annie. She liked to get her way by fair means or foul. Her way when I got home from France was to feed me up. Poor Da and Martin never got a look in and discussion about their 'bellies thinking their throats had been cut' seemed to quadruple by the day.

Patrick and Elizabeth were married now so our Pat, the apple of Annie's eye, was not denied rations for my benefit like the other two men folk on the home front. The couple, Patrick and Elizabeth, had had their first and second child by now – Alice and wee Paddy – and seemed happy – no – more like content, I envied them. Martin was courting a nice girl, Sarah, our Mary was still working away at the house as a personal maid to your mother now and my younger sisters were as innocent and skittish as ever. They were all so normal and there I was in amongst them making these good people increasingly hushed and miserable, or so it seemed to me at the time, by my mere presence.

Our Mary turned up at the end of a tense week for me and no doubt for the rest of my family – it must have been a Sunday. You people only give the staff a short time off on Sunday to see their family and go to church – good of you toffs, eh?

Mary had a letter from your mother which I've tucked in here for you to read. It came beautifully written on posh paper – I treasure that letter. I can't tell you how happy and suddenly full of life that communication made me feel.

I hoped that maybe my silence would lift after I got the letter from your mother and that I'd find something to say to my folk, other than "Aye, the tea's fine". I knew my behaviour was alien to them. I hated myself for it. But I was exhausted and had nothing left to give by way of comfort to them. Bad, eh?

I looked at your mother's letter again and again, with the pages sitting there in my lap. Finally, I was to be given a chance to see you. My mother was glad to see me smile at last, I think she thought my smile revealed that I somehow felt privileged to be asked up to the posh House to be patted on the back for my so called courage. And all I could think of was that I was to see you again!

As I say, your mother's letter came beautifully written on posh paper – I treasure that letter still.

***

Pte Daniel Cassidy c/o Miss Mary Cassidy

Dear Mr Cassidy

Your sister, Mary, who is a treasured member of our household staff, has told me of your safe return to your family here in Glasgow.

I know that your stay is temporary, hence the urgency of this letter. I must say that I am much relieved to hear that you are in good health and I hope that you will enjoy a deserved rest in Scotland before returning to duty with your regiment later this month.

Mr Cassidy, it is apparent that your actions saved the life of my son, James, whom I believe you know.

There are not words to thank you for your courage in removing James to safety in what must have been the most difficult of circumstances.

I understand that you will be decorated for your efforts. I must say that we are most pleased to hear such welcome news.

Thank you seems so inadequate a phrase with which to convey the depth of our appreciation. We should, therefore, very much like to be able to thank you in person and would be grateful if you might join us for afternoon tea on Sunday at four o'clock.

Do please accept this invitation.

With heartfelt regards,

Isabelle Lochdarnock

***

Danny Cassidy's writing continued to tell their story:

***

That Sunday, I had been polished to within an inch of my life having had my ma' lavish almost brutal attention to my face and neck especially. It wasn't so much that 'cleanliness was next to Godliness' as that in my ma's opinion a good thrashing was due to us all collectively at the hands of Annie Cassidy for the crime of us being poor and shabby and not at all up to the standard to which she aspired and to that standard that she imagined your mother lived.

I walked back to the house with Mary who had been visiting Shamrock Street that day. Mary disappeared into the kitchen – we'd come in the tradesman's entrance to the big house.

Bob MacKenzie told me later Mr Jillings got into trouble for not taking me in through the front door as was befitting the entry of a 'most welcome' guest. To Jilling's surprise, Lady Isabelle was extending full gentility towards a weeyin like me. I have to say, my feelings of being welcomed and esteemed deserted me when I came face to face with you, James.

Your mother was more than polite and took a lot of trouble to put me at my ease.

I, however, was feeling arrogant and put out having to look around at the opulence of Lochdarnock House. I wanted to torch the place, thinking how dare they live like this… Well you know how I felt and still do feel about such pompous displays of privilege.

In spite of my feelings of distrust and disgust, I could not help but like your mother and I could tell she loved the bones of you, and that gave me and Lady Isabelle more than a little common ground.

I spent most of the time with her marvelling at the look of her perfect skin and her resemblance to you. After she'd plied me with tea and silly wee sandwiches which wouldn't have filled a hole in yer teeth for about half an hour, she rang the bell.

It was Jillings who answered and she requested that he tell 'Master James' that a guest was waiting in the 'Morning Room' for him.

Jillings looked me up and down as if to say "What kind of guest might this be?" but I stared straight back at him in defiance. I didn't see a sign of a soldier about the man and I wasn't about to be taking guff from the likes of him, that was for sure.

When you came into the room, walking unsteadily with your stick you looked at me as if you'd seen something despicable. Part of me wanted to shrink into the overstuffed, over-comfortable chair my bony backside was occupying. I think your mother was the more shocked by your reaction to the sight of me.

"And why are you here, Private?" was all you could muster with a snarl when you saw me.

"James!" your mother rebuked you with a tone and a look usually reserved I imagine for anyone in the world but you.

You walked over to a sideboard and poured yourself a drink, failing to offer either me or your mother a glass – very bad manners for a well brought up boy, I thought.

You turned towards me. I could see you were struggling to keep your temper. It hadn't occurred to me that you'd be embarrassed, ashamed even, by your predicament. It never occurred to me that any man should be ashamed of the loss of a limb caused by war – stupid of me. I've to admit it has taken me a while to understand that men, the good men of the war, feel like this. As you know, I've never been blessed in my abilities at guess work.

"You were ordered to leave me!" you almost shouted.

"I was, sir," I said, now standing to attention in front of you.

I admit that I was, though, more bothered about your poor mother who had by now slumped into a chair and looked as if she needed help more than you had that morning in France.

'Fuck him.' I thought. 'Ungrateful bastard, treating me and his mother like this.'

My face, however, betrayed nothing. After dealing with the Andersons and other sadists in the army, you were easy to cope with. After all, what were you about to do – have me thrown out? I knew your mother would never allow that – I could tell that the last half hour of my time had been spent in the company of a woman of decency. You, on the other hand, had one of what I've come to recognise as 'your outbursts'.

"You will go this time, Private," you ordered and then you lost your balance.

The glass fell from your hand as you attempted to correct yourself and I found myself at your side holding you up. It was then I saw you had a temper and a half, for the first time, and I've to admit I liked what I saw. It showed you had spark, that you were real.

You made an attempt to hit me in the face. All I could think of was my ma's look when I walked back to Shamrock Street with a black eye.

I ducked or you misjudged the punch, and you, instead, fell on me. I tried to stand you upright but you weren't budging from my shoulder which you clung to, hurting me, you dug your fingers into me through the serge of my uniform. All I wanted to do in response was hold you, just hold you and let you know everything was all right.

Your mother just sat there watching us. I didn't care. This was where I'd wanted you to be for so long – your head on my shoulder, the two of us holding on to one another for balance as well as dear life, just as we'd done on the battlefield in France that day. It's a strange thing to say that it felt right, but it did.

It was your mother who spoke first.

"Mr Cassidy, would you be so kind as to escort my son to his room? I fear he is feeling rather unwell."

Do you think she sensed it? Do you think she knew of our love of one another? I like to think so.

Whatever the truth of it, she seemed unperturbed by our closeness, even glad of it. You came upstairs with me like a lamb. I didn't know where I was taking you. I was half concentrating on holding on to you and the other part of my mind was taken by all those portraits and pictures hanging about us – showing many of your ancestors, as well as the old Spanish nobles looking down at us – dour men – young and old alike – I imagined they knew what was about to happen between us and disapproved.

You directed me to your room, clinging to me. We finally sat on your bed, the biggest bed I'd ever seen up until that point in my life. I remember stroking your face, wiping away the tears that were streaming down your cheeks leaving little canals of silvery fluid on your face.

Hoarsely you said, "I just want to die."

To be honest, you can be a wee bit dramatic and wearing at times.

"No you don't," I replied. "I'm no' gonnae allow that, sir."

You laughed at the sarcasm in my "Sir." And that's when you leaned over and kissed me. It was the velvety kiss I've come to recognise, soft and restrained, no urgency in it. I responded gladly. I can't remember how we both came to be naked but I do recollect stroking your left leg, or what there remains of it after that artillery shell hit you. You began to cry again.

"It's fine," I said.

There was a pleading look in your eyes which asked, "Do you really mean that?" You know now that I do, that I always did and always will.

I pushed you back on the bed. Your head was on the pillow now – your long body outstretched over the massive bed. I ran my tongue down your body from your neck to your right foot and then up and across your torso and down your left side, as I had done a million times *in my imagination before. I felt you shiver as I repeated this contact again and again. Our love-making lasted an hour or so until we were both totally worn out, having kissed and touched and held one another in moaning embrace. You asked me after if you were my first.*

I replied, "Yes."

You smiled and asked me if I meant 'boy' and I told you 'either'''. Of course, I knew that I was not your first but the fact is that it did not matter to me. On my reply, we both said "I'm glad" at the same time and laughed.

When I got to my feet, you directed me to the washstand where a jug of cold water lay ready for me to do my ablutions. I was reluctant to wash the traces of you off my body. You watched me the whole time, smiling. Eventually, you apologised for the coldness of the water and started to explain that it would be hard to ask a servant for hot water in the circumstances and we both laughed again, nervously – me shivering this time from the cold. I told you that normal people were used to washing in unheated water. "The servants bringing hot water for yous – Christ!" I said, and pulled a face.

You replied, "I imagine you're right."

It's funny but you always watch me that way, even now when I'm washing myself. Have you noticed you have that habit?

When I'd finished getting myself ready, I brought a soap-laden cloth over to the bed and cleaned you up. I watched goosebumps appear on your skin. The appearance of the marks made us both smile so we kissed again, rid now of the evidence of our love-making but looking at one another, talking, making plans for our future. A future that all seemed so ridiculous – that day, a dream – the dream of going up to Braeside and walking with dogs and jaunts in a car and writing our political pamphlets and reading books. So stupid our thinking then, so stupid to think it would be easy. A war was going on around us, death and destruction were everywhere and yet we dreamed on, mapping out our easy life – and so far, so far it has been just that, do you not think?

You drew me closer to you, touching me. I remember those feelings as you touched me. I was aroused again, hard for you and wanted to stay all night making love to you, licking you, kissing you, our creamy fluids mixing blissfully on our warm bodies once again. But I knew I had to leave sometime and I went, leaving the room, all the time looking back at you lying naked on the bed, naked and ready for me if I had chosen to stay – I was so glad of our closeness that day.

Three days later I was departing Glasgow to go back to hell – leaving you and this heaven our minds had invented far behind.

22

The atmosphere was prickly now. I was on edge as if I knew, somewhere in the deep recesses of my mind, that I needed to get my material together, to put things in order so the story as I knew it could be told. It was as if this were my last chance to make the Lochdarnock story coherent.

I was aware when I was sorting out the mess that was my study that what I was driven by was a certain feeling of dread – well not so much dread but a sureness, whatever the events, that I needed to get my life's work (if I were pompous to call it that) organised.

Hetty had headed out with her friends that afternoon to have tea at The Burrell. 'The Ladies', her 'pile of biddy buddies' as I called them, had gone off as a group to Spain for the New Year – can you imagine it? A bunch of widowed octogenarians quaffing the sangria and dancing flamenco badly – and with what the young call – attitude! I had no doubt Hetty'd be reporting back to them on our wee holiday at Braeside, transforming herself into quite the raconteur and country dance expert into the bargain. The time spent at Braeside seems to have been poor Hetty's attempt to make her New Year celebration as 'thrilling' as the 'piles'.

Me – I took the opportunity not only to tidy up stuff in my

office but to go over some files from decades back – the 1960s and 1970s – when it was quite the new thing to delve into social history, as opposed to researching kings and queens and the Nobility of old. Aye, folk like me became keen to have *our* story told – believing that the lives of ordinary men and women were just as significant as the lives of the toffs. It is funny how you forget the changing fashions in academia and just 'how times have moved on'! Yes, men (and women for that matter) like me became fairly determined that *our* people would have, at least a cursory, mention in the story of how times rolled and came about in what we thought back in those heady days may become a truly equal society. Wrong again. Have you noticed, I've made a career out of failure to get things right?

That generation – my father's and grandfather's to be precise – seemed to me then to be a step above the mere mortals of my heyday. What those souls suffered in the First War would make me weep, silently in the privacy of my own home, away from Hetty and her campaigns for the purchasing of new-fangled turbo dryers and colour TVs. All her consumer ambitions were to me an insult to those men, and no doubt women too, who had preceded us.

As you'll gather, I'm a Puritan at heart – and, no, I was never ambitious with the writing I'm about to reveal. I was penning it more to keep my mind active than anything else.

I suppose the truth is that I was just plain bored that day stuck up in my wee room I'd the cheek to call my study, due to the lovely Jenny and big Gil going off on their separate roads to track down the Lochdarnock story. May be I was also putting what those two and I had so far gleaned into a wider social perspective – or am I just kidding myself?

Whatever the case, I was definitely keeping occupied with the task in hand and I was glad to have the peace to do it with Hetty conveniently carousing out of my way.

Here I go again, avoiding the truth, the fact of the matter is that I had a kind of inkling that things were about to undergo a dramatic change and I felt a real urge to put matters, my things, in order – this is the kind of stuff I hate to admit – that kind of thinking seems so primitive, does it not? So I began sorting out 'my material' as I've come to regard it, making a damn mess of the wee upstairs office in the process. I knew there would be hell when the old woman got back from her jaunt but I simply did not care a damn, the urgency I felt was so great.

Reading through the old material I produced, I am not sure about the style of my own writing (self-conscious stuff to say the least.) Thinking back I may have embellished some of the details in the accounts I wrote back then but when I found out about that rail disaster, the worst in British History, it stunned me, it really did. I was left feeling sick to the stomach and in the mood to humanise the tragic event and immortalise it's heroes as soon as I became aware of all the details. Ah, the enthusiasm of youth!

Do you think this need to organise the past has any true significance and if so, what might that be? Ach, ye'll make up your own mind about that stuff as you read it. The truth is I was determined now with the latest revelations, to make my material (the general stuff I'd researched way back when) available to Jenny and Gil. In my mind I was sure they would be interested in it, once they'd completed their ever expanding task in assessing all things Lochdarnock around the First War, right enough.

As if it hadn't been enough that I was so involved in unlocking the Lochdarnock's story, I had had to delve into the criminal negligence of governments which forsook the ordinary men and women back in the day.

I suppose that's why I had been arrogant enough to write up the historical material.

At the time, I remember, my purpose was to let people know just how little regard for human life had been shown on all sides at that particular point in time and how 'they' (the ordinary people) suffered as a result of the despicable disregard there had been for human life by society's masters.

Is it any better now, I wonder.

Given what has come out about recent wars and conflicts, I doubt it. I suppose the social conditions suffered then, the discomforts and humiliations seemed worse – well to me, anyhow.

The dead were, as now, turned into heroes. The maimed were merely ignored. We seem to be doing a bit better on that front, at least. But on we go. Sending the poor (poor) sods off to war – again and again. For what purpose, you might ask.

As I say, the original piece I'd come across which had shaken me up was that rail disaster.

23

Pt. Walter Walker 7th Battalion Royal Scots came round, his head pounding and his vision blurred. The sight of twisted metal and a terrible smell – a burning smell – assaulted his senses. He passed out again. The next time Walter became conscious an officer was standing over him pouring water on his face, which caused Walter to struggle unsteadily to his feet in response to the officer's urgings.

"We've corpses to carry, soldier," the officer commanded, ashen-faced.

The officer, too, had sustained an injury to his leg or foot, Walter's blurred vision made it difficult to tell which part of the fellow's anatomy was affected, all Walter could really see was that the man's right lower limb was doused in blood.

The young captain limped painfully amongst the bodies ordering Walter to heave the corpses "as best you can". The two carried the bodies of several dead soldiers and a train guard away from the wreckage and lay them on the trackside. Walter realised neither he nor the officer knew what they were doing let alone why they were doing it.

After what seemed an eternity, Walter felt suddenly overwhelmed, fighting back tears. The young private hadn't cried in many a year and didn't intend starting now he was a man of nineteen.

It seemed hours before fresh men arrived to aid them (Walter and the young captain) in their mission. The rescue soldiers did their best to comfort those still living and remove casualties and bodies alike from the midst of the scene but it was a tricky and exhausting task.

A woman was weeping and Walter heard a blackbird cry – he'd always loved the song of blackbirds. When he passed out for a second time Walter Walker would not awaken again. The young captain, injured and as yet dazed, bent over the corpse, closed Walter's eyes on the wrecked world and proceeded to organise the walking wounded and encourage them to further feats beyond their physical capabilities. At the end of the long day, Captain Perth found himself wandering like a ghost amongst the wrecked trains and debris.

Peter Perth was eighty-six years old when he died and had remembered Walter Walker's face and the man's courage and determination every morning on waking for the rest of his long life.

In Liverpool that night the 7th Battalion (Royal Scots) arrived allegedly ready for embarkation to Turkey. The ragged men were dazed and tired, their uniforms charred and filthy. Captain Perth approached an M.O. he recognised and called out.

"Charles, Charles," the young man insisted. "These men are… they simply are not to be sent abroad. You can see for yourself."

Charlie Hathaway looked up as he spoke. "The 7th. Bloody fiasco."

Perth found himself relaxing, having at last encountered a man willing to pay attention to him.

As Charlie Hathaway re-bandaged Perth's right leg, assuring him that the 7th would never be deemed fit for transportation, Hathaway pulled a face in lieu of a smile, a smile that would not, could not, come at a time like this.

"We'll have the men back in Scotland by morning," Hathaway continued determinedly, strapping Perth's ankle tightly.

Major Charles Hathaway was a decent man and a good doctor. There was no doubt of that. He died in November 1917 from gunshot wounds – face-down in a filthy ditch somewhere in France. His body was buried in France in a marked grave and stone-faced visitors still view his headstone to this day with due reverence and respect.

***

Self-conscious, yes. But the interview I had with Captain Perth in the 1970s had had a profound effect on me at the time.

I attended Peter Perth's funeral some years later, uninvited. I just had to be there to make sure they gave the old man his due at the last.

In the event his family was solemn and dutifully respectful. It appeared that they had genuine affection for the old soldier and I was glad to be able to fill in some of the gaps in their knowledge of his heroism for them at the wake.

I got the impression that his son felt a little envious that the old man had opened up to me, a stranger, during what was only a short visit I had once paid to him when I was doing a project on the First War – but his daughter was delighted and smiled through her tears to hear of her 'dear daddy's exploits' as she called them.

On the occasions I feel jaded by life, I remember the Walter Walkers, Peter Perths, and Charlie Hathaways of this world and spirits lifted I go back to my own soft life gladdened that they came before us sappy mortals, in the heady chronology of time.

Generation on generation we are becoming softer and more cosseted. What would happen now if we had to face the sort of trauma those men of the twentieth century endured? Christ, we'd all be sitting in TV studios waiting to be interviewed tearfully on camera and allocated a psychotherapist paid for, of course, by the production company filming us.

I've views on that kind of thing too – you'd never have

guessed, I'm sure! Modern freak shows, that's what I call them. The poor souls of today, the impoverished spirits with their tattoos and toothless mouths, drug and drink problems and jelly-bellies are exposed along with the lurid details of their chaotic lives just so that bored housewives and part-time workers earning nothing more than minimum wage (and on 'zero hours contracts') can feel superior to someone – anyone – at last.

Aye, well – it's not so much the viewers I take issue with as the be-suited hosts of these programmes who berate the angry messes they interview whilst having the bare-faced cheek to refer to the poor souls as 'my friend' – if those duped folk think for a minute that 'friendship' is what they're about to get then that misrepresentation and exploitation is doubly cruel.

Imagine making a trade like that! Fifteen minutes of fame in exchange for an eternity of your worst faults exposed for public scorn and pleasure is surely not a good deal in any man's calculations. Oh! Aye, I've a hunch that wee Danny Cassidy would have something to say about that kind of stuff, loudly and with gusto. And James Lochdarnock – my God that articulate and driven sod would have taken the show's producers and hosts to pieces on camera without a hair on his handsome, patrician head moving out of place in the process. Those boys were quite a pairing in their time, I'm damn sure of that.

My research into their war (Danny and James') was not extensive so a lot of what I've written was supplemented by imagination and best guesses and the certain knowledge I had managed to glean from my father before he passed away. The relevant facts about battles and the men's bravery are, as the American's would say, 'for real'.

YPRES – FRANCE – 23RD MAY 1915

"Whit the hell are you doing here, Billy Johnson?" Daniel Cassidy asked, berating himself rather than the boy who stood in front of him

uniformed on a French field. Each of them wiped the mud from their face. Danny Cassidy continued berating the boy. Hating himself for making wee Billy's miserable life even worse.

"Christ, I shoulda told them at the start when ye came te Maryhill ye were a wean."

"Come on noo, Dan. I'm seventeen," Billy replied, puffing out his chest in a way he thought manly.

"I worked wi' yer da, Billy. Yer just sixteen, if that, and should not be here." Daniel wondered why he was torturing Billy with this scolding, sometimes he heard his mother in himself. He tried to stop. What was the use? It was too late. Like it or not the boy was here – in the trenches ready to die with the rest of them.

"You know why I'm here. My ma has four weans te keep and nay wages comin' in. Ewart widnae take me on after ma da died," replied Billy Johnson, over the noise. Danny Cassidy's head dropped. He couldn't help feeling responsible for making the fuss he did. He told himself he had to face the fact that what he'd actually done had made things worse for Violet and the children. A picture of the boy's father's dead body lying spiked through entered Danny Cassidy's mind as it did so often. He took a breath and tried consciously to remove the image.

"Bastard!" Daniel spat, closing his eyes. "No, no' you, Billy son. My heid is full o'... Just you keep close to me. Ye hear, Billy? Nay heroics, heid doon and oot o' this mess quick, right!"

Billy smiled and replied, "Me, I'll be running like fuck, Dan."

Danny Cassidy patted the boy's shoulder. Further discussion seemed impossible – the strain of trying to talk took up too much energy that would be needed later. The men contented themselves with smiling or grimacing at one another or gesturing wildly or quietly depending on their character. Eddie Sanders was close by handing round cigarettes and an awful-smelling concoction which passed as tea here in the trenches. There was little to eat and what there was tasted vile and corrupted.

James Lochdarnock was a few yards away, awaiting instructions from the Generals organising strategy for the conflict – miles behind where James and his men were posted in this hostile landscape. The whistle to call the men to action hung about James Lochdarnock's neck like a rigor mortised silvery minnow.

The men and officers alike were lying on hard, saturated sandbags. James' thoughts turned inevitably and unoriginally to Dante's Inferno and Bosch's pictorial representations of a particular kind of modernist Hades which the precocious artist had delivered century's prior to Europe 1915 and the current hell being played out here.

James wondered why at a time like this, a time when the practicalities of keeping his men safe, should art be uppermost in his mind. The young lieutenant wished often he was more like Coburn – a career soldier intent upon dealing with each matter as it arose in the hideous conflict, practically and clearly. James' own mind wandered perhaps in an attempt to escape this, this unmentionable, unnameable Hades.

James Lochdarnock longed to see Braeside – his 'Eden' – and he checked himself yet again, realising too much longing might well lead to the wrong kind of paradise being realised. Young and inexperienced as he was, he knew that much. He smiled at the thought of death – what else could a man do? He and his men would simply have to endure the horrendous tension, the soaking conditions, the mud, coldness, stench and the ugliness of it all. It would, after all, be over... soon. Quite soon he would end up in one kind of paradise or another. Whether that would be Braeside or a Bourne from which none of them might return was not yet calculable, he knew. The corporal's phone registered that there was the expected call at last and it was this shrill noise which shook James from his musings.

Corporal Klein, Israel Klein, was a thin young man, bright and alert and a considerable asset to Lieutenant James Lochdarnock. Klein's technical expertise and his ability to improvise with machinery had proven invaluable thus far on James' hideous war journey. It was obvious to James that putting Klein in charge of communications was a wise idea, if not one supported by Lt. Lochdarnock's NCOs.

The barbaric Anderson hated Klein with almost as much vehemence as he reserved for Daniel Cassidy, which was a hatred to be reckoned with. James failed utterly to understand the old sergeant's venom for either man.

"A mere Yid, sir," Anderson had yelled when James raised the issue of Israel's involvement in communications. "A clever one mind, I'll grant you, sir. But, aren't they all those children of Abraham?"

James found it hard to mask his distaste for the anti-Semite – the inhuman sergeant – he had been saddled with.

Lt. Lochdarnock and Klein sat close together, taking incoming instructions as they leaned over the heavy lump of machinery which then passed as a radio. James heard the orders and was trying not to over-think them before being suddenly struck by the thought that if he didn't think then nobody would.

"Christ!" said James loudly on receiving instructions that the men were to push forward as day fell – they, their superiors, would call again to repeat the order in good time, he was assured.

Klein, though not an orthodox Jew, wasn't sure if Christ was listening even if he could be proven to exist in some spiritual Valhalla as yet unrevealed. James atheism, his religion of non-belief, was taking a battering also. He, too, was unsure if Christ was listening but somehow, of late, he had begun hoping that God or Christ, or at the very least someone with earthly authority would pay heed to all this suffering.

Klein smiled at James. "What are you thinking?" asked the lieutenant.

"Same as your man at Calvary, sir," answered the quick-witted Klein feeling similarly forsaken.

"Have you an answer?" James asked.

"I've an argument," replied Klein, "but it would be a pointless one. We're in the shit and that's that."

Israel Klein was married with three children. He had worked in a foundry before the war and was resilient, or had thought he was until he turned up here. This place where he had taken to asking himself what this bloody thing was all for seemed absurd in every definition of that word.

He consoled himself with the thought that the war was something to do with creating a better future and keeping his little family safe. Sometimes Israel became exasperated by himself, his people, and their constant referral to tomorrow, when somehow things would be magically easier. His people! Hadn't history shown them over and over again that things never became easier – only awful in different ways? Were they ever to learn the lesson? Yet, Klein – somehow – like the rest of his clan continued to strive. Israel wanted a better life for his children, a better life and a better world. Klein's problem was that he was unsure that warring with Germany would achieve the kind of world he craved but there was, at the present time, he reasoned, no alternative but to be here and ensure the Allies won.

The other men liked Israel even though he prayed to a God so clearly unseated by Christianity – yes, Israel Klein could be counted on. So, in the minds of the men around him, Israel Klein was one of their Clan too.

In the dark of night, Israel sat alone arguing with his God and feeling a certain sympathy for the children of Christ who were simply expected to endure whatever their god chose for them, in the hope that their afterlife would be better.

At least, he reasoned, he Israel, was not duping himself as completely as his Jesus loving counterparts – not in his own mind anyway. His unmerciful god allowed analysis, criticism and fury. Perhaps this was his people's strength? Yes! They could argue the odds with God. They may never win the argument but they had a freedom these poor Christians could not imagine.

Israel liked that idea, his freedom was in his thoughts and that would endure, that knowledge would help him scramble up the mountain and take him to the top. He laughed, flicking an annoying louse from his shoulder.

"What's the joke?" James shouted across at him.

"I'm beginning to think like a Christian, sir," replied Israel loudly with a smile.

"Seems I've been listening to too many of yer bloody hymns," Klein breathed in before smiling again and singing loudly "Onward Christian fucking soldiers and all that…"

Daniel Cassidy interrupted the corporal. "What's goin' on here?" They men are done in. Are we movin'?"

James saw Daniel but hadn't heard his question. The officer struggled sideways on his backside to Cassidy's position.

"Tell the men to get some rest," said James loudly over the din of sporadic incoming fire, which had started as the daylight came. "I'll give…" James words were drowned out by a scream from one of the men. Coburn checked to see if the private had been hit by shrapnel or bullet.

"Is that man hurt?" demanded James.

Coburn moved on his hands and knees toward James, whose uniform was covered in sweat. The young lieutenant hated all of this but he was determined to discharge his duties fairly and honourably and with humanity.

"The man is unharmed but gone mad, sir," Coburn replied. He looked along with James, Daniel and Israel as Anderson struck the screaming soldier, who was no more than a boy, hard with a rifle butt. James yelled at Anderson, who simply shrugged and thought to himself that the screaming brat of a man was quiet now and that was all that mattered.

Sgt. Anderson had no time for these cissy boys, always complaining and crying like children. What was the matter? Didn't they know they were in a bloody war?

"Jesus Christ!" responded James to Anderson's arrogant shrug.

It was a while before Danny replied. "Christ's no' fucking here, sir."

Danny Cassidy crawled back to his position.

24

I'd been staring at my gauche musings for about half an hour deciding on whether I should update them in the light of recent events but so far nothing seemed significant or new enough to make me go to the bother. I resolved to pick up the thread of Jenny Munroe's entry to the scene once this part of the journey with the Delaney boy and the girl was complete.

Just as I decided to put the mountain of papers away (Hetty was due back and I didn't want her poking her nose into my stuff like she has a habit of doing) the phone rang.

Gil Delaney IV sounded as bored as I felt (hanging about in Edinburgh waiting for the results of his inquiry into Angus Lochdarnock's antics from Scotland Yard was not proving to be that much fun for the boy.)

He has invited me over to Edinburgh (he pronounces it Edinborroh) tomorrow to visit the archives over there.

Of course, I'll tell Hetty when she gets back and hope to God she doesn't want to barge in on our meeting. It won't be much bother to persuade her of how bored she'd be. Unless there's a retail opportunity involved she'll show no interest – except she may actually want to see the Delaney boy again! No! That's right. Tomorrow is her sauna and massage day at the over-sixties club she joined last autumn. It sounds to me like it's a lot of giddy gossiping and five minutes of attention from a girl called Cheryl who "squirts a lot of really lovely smelling stuff – 'Heavenly Cougar' all over me". – (according to Hetty that is.)

I hope to God Cheryl's got enough stuff in! Hetty can be awful easy to please as long as there's a price involved – my mother achieved the self-same result with a quick sprinkle of 4711 (or whatever it was called back then) at a fraction of the cost my daft woman's paying out today.

Hetty has become, not so much a convert to consumerism, little conversion would have been needed, as a poster girl for the over-eighties with too much money on their hands and too much time, to boot. She has developed a delicate and elaborate strategy for 'buying' which she treats reverentially as though it is some kind of sacred ritual – the Presbyterian teaching she was subjected to in childhood falling short on firebrand anti-materialism as well, I've noticed.

I wondered if I should take my paperwork with me in case there is an opportunity to set Gil Delaney off on the right track again – but thinking about it that would be unfair to Jenny Munroe. There would be no guarantee he'd tell his competitor (though I have no reason to think that is how the two see one another) and then she'd not like that (competitor or not) – the Delaney Boy having the better of her, no that would not do for Jenny Munroe, however the woman likes to explain her relationship with Delaney or others.

So, I've decided. I'll pack my bag and check the car – tyres, petrol – the works. I fancy a longer drive than I've had in a long time.

I was due to meet Gil at 11 a.m. at The Old Waverley Hotel in Edinburgh – where Alistair Lochdarnock and Fiona Ewart had their assignations. Nice word assignation – makes the business of illicit sex sound less sleazy and more furtively romantic than it probably should do or indeed more sanitised than the actual affair must have been.

'Och,' I thought, 'that's the door now and I can hear my nimble-footed wife making her way up the stairs, clambering puffed-out towards me'.

"Oh, yer in?" said Hetty.

"Aye," I replied.

"Are you not going to ask me how I'm doing?" Hetty barked ferociously.

"How are you doing?" I returned flatly – grumpy old sod that I am.

"Och, don't bother then. Have you done the dinner?"

"I have not. I'll get it now if you insist. Oh, by the way – I'm away to Edinburgh tomorrow to do some Lochdarnock research."

"Suit yerself and I'll get the dinner since you're so obviously busy."

Hetty nearly took the door off its hinges as she left the room. That woman can be awfully easily annoyed sometimes!

When I tried it, the car started no bother but I decided I'll need to get the battery checked when I get back, it's overdue for renewal. That is, according to Jack – the middle aged and portly mechanic at the local garage, but I'm sure he's been *doing* me for years.

The drive to Edinburgh was uneventful and I enjoyed my time listening to 'Woman's Hour' and the dulcet tones of Jenny Murray or her counterpart – I never can tell them apart – is it Libby Purvis?

I pounded the roads up to the capital, taking the usual route from Glasgow to Edinburgh – M8, A71 then the A7 via the A700. I have to keep writing the details down these days just to keep the poor old memory vital. It's easy to forget this stuff regardless of age – or so I keep reassuring myself. Of course, if I could be bothered I would get one of those Sat-Nav contraptions but – there we go again – another thing to learn to shout at! I decided to do the handwritten map and commit the details to memory.

Of course, as a young man my memory was, as young William (not so young any more either) used to say, 'legendary'. But time takes its toll and has even had an effect on my 'rakish' good looks, so our Heather tells me. Heather suffers a wee bit from sarcasm sometimes and is definitely *my* girl, in more ways than one. At this stage of my life, I'll take a compliment regardless of there being sincerity behind it.

Gil was in the bar when I arrived at the hotel and asked if I wanted coffee. I told him I'd take a tea and he obligingly ordered a cup from a drippy looking creature behind the bar who, as it turned out, must have just waved the overpriced teabag at my cup.

"The tea OK?" enquired Gil seeming genuinely concerned for my comfort.

"It'll do," I replied, making a face – a twisty face my mother used to call it – at the beverage.

Gil beckoned at the barman/waiter to come over and asked for a 'pot' which seemed like a better choice than ordering a cup, right enough. The boy trotted off looking put out. Well, what do I care? The big Yank shrugged, obviously feeling the same way as me only he, as a cool yank would do, smiled.

"The guy's probably only paid a coupla bucks an hour." Gil said by way of excuse.

"Is he worth more?" I asked in return, very quietly thinking, 'Och, Gil is probably right. Kids!'

"I wanna look up some more Ewart stuff." Gil explained, sensibly changing the subject.

"Aye," I replied, blowing the tea newly poured from the pot which was piping hot at least.

"Your grandfather worked there in the yard. Do you know anything about them, the Ewarts?" Gil asked.

"Bastards," I replied.

"That was Gil 1st's view of them but he never elaborated. I might as well get on with that piece of research while I wait around to hear about the dead girl and her alleged connection with Angus."

"I've got some stuff I wrote up back at my house about the Ewarts."

"Could I get a look?" asked Gil, quietly sipping his coffee. "Before I go to London?"

"Aye, Hetty'll do us some dinner. I'll give her a wee call. How does Saturday night suit you?"

"Sounds great."

We jabbered on, obeying the social niceties, but I could feel that he was as keen as me to get on with the real job. I didn't know what we'd find out about the Ewarts that I didn't already know but the American wanted a look at the Naval Records from WWI and to double check the dates of family deaths.

"Making sure all the Ewarts are six feet under? Where they should be," I enquired with a smile.

"Something like that," he replied.

We arrived at the archive – the American stalked about like John Wayne and about to go all guns blazing, and me, well, I was a wee bit subdued I suppose.

"What about Jenny Munroe?" I asked.

"What about her?" asked Gil, who was by now squinting at a computer screen with an authoritative look on his face – I stopped to consider this look for a moment. I was bearing in mind his approach before I commented.

"Jenny's missing out on the action."

"But I'm not so sure she's keen to know much about the Ewarts unless it involves Fiona and the house."

I looked at the big Yank expecting some kind of reaction but Gil kept staring at the screen. What was he trying to hide, do you think? Ach, maybe it was nothing and I really was turning into Hetty, speculating on the course of 'true love' like some kind of mad auld biddy.

"Ah, well you'd know best but she'll be fascinated about Angus Lochdarnock and the connection to the dead girl," I answered.

Gil simply looked up the naval records for 1914/18. They gave nothing away that I wasn't already aware of.

"This Kenneth Ewart guy had two kids. Do you think they may be alive still?"

I found it hard not to tell him the Ewart story – but, I decided, the information about the Ewart clan was his to find out, even if he was taking an unnecessarily long way round finding out about it.

I thought, berating myself, 'And just how long, Bill Johnson, have you spent dealing with the matter!' I decided to play along with the American and to try to enjoy his obvious enthusiasm for the task.

"How old would they be now, Kenneth Ewart's kids?" I asked.

"1919 and 1921. Pretty much sure they're gone by now." Gil sucked in air and then blew out his cheeks. "And there is no evidence that those kids went on to produce family."

I could have told the fella that these *kids* ended up in New York with their mother after she left the vile Kenneth and that their childrens' children were probably now his own neighbours back home in the States, for all I knew, but that was for Gil to ascertain.

We left the records offices and wandered out onto the cold Edinburgh streets after what had been, in the end, a fruitless afternoon's research session.

It was looking like rain again. I noticed Gil brace himself and wrap his coat about him. It was hard for me keeping up with his long legs and after a few paces I gave up trying.

The American got the message and slowed to my speed. And then the rain started to really hammer down.

By the time we got back to the Old Waverley the two of us were soaked to the skin. We made our way up to his room and he hung my coat, jacket and jumper over a radiator and ordered something from room service for us to eat.

The American kept looking at his research material as if for some kind of inspiration.

"You don't look as if you're enjoying yourself that much here in Edinburgh. Braeside suited you better?" I asked, knowing the answer. "It's a pretty lonely existence researching this stuff for you, I suppose," I added.

"Engineering, the building of bridges is more team work based," he muttered quietly.

I sort of recognised what he was talking about but I'd become so used to my secretive way of researching and, if the truth be told, I am no team player. I never have been, I suppose. I've always preferred working under my own steam, getting more done and feeling more content as a result. Is that a bad thing to admit?

The Yank was interested and happy with my meagre excuses about getting more done when you fly solo, which was the only justification for my selfishness that I could come up with on the spot.

"You may have a point there," the Delaney boy smiled.

"Aye, well it's always better to have a partner," I said, half lying. "Even for a miserable old sod like me, this whole thing has been better fun with you and Jenny on-board."

I *was* obviously beginning to turn into Hetty, worse still – Hetty in full flow as 'the matchmaker'.

As if he'd partially read my mind, Gil piped up. "You and Hetty are still pretty good together, after all those years."

I rolled about laughing and couldn't stop. To give the American his due he joined in – he is definitely a man with a sense of humour.

"That's a good one," I managed to splurt out at last.

"She's a lovely woman," said the American, trying his hardest to be serious.

"She's a nosy auld biddy," I replied, half-serious, "but we put up with one another for want of something better to do."

"So you don't recommend marriage?" Gil asked, looking directly at me.

"Recommend – no. Och, well! It's not a matter of recommending this or that. What else would I have done? The truth is, like all men, I'd probably be dead by my age without her. But then I'd be a very rich corpse."

"You know what you're saying is true. I read that single women live longer than married women and married men live longer than single men. So even if women are high maintenance creatures, we still come out of the crisis with them better off. Or is my information wrong?"

"You've been married yourself, man. What do you think?" I asked, genuinely wanting to know his take on the matter.

Gil looked hangdog. "*I* screwed up my marriage," he confessed. I was surprised.

"Another woman?" I asked, feeling emboldened by the drink he'd plied me with from the mini-bar in his room. I'd forgotten, of course, that I was supposed to be driving back to Glasgow that night.

"No. She wanted kids and I couldn't have them." His reply was honest and his expression forlorn.

"And how is that your fault?" I asked.

"No, not *fault*. Jesus, I've had enough therapy to know that. But that was what she cited as the problem – so we ended."

"Did you love her?"

"I honestly can't remember. I must have done," he said quietly.

"But you don't now?" I asked.

"No. I can definitely say I'm completely cured of Gale. I believe she's a fat mother of four with an alcohol problem and a husband who's screwing his secretary," Gil laughed.

It was nice to see the boy smiling again.

"So you're well rid of her then?" I replied.

"I could cope with the kids and the fat," Gil replied more seriously than I'd expected.

"Aye, well it's funny how it turns out," I replied. "Our William and his wife don't have any kids but Heather has two.

Families are getting so small that the average gathering of the clans can be held in an SUV. When I was a boy we lived in two rooms and kitchen and were crammed in, the place splitting at the seams with bodies. Now-a-days filling one room in an average three-bedroom semi is a challenge." I felt quite sad as this thought occurred to me and Gil (sensing this) filled my glass again – good man.

It looked like I was not getting back to Hetty that night and I asked Gil if I could ring her, followed by a call to the reception to see if I could get a bed for the night in the hotel.

The poor boy apologised and insisted on paying my bill *and* calling Hetty, both of which I felt were way beyond any expectation I could reasonably have of him.

Suitably checked in to the Old Waverley, and Gil having done what he referred to as 'a number' on Hetty, the pair of us really got going on the stock now in *my* mini-bar – we had taken our business to my room now, having pretty much wiped out his stocks mini-bar-wise by the late hour.

The room I'd been checked into was identical to the one the Delaney boy occupied but my quarters were at the back of the hotel and two flights higher up.

We talked until about two. It must have seemed a good idea to me at the time but I told him some of the details of stuff he might be interested in that I held in my wee study back in Glasgow. Gil Delaney IV, eager as ever, jumped at my rash offer to put him up a couple of nights so that I could share my bounty with him.

I was deadbeat, of course, when we checked out of The Old Waverley the next morning.

Thankfully the Delaney boy offered to drive my car back to Glasgow. It's a funny sight, a big man like Gil driving a wee V.W. Polo. Thank God the car is an automatic or the poor lanky, long-legged American would have been really struggling. Can you imagine it if the car had gears? His attempts at gear changes on the motorway with those long legs going?! My poor wee Polo would have been knackered beyond repair, just by the one journey, had I had what Gil would have called a 'stick-shift car'.

As it turned out, Hetty greeted us with open arms – well, the Delaney boy got the royal welcome and I was received with the accustomed grunt, not that I expected anything better.

I noticed the old woman sniff in at me with that knowing look in her eyes. I'd been captured. Hetty knew for sure I'd been on the whisky. She made no comment, storing up my misdemeanour for later interrogation, no doubt.

Gil trotted lightly up the stairs to the spare room which had been prepared by Hetty who seemingly wanted to give a professional touch to her housekeeping.

The Braeside experience had obviously inspired her and the corners of the bedding were turned down crisply, towels – the best new bale she'd bought in the January sales – sat plump and inviting on the chest of drawers. There was a jug of water and best crystal glass on the bedside table, to boot. I shouldn't have rolled my eyes as I did, but honest to God!

Delaney was, of course, gracious and grateful as would be expected of any visitor and the two of us followed Hetty down the stairs again for dinner.

As we reached the bottom of the stairs the doorbell rang.

"Oh, that'll be Miss Munroe. Would you get that, Bill?" Hetty simpered in her best Edinburgh-style voice, though what would have been wrong with the usual Glasgow – I've no idea.

Of course the Delaney boy looked a wee bit shocked. I remember thinking, 'Canny auld bitch.'

The lovely Jenny Munroe stood leggy and beautiful on the doorstep with a nervous expression on her face.

I invited her in to the house. Gil and Hetty had disappeared into the expensive kitchen dining room I'd been coaxed (well railroaded really) into having in the new extension.

I took the girl's raincoat, a lightweight affair that could have afforded absolutely no protection against the outside January elements. Underneath this skimpy affair she wore a bright red blouse which suited her, and a pair of black slacks which hugged her good figure.

"Come on through," I urged. "Hetty's in the extension with Gil." As soon as the words came out of my mouth I realised that Hetty had not told Jenny of the American's presence. Jenny Munroe's face! It was a picture of a different sort. I couldn't gauge whether she was shocked or horrified. I've a feeling it was kind of both!

"Oh, I hadn't realised I was not the only company," said Jenny as evenly as she could manage.

"He'll be surprised to see you too," I offered by way of placating her.

When we reached the extension the American jumped to his feet and he had what Hetty was later to say was an unconcealed smile of joy on his face as he confronted Jenny.

Hetty told me she thought that his springing to attention was 'awful sweet' and 'a good indication that the boy was keen'. I've my doubts about the nosy woman's interpretation. The man seemed just ordinarily polite to me but then what do I know?

As Hetty put the casserole on the table (she called it something fancy but it was just beef and vegetables to me) Gil told Jenny of my hidden Lochdarnock bounty – my lovely secret material, the existence of which was now out of the bag due to my drunken stupidity. The two entered into quite a discussion and were clearly excited about delving into my boxes of yellowed, old papers.

"Oh, that man has had a fair forest of trees down for the Lochdarnock story," Hetty interjected.

"Has he now?" Gil smiled, looking directly at me. "How long have you been holding out on us, Bill?"

"I wouldn't say it was holding out," I snapped.

Jenny Munroe looked at me sympathetically. "I'm grateful for your help," she murmured. I told you she was a clever one. It was not exactly charm she was using but whatever you would describe her methods as, I was eating out of her hand.

I like this girl more and more and I noticed tonight just how lovely she is – she's one of those women who seem to put so little effort into looking good. So natural – but may be looking that natural takes hours – I'm only a man and can't tell, after all.

Hetty overdid the whisky in the Cranachan and the raspberries were obviously defrosted affairs from our over large freezer. Ach, the pudding was a passable effort. The company gave no indication of noticing her culinary blunder and scoffed the lot greedily, although I've to admit my own appetite wasn't as good as it should have been.

I took what Hetty had left of the whisky (after her attempt at making the pudding) and poured glasses for the four of us.

Hetty was as unenthusiastic about the amber magic as always and Jenny poured her share into Delaney's glass thinking I hadn't noticed.

Hetty broke out her new bottle of Baileys which Jenny declined – the girl was right to refuse – it's a vile aberration of a drink and a waste of good liquor in my opinion.

After an hour, I was ordered up to what passes as my study – Hetty had a sign made in wood, a few years ago now, to put on the door which reads 'Silver Surfer's Paradise'.

If you saw the state of the room you'd get the joke. I was to bring down the paper hillock I've amassed on Lochdarnock and the various goings on about it that I've uncovered but lifting it all up I felt suddenly jealous and wanted to keep the whole lot to myself now, as I'd had the pleasure and privilege to do for many a year. However, I, manfully, took a deep breath and shoved the mass of reconstituted tree all in a basket I keep empty under my computer table and slowly descended the stairs with it feeling as if I was heading toward the furnace at my own cremation.

I dumped the stuff on the dining table and it was then that I felt the pain, at first a stabbing pain, in my chest.

Gil was the first to notice my distress.

"You OK, buddy?" he asked.

I gasped something, I can't remember what. Hetty was fussing about now and I watched as the remains of her good dinner lay on plates with the unfinished gravy beginning to congeal.

I don't know which of them called the ambulance. I'm guessing it was Jenny as Gil seemed to be holding me as I was laid down on the floor and Hetty was doing an impersonation of a hysterical biddy with her head in her hands at the table. Her face was red and blotchy in no time. Anybody would have got the impression that she cared.

The A&E was a terrible mess even that early on a Saturday night with brawling drunks and junkies littering the place and demanding attention from a staff too pushed to even attempt pleasantries.

It was six o'clock in the morning before they found me a bed.

Jenny and Gil took a shaken up Hetty home.

On their journey back to our house, Hetty was probably moaning about what a stupid old sod I am eating 'all that fatty food' and drinking whisky. Poor Gil probably carries the scars of guilt on him to this day. God love us all, I'm eighty-five and entitled to have a dickie ticker, a body's got to go from something after all. Well that's what I think, but they seem to want us to go on forever these days getting increasingly dited and inch by inch a greater burden than the younger generations are equipped or happy to deal with.

Heather visited me the next day saying that Hetty would be in that evening with Ms Munroe and Mr Delaney.

"Very formal," I commented gruffly.

"I see you're still yourself, Dad." Heather smiled. "That's good. Anyhow, the doctor said it was just a wee episode of angina and you'll be home in no time."

I've to admit I was glad to hear it. Getting attention in hospital used to be the norm with bedpan rounds and doctors' rounds, and medicine being offered at strict intervals. Oh, the glory days of the NHS!

As it was now in hospitals, being fussed over by the daft old woman seemed a luxury by comparison to the humiliation of peeing yourself in a modern hospital bed – a bed which could be transfigured into any position required but which could not produce the necessaries – a urinal for example – without human intervention for either love or money. Just shows that for all their technology, they cannot replace the human touch and the staff seem to have lost the will or the knack of getting to patients with any degree of urgency.

Later that night, I was greeted by a warning from Hetty, "And that'll be an end to all this research nonsense, Bill Johnson."

'Aye, that'll be right.' I thought but said nothing, preferring to look pathetic in the hope of receiving the womanly warmth that Hetty must be capable of in some circumstances, surely.

Of course, the Delaney boy brought Jenny along to see me that night just after the daft old woman left with Heather.

"Did you get anywhere with the material?" I asked.

"You're incorrigible," Delaney laughed.

"We're not discussing Lochdarnock, the Ewarts, or the Cassidys. Sorry Bill, but it's all about you today," said Jenny.

I looked at Delaney and muttered, "Has she been getting lessons from Hetty?" I asked.

The two of them laughed.

"This is a spot of angina, that's all. I'm no' about to kick the bucket just yet," I assured them.

"May be not, but you'll have to do as Hetty tells you," Ms Munroe said firmly.

I looked to Gil for support but he simply shrugged,

"A guy has to know when he's beat," the American told me in response to my pathetic search for support.

Jenny kissed me gently on the forehead and Gil squeezed my shoulder firmly in a manly kind of way before they ventured out into the cold night, looking cosy together – a wee bit too cosy?

I was left lying there when they went. I remember musing on how the two of them might be getting on both with the research and each other. It was hard to tell for sure about them or the work.

I'll have to somehow get Hetty's opinion without making it too obvious that I'm actually interested in the potential for romance. Am I turning into a woman, d'ye think? Must be all the drugs they're pumping into me.

I do remember demanding that the old woman bring in some of my Lochdarnock stuff. I was keen, having had this scare, to pass on as much information as I could to the younger pair. Odd I know, having kept things to myself for so many years but Gil and Jenny were enthusiasts like me and I didn't want that daft auld biddy throwing out my life's work without the right people getting the chance to see it.

Let's face it, William had never shown an interest and as for Heather, she was busy in her middle age turning into her mother. I noticed Heather was putting on a fair bit of weight but that's what happens to a lot of women of a 'certain age' I suppose. Heather told me that I was not thinking right. And she's not that wrong – I must be a pain to live with. It's a good thing for me that the auld biddy cannot imagine life without me.

Being fair to Hetty, she'd had a fright and she was good enough to bring the exact material I'd ordered, as a result of trying to keep me calm and alive.

When I passed the bumph to the Delaney boy he was thrilled with it.

Gil was, after all, looking for news of the Ewarts and I had it by the bucket load and I was now more than willing to ensure that Gil Delaney IV got what he came to Scotland to find.

If I'd realised at the time that all this information I'd parted with would send him scurrying back across the Atlantic would I have done things differently? Who's to say?

25

I thought it was only fair to give Jenny this Lochdarnock find.

Delaney had his material, after all. I suppose I was trying in my own crass way to get the girl into the romantic mood with the Delaney boy, so I didn't feel that he would miss out on much in the end, as a result of my interference.

I'm a fool expecting her to take a historical romance and impose that stuff on her. Some of *them* (women that is) at least are not as daft as my Hetty, it seems

Jenny, in spite of my hopeful silly thoughts, still shows no discernible romantic interest in the Yank mores the pity. Or does, she? I cannot make up my old mind on that score. The truth is that Jenny Munroe is very good at 'playing it cool'.

Well, what else do I have to occupy myself with? Is it boredom that's made Hetty so damned nosy, d'ye think? Is it boredom that's doing the same to me?

As I say, it was easy to part with more of *her* story than I imagined it would be. They were all too polite to question me too much due to my ill-health and I wanted Jenny to know as much as possible so that she could... What?

I will never forget my war coming to an end in early 1918. The gas attack had been anticipated but when it came about I just didn't get my mask on quick enough, so they say. Sure enough even some of the boys that did still ended up with 'corrupted lungs' and had to be put in the hospital.

The honest truth is, I felt as if my chest had been put on fire after the gas attack. When they got us out – and that was no easy feat – we were in the hospital for weeks. So many of the boys died – slowly – it was a cruelty beyond imagining. If folk think that Owen exaggerates, I can tell them they are wrong.

It was while I was in the hospital that I became determined to have something done for the men who were suffering like me. All these years after and I fight on – and so do you – trying to get justice for those men the world would rather forget. All those young lives ruined and how would mine have been without you there to help me? God Almighty – without you…

Part of me was terrified when I left the hospital in France. I had no idea if you would feel the same way about me when I got back. We had had to be so careful in our exchange of letters that it seemed to me that you could not care less. You had written so many 'Well – Cpl. Cassidys' and 'How are my men?'

I was jealous that you even mentioned them.

I suppose my letters filled you with the same questions but the letters kept coming for both of us which had to be enough proof, I suppose, to each of us that we still cared about one another.

I had to go home to my family. They had been distraught, their nerves a mess when I was at war. My mother had always been overprotective with the lot of us but since I'd been sent to France, the poor woman was especially so with me.

It was good to get home to see them all – and the new children that Patrick and Elizabeth had produced during the course of the war. The wee babies were lovely but I had a special fondness for Alice and wee

Paddy. They were of an age that was interesting. Wee Alice had plenty to say for herself even at that age.

After a week of non-stop Cassidy attention (Annie was beside herself with worry about my chest, which I have to admit was not good) I was ready for a change of air, I needed to be away from the thrust of family life I suppose, and you got word to me through Bob MacKenzie that we should meet.

Do you remember the day? The day we met again after such a long delay.

The war hadn't ended yet and the streets were miserable if not quiet. We met at the Botanic Gardens. I wore my uniform and you were waiting for me, dressed in your finest. The smile on your face! I've never seen you beam like that before or since. I was sure then – sure of you and of us. As I got closer to you the smile was replaced by a look of concern.

You talked and questioned me for hours on the state of my health. You sounded like one of the doctors. I told you to shut up and you said, "I can't. Your health is of the utmost importance to me."

I wanted to kiss you but, of course, I couldn't. I don't remember what tea rooms we drank in that afternoon as we mapped out our future together.

It was on that day that you described the lodge at Braeside in detail to me (expanding on information you had already given me) and making the life we might have up there, the two of us virtually alone, seem so special. I've to admit I was excited by all the promising things our life together seemed to offer – and I have to say I have not been disappointed.

The city, though quiet that day, was more frightening than the battle-fields I had just escaped. I don't know why. There were just so many people milling about totally unaware of what this unsafe, unfathomable, world was really like. I suppose the city, even our city with all its problems and injustices on clear view, just seemed false – a kind of fake universe that no longer existed for the likes of me.

When I got home I told my parents that you'd offered me a job.

Do you remember we agreed that was the best way to put it? You took some convincing. You were always a determined big sod. I told my folks that you needed help up there at the lodge with compiling your pamphlets – which was true and with household and estate duties – which was not.

It didn't seem to matter to me what they thought I was going to do. I just didn't want to shock or hurt them in any way – and they are the kind of folk who would be hurt and shocked by what we two really are. You were keen to be less careful.

The world will change one day, James – there will be a day when people like you and me can live our lives openly – but not yet, not just yet, I remember thinking. If you've taught me anything it's that a better future evolves – has to evolve. You are a giver of hope to me and I hope that's what our writings give to other people.

My folks were, of course, unhappy that I was to leave the city but they relented – my father easily and poor Annie with such a terrible struggle. That war and me have tortured the poor woman. I sometimes think Annie Cassidy might one day kill the Kaiser herself – if she put her mind to it she probably could – no, she definitely would.

So it was that you and I ventured up north to the frozen land we inhabit happily together – well mostly happily.

You will never know how sorry I feel about the fight we had, the fight we keep having but you do recognise that not everyone is ready to hear our truth – well not the truth about us and I can't – I just can't – inflict the fact of our being together in this way on my parents.

Like I say, you've only to blame yourself for convincing me of the power of evolution over revolution and I find it hard to understand how you can contemplate burdening your own poor sick mother with the knowledge of us, of who and what we are. I know you argue that love should never be secret but you need to know that in spite of the love I feel for you, I am determined to protect those others around me not because I am ashamed of you in any way but because they would, could, never understand. So protect them I must – it is the way I have been brought up. As I say, one day – James – one day!

Yes, one day people, people more advance than we are now, will find our writings and wonder what all the fuss has been about.

I know you have waited so long to hear or see these words written but I love you, James Lochdarnock, I love you now and always will.

26

There was, of course, nothing surprising in this for me but Gil described Danny Cassidy and James Lochdarnock as extremely brave 'for the time' and he's right. As I say, Jenny was as usual 'cool' about the whole thing and still seemed, in my opinion – which as you know is never humble – a bit too distant from the story.

I wondered if she wouldn't respond more positively to the trials and tribulations of a 'girl' and so I sent on another extract I had removed some years before, from Mrs MacDonald's now infamous diary, to see if that might 'hit the spot'. The Delaney boy was very interested in this for more than one reason.

MRS MACDONALD'S DIARY

We are fortunate, here at Lochdarnock House, that poor weak Bridget Riley was returned to us (in a very sorry state, I must say). The girl turned up this morning. We had just returned from church. I had gone directly to my sitting room and was mending petticoats (our seamstress, Miss Sinclair, is away at her sisters as is usual at this time of year for her) Bob (Mr MacKenzie) knocked at my door and coughed so I knew it was he who wanted me. I told him to come in. Poor Mr MacKenzie (such a good soul) was pale faced and trembling,

"Mrs MacDonald, you'll need to come into the kitchen," he murmured.

"What on earth is it, Mr MacKenzie?" I replied, feeling somewhat anxious and perplexed, as you can imagine.

"Bridget, it is wee Bridget. I think she needs your help."

I darted out of my seat, dropping the half-mended petticoat on the floor. I didn't bother to stop to pick it up and simply trampled over the garment with my as yet muddy shoes. I am not usually one to be so clumsy and remiss but my heart was filled with a terrible fear.

When I arrived at the kitchen, poor wee Bridget was bruised and filthy. I could smell alcohol on her breath. I must say, even in spite of the fear I had been feeling, I was shocked at the look of her. I managed to get her up the service stairs without either Lady or Lord Lochdarnock seeing her. They are both so pre-occupied since the death of Master Angus, I doubt they would notice anything. The poor girl could hardly carry herself. When I cleaned her up and bathed her wounds she explained her predicament in so much detail my head was reeling. I had thought I was a woman of the world and only realise now how sheltered my life has been, how lucky I have been to know service in a civilised household. Yes, the work has been hard but life away from this house – how can I tell it? The world is an awful cruel and wicked place.

Bob brought us tea and I had the girl sip at it while she told me her story. The details she recounted are so terrible I can barely bring myself to retell them. Oh, dear Lord – how can this man carry on with life knowing he has done such terrible, terrible things to an innocent girl like silly wee Bridget?

Bridget told me of the time just before she ran away. She smiled as she remembered, starting with the words

"I've been a right bad person, Mrs MacDonald and you should put me back out onto the streets. I only came here to see my pal Mary."

"Mary is helping out up at the lodge," I told her.

119

"Aye, she's a good girl. Not like me," Bridget replied.

"Bridget, just tell me how you got into this terrible state. No one is going to judge you. That is the job of God alone," I said, and then felt terrible in case the girl just clammed up and refused to let me know what awful times had befallen her.

"Oh, Mrs MacDonald! I was that stupid," she replied, crying once again.

"How stupid can stupid be?" I asked.

Poor wee Bridget hung her head very low.

"I went off with a gentleman. Or at least that's what I thought he was. Oh, Mrs MacDonald. I have been that daft."

"And who was this gentleman?" I asked. I have to confess I hadn't an idea of who it might be and assumed that it was a person not known to me or the house.

Mr MacKenzie says I should not do so but I blame myself for not warning the girl against the man, that bad man. One look at the sort – well what can I say? The only justification I can give is that I had been told that often since being in service that it was not my place to comment on the goings on of the gentry.

When Bridget told me who it was she'd been away with, I admit I was disappointed in both her and myself, for not being a better authority in the girl's life.

"Oh, Bridget! That man, did you not see through him at the start?" I asked and then regretted the question. I suspect many a young woman has been charmed by the likes of him.

It took me a full five minutes to stop her crying again.

It seems that poor Bridget had been taken to an apartment in the Cowcaddens and made drunk, taken advantage of and then kept barely fed and watered so that he might return at his pleasure to take advantage of the girl again.

Bridget's body is covered in scars and bruises but it is her poor wee mind that is barely in a normal state. I fear for the girl, I really do.

She tells of lashings with a metal chain, kickings, beatings and *abuses of which I cannot write. The girl has been molested and I thank God that there seems no chance that she is with child. Poor wee Bridget – at least she has been spared that indignity.*

I have spoken to Mr MacKenzie and he believes that we can persuade his Lordship to allow Bridget back into the kitchen to resume her old duties once she is physically well. I am, I have to admit, worried. The girl's mind is not what it might be. I would not be at all surprised if she were to go mad. I have heard of young girls losing their sanity after such terrible treatments. The asylums are full of young 'Bridgets', sadly, full of them.

Of that man, Mr MacKenzie tells me that Lord Lochdarnock has made it clear after Angus' death that he wants nothing to do with him. I am glad Bridget will not be forced to encounter the Godforsaken creature again. I am glad that I will not encounter the man (if that's what he can be called). I am not sure that even with all my experience in managing this house that I would be able to remain calm in the man's presence.

I will give poor Bridget a week to recover herself and can only pray to God that she stays well enough to prove herself of value to the house. I surely do not wish to lose the poor wee girl again. Kenneth Ewart will not be allowed near the girl – not on my watch.

I fished out of my box of tricks, extract after extract, that I thought could lead Gil and Jenny forward in their research on both the Ewarts and Lochdarnocks.

I had photocopied Mrs MacDonald's diaries comprehensively when the house had acquired them a number of years back now, and I wanted the pair, Gil and Jenny, to get a flavour of the atmosphere of the house when many of the main protagonists in the main story were gone.

These extracts seemed pertinent so the Big Yank and the girl got these shoved in their direction.

The 'find' of the Guthrie at the gatehouse is explained, I think best by these extracts, and the atmosphere in the house after Fiona

Ewart moved in explains Mary's determination to get away from Lochdarnock House once the new mistress got her feet under the table. Aye, you can see why.

MARGARET MACDONALD'S DIARY

Oh, this house leaves me with a heavy heart. Fiona Ewart married the Laird not a month ago and has returned here tearing the heart out of the place. I cannot tell you how many images of Lady Isabelle have been put on the fire, both since her early death and Fiona Ewart's unhappy marriage to Lord Alistair.

Young Mary (not so young now), Bob and I have retrieved only Guthrie's portrait of Lady Isabelle which Bob took by car up to the lodge for safe keeping with Patricia (my equivalent up at Braeside) who can be relied on to ensure the portrait's safety, Bob says, "to keep it always safe". I pray to God he is right and that God and Patricia can do what is necessary in order to protect the cherished portrait. The thought of her Ladyship's image ceasing to exist is an awful one to me – she is so sadly missed by so many of us.

That Ewart woman looks as though butter wouldn't melt in her mouth. At least her mother 'the old Ewart woman', as Bob calls her, is what she is and that brother of hers, the evil wretch Kenneth, in America stays well away from this town.

It's a wonder a body can bear the havoc that that crowd have created for this household.

I am not a woman given to pronouncing oaths but in the case of the Ewarts I seem unable to help myself, God save me from judgement!

Mary is very troubled by the introduction of a Ewart into the household. She is barely over the death of her brother. The girl seems to blame the Ewarts for Danny Cassidy's death saying that if it hadn't been for that family the boy would have been in a reserved occupation before the war and not then subjected to the gas attack that did for him in the end. We will, of course, never know.

Fate is a peculiar thing, as Mr MacKenzie is never done telling me.

I should thank my stars for Bob and my work here at the house but it is true that Fiona Ewart coming into Lochdarnock House to run things will cause me much trouble. Lady Isabelle relied on the staff so much for the running of the house that Fiona Ewart's interference seems doubly insulting. I have to keep reminding myself that it is her house now that she, Fiona Ewart (as was), is married to Lord Alistair now.

As I say, the one saving grace of the matter is that Kenneth Ewart is away in America and the father, Sir Douglas, dead of a heart attack. Nasty men, the both of them!

I've to admit, I look at the laird from time to time and think "What are you thinking of?"

I know it isn't my place to interfere with Lord Lochdarnock's decisions and I couldn't even if I wanted to – I can only think the poor man is lonely and easily swayed by the charms of this younger woman – who it is clear to see cannot hold a candle to Lady Isabelle either in terms of her looks or her temperament.

Mrs Laidlaw describes Fiona Ewart as a 'wish-washy wee madam'. I had to rebuke her for talking that way in front of the junior staff but I can't say I disagree with the cook on that one. Mr MacKenzie (Bob) warns me to say little or nothing to Mrs Laidlaw – a more gossipy body you couldn't meet but what a cook!!!

Wee Bridget, now a full grown woman but still with a tendency to be a bit giddy, seems that nervous at the prospect of a Ewart in the household, as I've said. I don't blame the girl after what she's been through.

I heard Bridget say to Mary that she's thinking of moving away to some folk she has in Dumbarton. I'm not sure that she should bother. I doubt that Kenneth Ewart would condescend to return to Glasgow after all his success in America. We're all probably far too dowdy for him now, even the laird and his sister. But there will no comforting a girl like Bridget in her worries and that I understand – for sure I understand that much. I must remember to tell Bob that there are one or two photographs of the Lochdarnock boys that I've hidden in a book in the library away from Fiona Ewart's beady wee eyes. I'll get him to take those pictures up to the lodge for safe keeping too – that madam seems to want to eradicate the memory of all Lochdarnocks from this house. It would kill the Laird if that, Fiona, one destroyed every memory of his boys as well as Lady Isabelle. Mary keeps talking about the Ewart's 'Evil Streak' as she calls it. I give her a telling off of course when she talks that way but in my heart I think she is probably right. There are just some people who lack common decency, as though the idea of the 'milk of human kindness" had never been made known to them in their sad and pitiful lives.

There are times when I am glad of this diary I keep and for the letters I write to my sister. It is in this diary that I can confide my true feelings about the goings on in this house. It is, as Bob knows, a terrible strain keeping my thoughts to myself sometimes. I can only hope that with God's help I can endure the troubles that Fiona Ewart is bringing with her.

Talking of Bob (Mr MacKenzie) he has asked me to do him the honour (once we retire – which may not be too long away) to go with him down to Ayr to be near my sister. He tells me that he has enough saved for us to have a comfortable wee house near the sea. I would love that. I look forward to the time when we can move away from the trials and tribulations of the life in this house. I confided to Bob that I thought that this was indeed a cursed place. Bob, in his usual way, told me not to be so daft and not to talk like that but the more I think about Lochdarnock the more convinced I am of the truth of the matter – the dread curse of the Lochdarnocks does, must, exist.

27

It was in the 1970s that I was most keen to get all my research into context and I made a half-hearted attempt at putting together a full history of the place. The writing didn't go smoothly.

Back then, I was working, had teenage kids and Hetty to contend with and to be honest I never finished the comprehensive work that I'd intended to produce. I'm glad to be able to pull out relevant bits of the work to show to the Delaney Boy and the Munroe girl. I wanted them to have the full flavour of what the Ewarts were about – what a crowd!

In all honesty, it's always interesting to see what that pair make of things. I updated this extract in the 1990s when the house acquired Mrs MacDonald's diaries. Oh, and I used several sources to come up with the story which I don't seem to have referenced – not much of an academic am I?

***

CONFRONTATON – FROM *THE HISTORY OF THE LOCHDARNOCKS* BY BILL JOHNSON

Mary had helped Lady Isabelle dress that morning. The young maid noticed the unsteady woman shake and shift around, knowing that her beloved employer was feeling agitated about something. Later that day Mary would know the reason for Isabelle Lochdarnock's obvious discomfort.

"Are you in pain?" Mary asked. "Can I get you your medicine?"

"No, it's quite all right, Mary. I will take my powders after lunch. Thank you." Isabelle's voice was odd, there was a distant quality to it. As Mary stood back from Isabelle at the end of her 'toilet' she noticed how frail the older woman seemed – Isabelle Lochdarnock was, indeed, a ghost already before her actual physical death.

"I will be taking morning tea in the breakfast room. I am expecting a caller." Lady Isabelle stated as strongly as she could.

Mary wanted to ask who the caller might be but waited a beat for Lady Isabelle to reveal her plans.

"Miss Ewart will arrive at half-past ten. Please make sure that Mrs Laidlaw knows."

Isabelle smiled gently at Mary who tried her best to disguise her shock at the news. Everyone in the house knew about Fiona Ewart and the goings on between her and Lord Lochdarnock.

Everybody in the house was silent on the subject and determinedly refused to engage in gossip on the matter. Alistair Lochdarnock seemed to provoke a loyalty which Mary found hard to understand. How could he, lovely man and good employer that he was, betray Lady Isabelle in this way? Like many others, Mary found the matter hard to fathom.

"Yes, Lady Isabelle. I will make sure that everything is lovely," Mary said as simply as she could.

The maid felt her throat closing over with anger at the thought of that trollop being invited here to tea. Poor Lady Isabelle – hadn't she suffered enough without being humiliated in this way, surely the older woman knew of her husband's affair with this flighty wee piece? But it seemed not.

Mary left Lady Isabelle sitting at her dressing table, as she was asked, and headed to the kitchen – pulling herself together and bracing herself for the raised eyebrows which were probably to be the only expression of distaste shown in the household that morning – save for the reaction of the cook.

"Lady Isabelle is expecting a guest for morning tea at half-past ten," Mary told Moira Laidlaw.

"Och, who's she expecting now?" enquired the busy, red-faced cook.

Mrs Laidlaw was annoyed as usual that her morning would be disrupted by the arrival of an interloper. There were to be guests to dinner tonight and Moira Laidlaw was a meticulous woman who did not like her plans disrupted.

"I think Miss Ewart," Mary said as simply as she could. There was a silence before the reply.

"Oh, aye." Moira Laidlaw's eyebrows raised, making her red face look even more comical than usual, as Mary had predicted.

The rest of the staff in the kitchen fell silent. Mary glared at nothing in particular to make her displeasure at the cook's comments known.

Mary briskly left the kitchen to ensure that the parlour maid had performed her duties to the letter in the morning room, getting the new youngster in the house to lay the tea table to a suitable standard. It was a summer morning and there was no need for a fire, Mary told the girl, besides Lady Isabelle found heat intolerable and preferred coolness.

"Titivating as usual?" Bridget said cheerily to Mary as she too arrived in the morning room to prepare for the arrival of Fiona Ewart.

"Visitor!" Mary gasped as she turned to see Bridget behind her.

"So I hear," said Bridget with eyebrows raised, the expression made the wee maid look vaguely insane. It seemed the whole household had donned odd expressions this morning.

"I didn't have you down as a gossip, Bridget Riley." Mary snapped.

"I see you're in one of your moods, Mary? Well, is the room up to your trying standards?"

"It'll do," said Mary with a smile. "It'll do." The two maids took the backstairs down to the kitchen and on arrival in the impressive space began arranging crockery to help Moira Laidlaw who was cutting into some delicious looking cake.

"Oh, I could do with a slice o' that," sighed Bridget.

"You mind you keep your hands off it. You're a pure greedy girl, Bridget Riley," barked Moira Laidlaw who stood with her hands firmly on her hips – her mouth was a tight pout.

Mary thought about the fact that in the eyes of Moira Laidlaw and Mrs MacDonald, she and Bridget were still seen as girls, grown women though they were by now. She'd even heard her own mother refer to women over twenty-five in that way and thought how strange that these women in their older age reduce everyone to a child. Mary determined that she would not behave in that ridiculous way as she aged. An adult was an adult after all.

The doorbell rang and Mary imagined the pompous Jillings opening the door to Fiona Ewart with lips pursed even more firmly than usual.

Mary made an excuse to leave the kitchen and scurried upstairs to see if she could help Lady Isabelle. Mary knew that it would be Bridget who would carry in the tray – most likely the plate would be missing one piece of cake which had inadvertently ended up in Bridget's pinny for later consumption in private.

Bridget, in spite of her terrible experiences, still had a tendency to wildness, thought Mary.

Shortly after, Bridget knocked on the door of the morning room and entered as asked.

The Morning room was a lovely place – Lady Isabelle's favourite. The pale yellow walls gave the room a cheery aspect and the gilt chandelier hung over the room, illuminating it at night time and during the day gave the room a kind of understated opulence.

Portraits large and small were arranged on the walls. Some of these were too dark, Bridget thought – far too dark and cheerless for such a room but they were of the Lochdarnock forebears and could not be discarded, Bridget knew.

Setting the tray down on the fine delicate table gently as she had been trained, Bridget lifted her eyes and looked at that horror – that Ewart – the sister of that bastard who had tortured her. Bridget thought that if she had had the opportunity and could have got away with it she would have poisoned Fiona Ewart's tea. The slut was no better than her brother after all – carrying on with a married man.

Bridget looked down at the fine rug in yarns of blue and red that lay beneath her feet and slowly began to leave the room. She decided though to lift her head as Mary had told her and looked again at the room and its adornments. The long windows with their shutters open, the fine cornicing, the old fashioned brown furniture and vases that stood upon it, blue and white and sparkling in the morning sun. There was an odd chair here and there in window recesses which could be pulled out for guests if the comfortable sofas in blue and white proved insufficient to hold the rich backsides of the now infrequent visitors who attended the house.

The maid was relieved when, at last, she closed the door behind her – having bravely completed her duties in an unhurried fashion with head held high as directed by Mary Cassidy. Being in a Ewart's presence, any Ewart, was a terrible reminder for Bridget of how far she had fallen. She was more determined still to prove to a Ewart, any Ewart, how she had survived, how she still retained her decency.

Even the distractions of all this opulence and beauty could not protect Bridget's heart and mind from the memories of her suffering, but her performance of her tasks as a grown woman and valued servant of the Lochdarnocks had given her a bloody-minded boldness which she enjoyed and which her friend Mary encouraged.

Bridget was relieved to see Mary in the hallway, hovering near an ornament which she was obviously just pretending to dust.

"Everything OK, Bridget?" Mary asked matter of factly.

"Fine," said Bridget. "I'll need to get back to the kitchen."

"Did you get cake?" Mary smiled.

"I did not," Bridget protested.

"Shame, I was gonnae ask you to gi'e me a wee bit!" Mary laughed.

Bridget considered this for a moment. "I suppose you need to find something in oor wee room. May be ye left your hanky there? Is that right?"

"It is right."

The two women proceeded to their room trying not to giggle like mischievous teenagers. The two maids closed the door behind them and scoffed the stolen cake hungrily, enjoying this re-run of their naughtiness of previous, younger years.

"I pure hate that Ewart one," Bridget said – mouth now cleared of all traces of the crime of stealing as she had cleverly eaten the evidence along with her co-conspirator, Mary.

"I'm no' surprised," Mary allowed herself to comment. "Bad bastards, the Ewarts. That's what my brother always says."

Bridget was quiet a moment and then smiled. "Well, I'm awful glad that you, Mary Cassidy, are still in that dour wee body somewhere. These days ye look shrivelled up and hardly part o' the world."

"Well, thank you very much." Mary affected a put-out countenance but knew that Bridget was right – she felt shrivelled, a shadow of the person she had been. In that respect at least she could understand Lady Isabelle, both of them shut down, closed up snails who had retreated into shells too small to contain the true creatures of their actual substance.

The Morning Room was aglow with springtime sunshine. Isabelle Lochdarnock had made the effort of small talk which was required. Fiona Ewart was hiding her trepidation. She had been startled by the invitation to morning tea with Lady Isabelle but had been unable to discuss the matter with Alistair who was, for once, genuinely away on business.

The lord was adding to the house collection of Spanish paintings which were heavy and dark and not to Fiona's taste. She looked at Isabelle Lochdarnock or at least the ghost of the woman who had once been the lady. Fiona knew it was unkind but her mind kept wandering to the fact that Isabelle could not last much longer and that one day, one day quite soon – all this (Lochdarnock House and its master) would be hers. She couldn't help but give a little smile as she looked about her, contentedly.

"You find the room pleasant, I hope?" asked Isabelle.

"Yes, most pleasant," Fiona replied.

"I'm sure it's a comfort knowing that you will be taking tea here frequently at leisure one day when I am gone?" Isabelle managed. She had practiced the line in her head all morning.

"I beg your pardon," Fiona muttered, trying not to show her shock.

"When I am gone, Alistair will of course do the gentlemanly thing and marry you, Miss Ewart."

"I'm sure I don't know what you are talking about," Fiona managed.

"I'm sure you do," Isabelle muttered, feeling particularly and unusually angry.

"No!" Fiona protested.

"Miss Ewart, I am not blind nor am I an idiot. You have been conducting an affair with my husband for quite some time. If I were a well person, this affair would never have begun and you have, most cleverly, taken advantage of your luck by providing my husband with… comfort. You will find it strange to know that I am pleased that Alistair has someone who can fulfil him in this way but be under no illusion that your liaison remains unknown."

Fiona Ewart's heart was pounding. Isabelle Lochdarnock had always been completely placatory. Fiona looked about her and fixed her stare on a marble bust which sat upon the mantle shelf, trying to gather her thoughts as to how she might respond.

Isabelle saved her the bother of trying by continuing on her trajectory, resolutely, clearly, and sharply.

"When I am gone, Miss Ewart, you will be the mistress of Lochdarnock. I am sure by your demeanour that you will be capable of running my house, relatively well. However, you should be aware that houses and estates like this are borrowed. None of it will ever belong to you or your family. James will inherit the entire Estate *when his father has gone and you, as tradition dictates, will be given a small residence which will return to the Lochdarnock family when you are finally gone." Isabelle took a breath. "I tell you this only so that you are aware of your fate. Being mistress of a house like Lochdarnock is a job of work, Miss Ewart, and not everyone is built for the task – though I am sure that you will prove yourself to be up to the job." There was a pause.*

"Can I pour you some more tea, Miss Ewart?" Lady Isabelle added with a smile, glad that her work was done.

"No. No thank you. I have another appointment which I must attend," Fiona managed.

"Be a dear and pull the cord. The butler will show you out."

It seemed to take forever for the butler to arrive. Fiona found herself shaking from a mixture of real fear and temper that this woman should confront her in this way and make her feel like – like – like a slut.

As the door closed behind the Ewart girl, Isabelle gave in to the drained and exhausted feeling she experienced regularly. She managed to cross the room to pull the cord once again. She needed dear sweet little Mary to help her to her room.

The task was completed now. Isabelle wondered what she had hoped to achieve by her actions and words – had she wished to rid Lochdarnock of the threat of takeover by a Ewart or had she been honest with herself when she had made the decision to invite the girl that her only intention was to direct Fiona Ewart in a way that would help her husband in the long run. Would Fiona Ewart now tell Alistair? Would Alistair be embarrassed and furious that she knew of the liaison? Isabelle decided that the little louse of a girl would not dare bring the matter up, fearing that Alistair would end the affair immediately when he knew it had been discovered.

Isabelle despaired for a moment – sad at the thought that a man like Alistair had been drawn into such treachery but then he was a man, after all, dear Alistair, even he was a man – as good in many respects that he might be – he had been tempted and had fallen under the spell of this rather ordinary looking and insipid creature.

Mary knocked on the door. "Can I help you, Lady Isabelle?" she asked gently as she entered, noticing the older woman's drained and ashen demeanour.

"I'd like to lie down now, Mary. I would be grateful if you could help me to my room."

The two women ascended the stairs slowly passing grand portraits which adorned the staircase walls. Pictures of dukes, earls and baronets, of Spanish kings and Infantas hung over the two women as they walked upwards. The characters in the paintings all seemed to be looking down upon the two women who were now struggling to the top of the stairs. On the way up Mary and Isabelle passed niches which held impressive looking vases and other adornments. Even so much wealth and richness could not help Isabelle Lochdarnock in her struggle, in her physical trials which had never been identified.

Even such wealth and richness as this would never bring back beloved Angus, nor would it restore Isabelle's health or hope.

As the two women clung together in the tortured assent, they reached the top of the stairs and processed in jerking motion along the brightly carpeted hallway – red carpet lay beneath the red walls of the music room, and they proceeded through another two rooms before reaching Isabelle's bedroom. The dark brown furniture sat against the floral paper of the walls. The yellow of the paper saw birds and flowers in greens and reds playing against the sunny background. The four-poster bed draped in rich red velvet looked inviting to Isabelle who simply flopped on the white coverings, too hot to be covered, too exhausted to find comfort even in the company of Mary. The maid settled Isabelle and left the room, feeling sad, feeling as though – somehow – she was about to experience yet another loss.

***

Some of the extracts, as I say, were taken from my work in the 1970s which were based on evidence from Margaret MacDonald's diaries. Good woman that she was, she could be a wee bit of a wind-bag so I 'adjusted' the writing and worked on the hints she had given to make sense of events, och, and I've to admit that in the light of what I already knew I was piecing things together as I thought they might have happened. Where I could, I stuck to the source material, of course.

I'd read *The Tale of Us* many times over and I knew the outcome for all the protagonists. As you know, history is not an exact science – you'll excuse my literary style, if you could call it that. I imagine Gil will be impressed and Jenny, perhaps, appalled by my attempts – ach well!

***

ISABELLE IN GRIEF – FROM BILL JOHNSON'S 1977 *HISTORY OF THE LOCHDARNOCKS*

Bob MacKenzie looked towards the board which showed a ringing bell at the main entrance to the house. Jillings was away and MacKenzie was expected to act up as butler in the doddery old retainer's absence.

Bob sighed and reluctantly shoved his newspaper to one side, straightened his tie and jacket and walked up the stairs. No-one was expected and Bob hated receiving impromptu visitors – especially at this time of year when he was more than due a rest.

Lady Rowena and Sir Henry sat in their car – a hired Rolls Royce (it seems), hiding from the fierce cold which had descended on the grounds in this part of the world. Their chauffeur, a rough-looking chap they'd taken on whilst here in Scotland, did his best to formally introduce the pair to Bob MacKenzie in what the poor man had assumed was the proper manner.

Lady Rowena, a stout and forceful woman with a keen sense of fun, dived out of the car as soon as MacKenzie opened the door and pushed her way passed the stammering man she'd taken on as her driver in Scotland.

"That's OK, Malcolm, I'll explain all to Mr …?" she looked quizzically at Bob.

"MacKenzie, Mam," replied Bob, looking at the loud woman who was fairly bouncing up each step toward him and the main entrance of Lochdarnock House, her heavy coat looking liable to load her down and send her toppling backwards to the bottom again.

Fortunately, Lady Rowena was known for her nimble-footed charm, which was among many of her other physical attributes and she continued bouncing upwards confidently if breathlessly.

"Sir Henry's in the car. Malcolm here's gonna bring in the bags. I know I should have written Lady Isabelle but we were already here so all this English politeness seemed crazy to me."

MacKenzie wanted to remind the woman she was actually in Scotland and the use of the word English was at the least unfortunate, but knowing his place he merely raised his eyebrows at the short woman from across the 'pond'.

Sir Henry, a spritely looking seventy-something was now bounding up the stairs after Rowena, making MacKenzie feel doubly nervous. The old man wore a tweed suit, which he had sensibly covered with a Harris Tweed coat. His eyes could be taken for Lochdarnock blue but MacKenzie knew that particular blue-eyed look came from Lady Isabelle's family the Farquarson's and was only partially responsible for the blue-eyed family look which was common amongst the Lochdarnock clan.

"Tell the darling girl to come down and kiss her old uncle," the old man twinkled.

"Yes, and do you think you could stretch to some tea and say… sandwiches? We're both starved, aren't we, Henry?" Rowena chirped as the trio walked up towards the morning room where MacKenzie had decided to put them. The fire had been started up in the room for Lady

Isabelle earlier in the day but she hadn't yet come down. MacKenzie wished little Mary would get back from her New Year break, it was an added responsibility for the man, having, Isabelle, the grief-stricken-woman on his plate.

None of the other servants dared go near poor Lady Isabelle's door, not even Mrs MacDonald.

"I'll have the maid inform Lady Isabelle that you're here," Bob said as sing-songily as he could as he left the room.

The liveliness this newly arrived pair was showing hadn't been seen at the house for quite some time and MacKenzie wondered how Lady Isabelle might cope with their enforced jollity which seemed so out of kilter with the atmosphere which existed currently at Lochdarnock House, which had become an eerily quiet place since the death of young Angus.

Rowena sat on a sofa. She spread out the loose material of her voluminous dress, with which she covered the furniture carefully.

"I just wanted to thank you for coming here with me, Henry," Rowena said quietly when the two were alone at last. MacKenzie, having carried out his duties in getting the kitchen staff to prepare food and drinks, had disappeared in order to inform Mrs MacDonald of the latest news. Bob was hoping that the experienced and clever Mrs MacDonald would know how to handle this unexpected situation. MacKenzie himself was quite at a loss.

The older couple continued their dialogue once alone which showed the care and genuine concern they had for Lady Lochdarnock.

"No, no. You're quite right. We have left Isabelle to her own devices far too long and must be here with her. Poor girl. I can't bear to think of her languishing in such pain, unaided by family, for so long now," continued 'dear old Uncle Henry'.

Rowena replied, "After speaking to Alistair in London I'm convinced we should have come at the end of the war. Why did we leave it?"

"I won't have you blaming yourself. Time rushes past us and before we know it one year is gone and then the next."

"Look at Guthrie's portrait of her," Rowena said softly, scrutinising carefully the beautiful diaphanous image of Isabelle which had been captured not so long ago.

"She was already quite ill by the time this picture was painted. I remember she actually 'sat' for the portrait at first but Sir James had her stand. I think he wanted to display her in all her elegance. She is, after all, both tall and slender in what has become a fashion for women these days. I, for one, regret that, preferring my ladies to look more substantial.

I do remember, Isabelle told me at the time that she found it quite a trial sitting or standing for the portrait, though you would never guess by her demeanour in the picture. I think that Guthrie chap got her quite right," Henry finished.

"Henry, I don't want you to be too put out if she looks quite different to the last time you saw her. Years have passed and she's endured so much, poor little thing," said Rowena.

There was a knock at the door and a maid served a tray of tea and sandwiches at the Morning Room table.

Henry and Rowena obediently stayed seated whilst the maid moved tables and arranged their longed for sandwiches and cake.

"Thank you so much," Sir Henry told Bridget, the maid, who bobbed at him and left.

"No one in this house has a smile. Did you notice?" asked Rowena.

"I'm absolutely certain you will change all that misery into mirth of a sort, soon enough. My wife – you've become quite the queen of consolation. What with that dreadful war and those around us finding themselves almost penniless in its wake," Henry added, filling his face full of food.

Rowena smiled but was glad to change the subject back to the matter in hand.

"Isabelle will be thrilled to see you. You were always her favourite old uncle. Do you remember her as a child? When she saw her uncle Henry she broke all those rules and dashed towards you, nearly bowling you over when she jumped up at you," Rowena smiled.

"She was quite the little tom-boy, I remember that and she was so very bright."

MacKenzie knocked at the door and coughed as he entered.

"Lady Lochdarnock will be down in a few moments. She's asked if you will begin lunch without her," said Bob, noticing that the two had indeed already begun the repast.

Rowena laughed and spluttered. "I will never get used to this kind of formality."

"You do pretty well, most of the time," Henry assured her, "For a girl from the Canadian backwoods."

"You think so, do you?" Rowena laughed. "I just hope I don't embarrass you too much this time."

"I've never been embarrassed by you," Henry said gently. "Ah, except for that time in London when you told the incumbent Lord Mayor what you really thought of all the pomp and ceremony. That was quite naughty of you."

"The man nearly died." Rowena chuckled. "I'm sorry for you. I just don't know why you stay with me. I think something and the thought is straight out of my mouth like a bullet before I have even given any consideration."

"And you're getting worse not better with age. It is, of course, just as well you are completely adorable in every other way." Henry laughed.

The two chomped on their food, finishing the plate of sandwiches in double quick time.

"I'll ring for more tea." Henry smiled.

As the two chatted and waited for their tea they heard a gentle knock at the door. Isabelle appeared a second after, stumbling in through the door – ghost-like.

"Uncle Henry, Rowena – what a pleasant surprise," Isabelle said, unable to hide her misery.

"My dear, do sit down," Henry ordered, taking Isabelle's arm and guiding her to a comfortable sofa.

Rowena was shocked at the sight of her niece. "My dear!" she said. "Can we get you some tea?"

"No," Isabelle replied. "I'm so sorry. Alistair is in Edinburgh or London, I can't quite remember which. I'm afraid I'm not much company for either of you."

The older couple exchanged a concerned look before one of them replied.

"We're not here for you to entertain us, Isabelle. We want, simply, to help in any way that we can." Henry looked into her eyes as he said the words, trying to pour as much in the way of what energy he had into the younger woman.

"I'm afraid, Uncle Henry, that I shall be something of a bore for you and Rowena. You will have to excuse me…"

"It's all been so difficult for you, Isabelle. Please let us help." Rowena's voice was quiet for once. She felt a compelling need to show gentleness. It was as though Isabelle might break if anyone dared as much as speak loudly. As it was, Isabelle started to cry.

"I must show you Angus' medal. We have it displayed in the Music Room."

"We'll see that later, Isabelle. Now you must have the maid help you into outdoor clothes. We must take you for a walk in the grounds. It will clear your head." Rowena noticed that Henry was being unusually dominant with his niece as he made his announcement.

"Henry's right, Isabelle. Fresh air is what you need. In fact, hang the maid, I'll help you get ready," Rowena chirped.

The rotund Canadian all but marched Isabelle out of the room and up the stairs. The older woman felt her niece's fragile body cling to her as they walked into the wide and spacious hallway and then up the graceful staircase.

In the next three days Isabelle gradually became a part of life once more. When Alistair returned he was astounded.

"My dear, you look wonderful," Alistair enthused.

Isabelle managed a faint smile at her husband in response. He was home. That was important to her now. That night the couple lay next to one another holding hands and talking of their boys.

"I think we might take Henry and Rowena to Braeside. I'll send word to James that we are to come." Alistair smiled. "You'd like to see James again soon, my dear, I'm quite sure."

The journey to Braeside was made by train and car. Isabelle slept most of the way as did Rowena, whose endeavours since she had arrived in Scotland had made her weary.

The two men sat opposite one another, saying little for most of the journey. Henry felt compelled to break the silence which he found uncomfortable.

"It's been a difficult time for you both," Henry muttered.

"Losing Angus has left us both quite worn and James' refusal to be at the house is something Isabelle cannot bear," replied the laird.

"The boy knows about his mother's condition?" enquired Henry, cautiously.

"I thought it best that we behave as though all is quite well," the laird replied.

"My dear man, your wife is in extreme distress. Her current condition is not simply physical. There are doctors who might help her. Have you thought of making such a consultation?" The older man looked down at his shoes anticipating the reply which was a long time coming.

"Isabelle will not hear of such things. It's as though by being happy she offends the memory of Angus. He has somehow become for his mother a symbol of failure – her failure. I think she may be avoiding James as much as he seems to avoid her." There was a tear running in a miniature river down the laird's face as he spoke the words.

"This all must end. So many young men were maimed and slaughtered, Alistair. You cannot allow Isabelle to continue in this way. It is quite natural that a mother's heart is broken by these events but we must all work to improve her situation." Henry paused. "I would not want to interfere but I am told that you are away at business in Edinburgh quite often. Perhaps you might delegate the work you do there to others so that you two can endure the pain of your loss together."

"Quite right." Alistair smiled. "You are indeed quite right, as always, Henry."

Mary, who had been sent for in order to accompany Lady Isabelle, fussed about the train carriage making the party of four as comfortable as she could on arrival at Braeside.

Mary's relatives had been put out that the Lochdarnocks had had the cheek to bring the lassie off her holiday in this way, MacKenzie having turned up at their door with a letter from the Laird but Mary had been only too glad to go back to what for her was home – and a comfort to her.

Seeing that the Laird and Sir Henry were talking and the ladies at rest, Mary got out her knitting. She was completing a jacket for her niece, her darling 'niece – wee Alice'.

"It's all right," Danny had shouted at James when they had heard the news that the Lochdarnock parents were to visit the lodge at Braeside with guests.

"I can assure you it is not," James replied, throwing paper across the room. "There is not the space here to accommodate a party of six including servants."

"MacKenzie and Mary will stay at the gatehouse, I'll be there too," Danny said flatly. "And before you say anything, that's my decision which is final, Lieutenant."

James began to laugh. Danny ambled towards him and the two embraced.

"It's only four days and I'll be back," Danny reassured James quietly.

"But you belong here more than any of them, with me. And your argument that there is not enough room is a bloody nonsense, Corporal, and you know it," James whispered.

"Aye, we both know I belong here – and we both know that neither of us can afford to..."

"To be found out?" James asked.

"It's just a matter of keeping things in perspective and our people don't have a perspective on – us!" Danny wiped James' cheek, which was flushed.

"You'll make a politician yet, Corporal." James kissed Danny gently on the mouth; Danny responded in kind. As they made love, an impromptu affair, the moments flew by quickly.

"You still have not said it," James complained as he put on his shirt.

"You need me to, do you?" Danny asked matter-of-factly.

"You know that I do."

"Just a word, just a four-letter word." Danny complained.

"One I need to hear," James replied. "My God, soldier, you use a number of four-letter words which are much worse – all the time in fact – as a matter of everyday speech."

"It's hard for me." Danny sighed.

"If you can't say it, then write it. That will have to suffice," James implored him.

The pair kissed again – this time passionately. Their love making was rapid and greedy once more.

"I never could get enough of you," Danny responded. He took a breath before adding, "I'll need to get my things to the gatehouse. Their car's due. Christ, it's due any time now. Fuck, man…"

"A letter?" asked James.

"If you'll keep yer hands off me and let me get ready I'll write you a whole bloody book," replied Danny with a smile.

The path to the gatehouse was a steep one. Danny knew that getting his things there would be difficult. Lillian and Patricia could be trusted to be discreet.

When Danny arrived at the gatehouse it had been decided that Mary would be staying up at the lodge to be on hand for Lady Isabelle and Rowena but there was no need for Danny to be up there and it may well raise suspicion if he were to stay at the lodge, considering that his official position was as an assistant to James.

Danny hated being away from James for even a night. He knew how much he was depended upon and liked it, Danny Cassidy really enjoyed being so wanted and so needed by the man he loved.

They were to take Alistair Lochdarnock and Sir Henry fishing the next day with Bob MacKenzie. Danny knew MacKenzie 'knew about *them' but could be counted on to say nothing to upset the Lochdarnocks. No, if anyone were to be the loose cannon it would be James, himself.*

"I cannot bear it if you are treated like a mere servant when you are… everything, literally everything, to me," was what James had said. Danny had smiled at the thought.

"You think you're no' to me?" he asked. "Mary will be here. If you think so much of me then for my sake just treat me like a servant."

"I can't do that," said James "I simply cannot."

"Then I'll go back to Glasgow 'til your folk go home," Danny said. "You think your father would be appalled, my God! Can you just imagine how horrified mine would be, not to mention the look on Annie's face?"

"You'll stay," James said sharply.

"Is that an order, sir?" Danny enquired, smiling at James.

"How can I order you?" James asked.

"Just think you're in the trenches. It came to you there wi' no difficulty, seemingly."

"There will be a difference this time," James laughed.

"Oh, aye, whit's that?"

"This time, for once – as we are not in the trenches – you'll do as I tell you," James replied, remembering how unco-operative Private Cassidy could be.

"Aye well, just as long as you don't get too used to me doing yer biddin'," Danny said, using the delivery that Glasgow people do and exiting the room with a knowing smile.

***

According to the Delaney boy Jenny went to bed the night after reading this extract, exhausted by her efforts.

She had looked at the papers in front of her worrying about *me and my condition* of all things. She wondered if it was her fault that I had ended up in a cardiac unit of the Royal Infirmary and cursed herself for pushing me too far – and just as bad –

cursing Gil Delaney IV for using 'the poor 'old thing' that way'. Aye, that is how the Delaney Boy reports Ms Munroe's feelings on the subject!

Jenny tried to get Gil on the phone but succeeded only in getting a recorded message on his mobile. The girl left a terse and annoyed message asking Delaney to call back to "discuss poor Bill and what we might do about the research in order to keep him well". (It's nice to know they care, do you not think?)

Delaney tells me he answered within a few minutes.

"Hey Jenny. You didn't get much sleep."

"And what makes you say that?" Jenny asked obviously feeling even more annoyed by now. She wondered, as she said this, why the pair of them had to get into these clashes and knew that she was just as guilty as him for *rushing* poor old Bill on the subject of Lochdarnock but how could she let this annoying American know that?

"Because you're usually just bitchy and today you're super-bitchy. Congratulations – you almost scared me," Delaney retorted.

"You need to take this matter more seriously, Gil. We cannot involve Bill in this matter again. The man is sick."

"You know as well as me that Lochdarnock is what keeps the old man going. What the hell do you want him to do? Christ, if it is Lochdarnock he's thinking about it's the quickest way to rid himself of his annoyance with poor Hetty."

Of course, I only found out about this conversation later as a result of a boozy night in (drinking) with the long-legged Yank. But ye've to admit it, sometimes that man has me pegged – on the 'Hetty' front at least!

"You really do not understand," Jenny had blustered on, "it is very obvious to any grown up looking at the situation that the pair are devoted to one another. My God, no wonder you couldn't keep your marriage together."

It was Gil's turn to feel slighted now; he told me he hadn't expected Jenny to mention this kind of personal stuff in the context of the research – but that just shows you how much the boy understands women.

"OK, you win. Let's do whatever you think we should do. In the spirit of modern international co-operation there has to be at least one dictator centre-stage," Delaney added foolishly.

"That's unfair," Jenny seethed. "I'm simply pointing out that Bill is a sick old man and that we are pushing him far too hard."

"Has it ever occurred to you that he's the one doing the pushing? My God, whenever either of us lets up he's there with a magical new piece of information," Gil answered – clever big bugger. "Just look at the stuff he wrote himself. The guy knows more than he's letting on, if you ask me."

Of course, I found this out much later and continued to play the innocent totally unnecessarily for many weeks – fool that I am.

Jenny was silent. She knew there was something in what Gil was saying and instantly made her mind up what to do.

"Come over to the house tonight. There will be things both you and I need to look at."

Apparently one of the pieces Jenny wanted to discuss was about Kenneth Ewart. Gil tells me he found it odd that she was that interested in the man. I suppose she was trying to keep the American feeling involved and content after her character assassination of him. Or maybe it was Jenny Munroe's way of apologising – I've seen women involving themselves in these kind of complicated stunts when a straight-forward "I'm sorry I was bitchy" would do.

28

I decided to 'release' even more of my archive and writings to them as I was feeling quite pleased by the way they seemed to be handling the material and my health 'situation'. I have to admit that I was enjoying myself and feeling better by the day as I bombarded the pair with more of what I considered to be pertinent information.

Hetty was by now, of course, driving me round the bend with her nagging about my health so I was glad to be involved with what Hetty was calling the 'youngsters!' and their vital work.

Where all this would get the pair, especially Jenny who should have been concentrating on finding out the truth of her forebears, I didn't know. But it was like a game to me, a grown up game but nonetheless I did wonder if the three of us were just wasting time with it all. As far as serious historical research was concerned our wee game was far from the mark.

I decided I didn't care – knowing that I was never going to write a definitive history of the Ewarts or even the Lochdarnocks for that matter. I suppose my thinking is that if *I* don't ever get round to putting the history together then Jenny Munroe will. I'm beginning to know what that girl is like, how she thinks.

That Gordon Barton was not far from the truth when he described her as 'merciless in her pursuit of whatever is in her mind'.

I wonder how she got that way? Is it just that some of us can't let an idea go, like the proverbial dog with a bone, do you think? Or is Jenny Munroe just avoiding things she doesn't want to think about? That often happens, I think they call that 'displacement' activity. If that's right I've been guilty of it all my life, you've only to ask Hetty for confirmation.

***

KENNETH EWART – FROM BILL JOHNSON'S *HISTORY OF LOCHDARNOCK* – 1977

I don't know where to begin describing this particular piece of humanity, if that is a way of describing him, at all. I am driven in my attempt to do so by the material I found from Mrs MacDonald's diary.

Oh, yes! I've come across a lot of commentary in my research but nothing that would stand up as proof on which a court of law could convict this man, which makes him either very lucky or very clever. However, in the interests of justice and because I can now, legally, say these things I feel duty bound to write down what I do know.

Were he alive I know that what I write would constitute libel and even though he is long dead many would consider the following reportage of him as an unnecessary character assassination. I have asked myself whether my fury at the man arises from his part in my grandfather's death and, to a certain extent, my feelings are driven by this factor. The point is that nothing I have found out about this man has in any way interfered with my initial knowledge of him and I feel justified in setting down all the stuff I can on Kenneth and the rest of the Ewart family. It might seem that I am portraying him as the 'Mr

147

Jasper' character with twirly moustache and all but that is what the material I have found on Kenneth Ewart suggests.

My fear is that there are plenty of Kenneth Ewarts still out there – only these days they seem to have been tutored in public relations to the point where their vile behaviours are masked and hidden beneath a well-managed heap of rhetorical self-justifcation.

The 'modern world' eh!

Kenneth Mitchell Wilson Ewart was born in Glasgow in late May 1889, the first and only surviving son of Douglas and Helen Ewart.

Douglas had already made his name in the shipbuilding world and proudly presented his offspring to genteel society by announcing his birth in both The Times *and* The Scotsman.

These days there would be a photographic record of the child from its first breath but the technology was still at a premium and the first image of the boy that still exists seems to have been taken when he was about a year old. The picture of the baby with his stiff-looking Victorian parents can be found in the archive.

Fiona Ewart has kept a few of the pictorial records of the Ewarts. I imagine that after she'd 'seen to' the pictures (both photographic and painted) of Isabelle Lochdarnock, she had an unaccustomed nostalgia for family – as long as it was her own biological unit, that is.

To all eyes, Kenneth Ewart looks like a normal baby of the time – a boy dressed in what appears to be a dress. The psychologists of today might try to argue that putting the wee boy in a girl's dress may have damaged the man but it was, after all, common practice in those days to put boys in dresses and that excuse for him will not stand up, not in my opinion. Gender did not seem to be an issue at an early age for the Victorian child – no excuses can be given for this man's behaviours.

Kenneth was soon followed by another brother who died in infancy – a not uncommon event even amongst the middle-classes in those days. It was several years before the Ewarts produced another child – this time a girl, Fiona. She was to be their second surviving and last child.

Douglas and Helen were determined that their new-found wealth would provide their son with an education which was second to none. They applied for a place at Fettes for the boy and were successful in ensuring his youth was spent at the 'Scottish Eton' as Douglas liked to refer to the school.

It has to be said that all the evidence shows that Kenneth Ewart's particular personality traits were firmly established before he arrived at the school – though it would be easy enough to assume that his public school education had a hand in shaping his personality.

His time at Fettes certainly ensured that Kenneth had a sense of determination and entitlement. The network which was established for him through Fettes helped him in the following years to establish and consolidate the family's shipping empire.

On leaving school, Kenneth moved South to England and attended Cambridge as a student of mathematics. The record is not clear but it appears that after his second year the young Kenneth never returned to the university – there were rumours (unsubstantiated) that Kenneth was no longer welcome at his college. As I say, the reasons for his return to Scotland are unclear and my over-ripe imagination conjures up several theories which I will not elaborate here.

So, it was into the family business that the young Kenneth Ewart was thrust. To be fair to him, he took to the business and engineering side equally well and soon (even at a very early age) became a force to be reckoned with, earning a reputation as a demon negotiator and a ruthless boss – the books balanced and the company flourished and that was all that mattered to the Ewarts whose fortune was increasing substantially year by year.

Kenneth seems to have taken up with 'certain types of people' (Helen Ewart's diary – p.p. 62) – 'hard drinking womanisers, gamblers and other undesirables'.

It seems that the young Kenneth was lucky not to be arrested for his misdemeanours or he was saved by paternal intervention from suffering his due deserts for the 'stunts' (both financial and otherwise) that he is rumoured to have pulled, on a number of occasions. It is sufficient to say that the young Ewart got away with 'blue murder'.

Kenneth was twenty-five years old at the beginning of the First War. It seems that his father made sure that Kenneth was given a safe job in what would now be termed 'Naval Procurement' and, as a consequence, Kenneth saw not a moment of active service.

I wonder how Kenneth Ewart would have done under fire? We'll never know but it may have been better, all round, if the young Ewart had met his end like so many young officers in that conflict. Certainly he would not have caused such injury to his own family but then history is odd – if you mess about with one strand of it a whole different blanket ends up getting knitted, don't you think? Certainly, his war time position would not have benefitted my poor grandfather one bit even if he had lived.

It can be seen from the 'Royal Navy' record of the time that Ewart indeed made some interesting deals which were beneficial to himself and more especially to Ewart's shipbuilders – now there is a surprise!

How he managed to get away with his particular financial dealings is a mystery. I can only assume that people in navy procurement weren't clued up from a business perspective in those days. Those old military types counted the cost of war in a different way, I suppose. Financial cost and body count weren't as important as the stiffness of the proverbial upper lip and a grand victory for the Empire.

In 1914 Kenneth Ewart met Harriet Beech, the daughter of an English duke. They married before the end of the First War and produced a couple of kids – who it seems Harriet whisked off to America in the early 1920s. It is alleged that the poor woman was determined to get away from her 'cruel and unfaithful' husband.

Harriet, a bit of a girl in her own right, became a member of the Church of Christian Science and died unnecessarily, as a result of her religious beliefs prompting her to refuse medical treatment at a fairly early age – poor woman.

Kenneth Ewart never married again.

(Post-script – 1994) What the record from Lochdarnock does show, however, is that this man was responsible for as much suffering *away from his business activities as he caused in the shipbuilding industry.*

Yes, Mrs MacDonald's diary (which was bought by the house in the 1990s) reveals the full horribleness of Kenneth Ewart, who picked on poor Bridget Riley – a simple girl who was guilty of nothing more than being pretty, desirable, poor, and tragically gullible.

***

Parting with the story – that of Lochdarnock (*my* story as it had always seemed to me) was proving simpler and less painful than I thought it might have been. I wanted to share the Lochdarnocks of the early twentieth Century period with Gil and I thought, "To Hell with it"

I was e.mailing extract after extract from my *History of the Lochdarnocks* and other sources – it seemed strangely imperative to me then, after I got home following my 'health scare' as Hetty now calls it.

***

MORE LOSS – BILL JOHNSON –
A HISTORY OF LOCHDARNOCK 1977

The stableblock was large. Lord Alistair owned a number of fine horses which his sons and he rode. Their competitive spirit meant that energies which were often expressed negatively by the boys could be channelled through riding. Alistair insisted that his sons learn to ride early, in spite of Isabelle's fears. Isabelle had been thrown from a horse when a teenager and believed without cause that the fall was the reason for her current illness.

Both boys were competent on horseback and enjoyed competing with one another. Isabelle noted that they were at their happiest together when riding and although she could not watch them, fearing for their safety as she did, she was pleased when they returned from their jaunts especially at the lodge where things were so much more relaxed than at the house in Glasgow.

Alistair was thrilled that these two fine-looking young men engaged with one another positively in their sport.

If only the war had not ruined everything for them. If only Angus were alive, life might be better for Isabelle – for them all but the war had happened and life would never be the same again.

The lavish parties were no more, money seemed to be drying up, income was low, the hunting lodge was occupied year round by James and his Batman (until the poor young man died ridiculously early as a result of wartime gassing) and only he and Isabelle lived a semi-dead life now here at the house in Glasgow.

Alistair felt guilty. Alistair felt half the man he had been before the war when everything had seemed possible, when there was greater certainty and more laughter.

The only laughter in Lochdarnock House now was when a servant would inadvertently lapse into happiness but there was an air over the place which forbad this and that made the servants nervous and Alistair sad as a result.

The situation meant that Alistair wanted to run from his beloved home into the arms of his lover (the ever-present Fiona Ewart) in Edinburgh. Little enough excuse, he knew, but there it was. He was human and one who had judged others harshly for the kind of behaviour he was indulging in now.

Ultimately, Alistair had convinced himself, we are all mere human beings capable of the most incredible selfishness. Perhaps, he reasoned often enough, that it was selfishness which allowed us all to survive life's horrors.

Alistair closed his journal, put his pen away. For a moment he hung his head, thinking of life and its small and large tragedies.

His valet knocked on the door. Alistair showed the man his small suitcase and rose, ready once more to lie to his ailing wife.

The valet carried his case to the waiting car, as Alistair made to move through his beloved House, a House which had been enriched by so many wonderful memories and so much and so many valued possessions, towards his wife.

Isabelle would, he knew, be withdrawn as usual. He would kiss her lightly on the cheek before descending the staircase. Alistair decided to stop off on his way in the Business Room and Morning Room and looked about him at the stuccoed walls and the Guthrie portrait of Isabelle in happier times which hung in an alcove. She had been a beauty, she had been so important and vital to his life. He could not have imagined when James Guthrie was painting the portrait that his beautiful Isabelle could succumb in such a way to life's horrors and to the mystery illness which seemed to stalk her so cruelly.

Alistair sat at his large desk and marvelled at the Raeburn which hung in a corner, dimly lit, in this, the Business Room. It was a fine portrait by Raeburn of a forebear, but it lacked the delicacy and romanticism of the Guthrie which was his favoured picture in this House.

Groupings of glass paste medallions by James Tassie sat either side of the fine Adam-style fireplace which lay to the side of his desk.

Alistair was a romantic at heart. He was not especially keen on the medallions but Tassie was a local man and Alistair had been determined when he bought the medallions to bring them home to the city, to their city, a city of himself and Tassie and many others whom he so admired – so many others who had bothered to keep alive creativity in the face of so much suffering over the years.

Above the fireplace hung a Ranken picture of flowers, beautifully mounted in a frame which complemented the stucco in white and gold.

Alistair Lochdarnock had spent the last twenty-five years running the Lochdarnock estates from this room.

He had spent much happy time here, deliberating with staff and tenants. The boys, when young, had run in and out from time to time, wildly and absurdly as children do.

Alistair knew the servants and tenants were horrified that his boys were not kept 'under better control' but their laughter and childlike joy filled the house with an essence of what he knew he and Isabelle were truly all about – above all their union was about life and living, which made the horror and tragedy of the last few years so difficult to abide.

The laird looked about him once more, pondering the unfairness of fate. He tried to take pleasure in the room and its beautiful treasures to lend him the fortitude to get off to Edinburgh where there was at least a chance to be light-hearted, as in the days of his relative youth.

The pictures around him made Alistair smile. The fresh and loving memories they brought to his mind outshone the misery of the passing of better days.

Perhaps Alistair's favourite piece aside from the Guthrie was the painting by Mengs of 'Girl with a Dove' – touching and again romantic – the picture showing innocence and tenderness which were qualities that Alistair craved now in his middle years.

Alistair sighed and wrote in his business ledgers as he normally did before rising and climbing the staircase which sweeps grandly upwards. Fine mahogany bannisters aided the walker up the stairs which at times had seemed impossibly steep to dear Isabelle these days.

It was on these walls that the house's fine collection of Spanish paintings mainly hung. Severe-looking grandees and pathetic infantas sat cheek by jowl on the walls. Alistair was not particularly fond of these dark and seemingly depressing portraits preferring the modern style portraiture he had selected for the house himself.

On reaching the first floor Alistair decided to enter the drawing room which had recently had its paintings rehung to his own specification, wondering why it was he felt compelled to make this inspection of the house at this time.

These paintings too seemed dark and sombre today sitting on the pale green stuccoed walls. Paintings of Jacobites, poets and other historical figures seemed to glare down at him, judging, always judging.

Alistair slumped in a comfortable sofa and tried to concentrate on his collection of maiolica, cheerful, bright and pleasant but it would not do. His mood was low, he felt a sense of foreboding and wondered whether he might cancel his trip to Edinburgh in spite of the obvious allure which beckoned him.

The laird looked at the fine rug beneath him which was Turkish, he believed – and he wondered at the beauty of the piece and of this House and how it might be preserved after his passing – Alistair felt an overwhelming sense of responsibility for all things Lochdarnock – the house, the lodge, the people.

James seemed not in the least interested in dealing with the Glasgow house preferring to secrete himself away in the North, writing those dreadful pamphlets of his.

Finally, MacKenzie knocked on the door and asked, "I was wondering if you were ready for the trip, Sir Alistair."

"Yes, of course," Alistair managed with a smile. MacKenzie was a pleasant reminder that some things did indeed stay the same after all, things which could be relied upon – the man was loyal and kind and thoughtful.

The two men proceeded to the car, the valet having already put the small suitcase in the front passenger seat by MacKenzie. Soon, too soon, the car took off with the two middle-aged men, Alistair regretting his situation but glad of taking his leave from the house and its heavy, sad atmosphere.

When Alistair arrived at the hotel in Edinburgh, Fiona Ewart was waiting for him patiently as usual. She knew his tastes well and had ordered dinner for them that evening and the correct whisky for him to drink – a whisky which relaxed him.

Their love-making had, as to be expected, become perfunctory but the closeness although not of the quality or loving passion he had once shared with Isabelle was satisfactory and helped him forget the recent terrible past.

As we know, I was in my sickbed pretty soon after getting this material sorted out – I know you'll think this obsession that's been growing in me of premonitions is strange for a man like me. I do myself!

So, I had furnished the big man Delaney and the girl with the story of Lochdarnock as far as I knew it. To be fair, especially with the Delaney Boy, the exchange of information worked well.

Of course, the big Yank had plenty to say about it.

"So Bill, you've known this stuff all along. You played Jenny and me for fools," he said, looking far from pleased.

"No, not at all," I managed, not blaming him for being annoyed. "Look on it as a game. I got you two involved in a game I've played on my own for a time and let's face it, Gil, the two of you enjoyed every minute of it."

"Smart! I suppose you think it was smart to get Jenny and me on-board. If you had told the two of us all this stuff before it may have saved a lot of time," Gil Delaney seethed.

"It didn't seem you were in too much of a hurry to get away from one another," I sulked.

"Point taken. But Jenny is as mad as hell with you. She won't say a thing because she doesn't want you having another heart attack but you can see her point. She has this job to think of and then you lead her on a romp!" Delaney added. "Knowing that you knew all this stuff by heart."

"The Guthrie has had us all romping. Remember, the point of the whole exercise is to work out how Jenny looks so much like Isabelle Lochdarnock. That's where her interest started." I paused. "I know I could have given you all the Ewart stuff well in advance but I wanted the two of you to play nicely!"

"Nicely?" Gil scoffed.

"It's the kinda thing Hetty would say, I know. But you've to admit, the two of you have had a lot of fun too," I offered, glaring at the man.

"OK! You got yourself off the hook," he replied after due consideration.

I was relieved and exhausted.

"So what next?" I asked.

"I was kinda hoping you would tell us," Gil replied with a smile.

29

Naturally enough, the pair decided in their own fashion that they both needed to give 'poor old Bill' (that'll be me!) something back – annoyed as they might have been. They are an easy couple to manage. I think that Jenny just wanted to keep me going, afraid that I might pop my, dodgy, clogs.

Jenny put together a couple of extracts from her mother's family history which filled in bits I had guessed (but never definitely knew) about the Cassidy clan and Gil gave me another strand to link the Cassidys, Lochdarnocks and Ewarts, which had turned up in his research.

I love this – putting the jigsaw together in my sick bed saved me the bother of having to be too involved with the biddy who was on a mission to 'save' me from myself.

William and his wife had come up from London. They were pleasant enough, as was only to be expected.

Of course, Heather was there at her mother's side and was nagging me,

"Slow down, Dad," she repeated over and over. "Och, I suppose there is absolutely no point in me telling you that. You've always been that stubborn."

I could not disagree with the girl, who had obviously been well briefed by her mother over the years.

William understood the matter better and asked me if I was still continuing with my research.

He and I discussed Lochdarnock, a subject in which he had feigned an interest over the years. William was taken by the excitement the inclusion of the American and Jenny had brought to matters. Of course, he was sympathetic to a point, but ach! The man has his own life to lead…

I've to admit I wasn't too perturbed to see William and Heather turn up but it was when the grandchildren rushed to my bedside from all points of the compass I got a wee fright. Were the doctors not telling me the whole truth? Was I about to kick the bucket? I suppose it is inevitable that a body of my age would think that way but, stubborn, yes! Stubborn as I am I was not ready to die – not yet.

I asked William if they all thought I was about to breathe my last.

"No, but mother does." And he told me to be 'understanding' of Hetty, citing the fact that she wasn't getting any younger as an excuse for her hysteria.

"Neither are you for that matter." William added, unnecessarily.

"Whit happened to *your* hair?" I asked trying to change the subject.

"Still using the old 'deflect the conversation away from matters I don't want to discuss' routine?" asked my boy who was looking to me like an old man himself what with the wrinkles and lack of hair.

I have to say that by the time they took the hint and took their leave, I was glad that they all buggered off and left me to my 'Lochdarnock' musings. Trying to convince them that there was little the matter with me that a bit of peace and quiet wouldn't solve had been a labour, I can tell you.

It was as soon as they all departed that I was able to take a good look at the material provided by Jenny.

Reciprocity in this lark was essential. Jenny Munroe knew

that even if my family was critical of the girl for what they called 'bombarding' me with material, I was happy. I'd hardly call what Jenny and Gil were sending 'information overload ', would you? A few wee family bits and pieces and Jenny's mother's own attempt at writing a family history including the following tidbit...

30

March 1933

Alice's eighteenth birthday should have been exciting. She was a married woman now but instead of a party, instead of a celebration, she was looking at her own mother's coffin, sitting in the living room. Elizabeth Cassidy was thirty-eight and had just had one child too many, had been through one labour too many, for her poor weak body to withstand.

Patrick Cassidy sat by the fire which was roaring. Alice wondered why they had bothered having a fire today. It was warm, so warm she felt stifled.

Alice had cried buckets over her mother's death and tried constantly to calm herself. She was in the process of becoming a mother herself, after all. True, it was early days and nobody but she and Brian Maguire – her new husband – knew about the happy event to come. Alice wanted things to stay that way. At least until the funeral was over and her poor mother was cold in her grave. Alice picked up Suzie – her little sister – just two years old, and cuddled the crying child. Little Maria sat quietly in the corner stroking the

161

arm of the chair. Alice had no idea what to do for any of her brothers and sisters. Johnny, Harry, Paddy and Ellen were old enough to fend for themselves but she'd already decided that she would need to take wee Suzie in hand and she worried on about Sally (darling wee Sally). Alice's father, poor Patrick, poor hardworking Patrick Cassidy, had not a clue about running a household, caring for babies and being without his beloved Elizabeth.

A trail of uncles, aunts, and friends had paraded through the cramped tenement – all wanting to show their respects and mumbling prayers, eerily around Elizabeth's open coffin.

Alice had been hard at work since morning ensuring there was a steady flow of tea and food for them all to have before and after the funeral which seemed to be taking a terrible long time to come.

Posh Auntie Mary was there. The woman was dressed smartly in black and Alice felt annoyed that her poor mother had never had all the nice things this spoiled old-fashioned woman took for granted.

Auntie Mary couldn't have been more than thirty-eight herself but had always seemed so much older, so much denser a personality than Alice's poor sainted mother who never raised an eyebrow, never mind her voice at anything. Posh Auntie Mary, on the other hand, could kill with a look. Strangely she had always been good to Alice and the other kids, of course, but Alice knew Mary had a soft spot for her – which she found annoying and suffocating at times.

"Are you coping well?" Mary asked. "Is there anything I can do to help you?"

"No, I'm doing fine," said Alice proudly, her chin held high and her nose pointing upward in defiance of her feelings of loss. "I've just to get Maria and Suzie into their coats."

"Let me do that, Alice. You look like you need a wee break," Mary stated flatly. It was obvious to Mary that the girl was 'in the family way' already even though she had been married only a matter of weeks.

'What can I say?' thought Mary.

As Mary clothed the two smaller girls she heard Alice sing quietly to herself. The girl was leaning over Patrick Cassidy trying to help the shocked man to his feet. Patrick Cassidy looked at his daughter Alice and then to his sister.

"She sings to me. My Alice sings to me, just like her mother used to."

Alice, long and slender and beautiful as ever, managed to get the man to his feet and helped him put on his black jacket. Gently, Alice fixed his tie and smoothed the man's hair.

"It's all right, Da," the young woman said gently. "Everything will be fine."

Alice knew in her heart that it would not be fine. Alice knew in her heart at that moment that she had lost both her parents forever and she wanted to weep and yell to the world about the injustice of it all.

Brian Maguire, Alice's new husband, 'the big farmer' as he was nicknamed, stood behind his new wife and whispered into her ear.

Alice tried to smile but couldn't. She was getting increasingly annoyed that Posh Auntie Mary kept staring at her. The interfering old fool had always wanted too much to do with her. Alice wondered why the older woman hadn't got herself married by now. Apparently she'd been a looker in her day. Still, Alice supposed, she was probably far too prim to be involved with something as disgusting as a man. Alice knew about the payments Mary had made regularly to her mother but just because Auntie Mary had helped her family out that didn't give her the right to try to take over their lives.

The room was full of Cassidys and her mother's family. Strange, Alice thought, that she herself didn't look like one of them.

"Aye, Alice my girl, y'er a throwback to the big farmers on my side from Antrim," Annie Cassidy, her grandmother, had told her when she was small. "Would you look at the long legs on ye."

Alice liked her Nanna Annie, who was nothing if not honest, and she didn't really mind being so tall. It could come in handy sometimes being the giant in a land of wee people.

Alice grabbed wee Suzie from Auntie Mary's arms One thing was for sure, Alice would not let this wrinkled auld yin take over her *family. Money or no money, Posh Auntie Mary was not in charge of the Cassidys and never would be.*

Alice looked again as the coffin was lifted, the coffin containing her lovely mother and unnamed little sister. Patrick had refused to name the child. Alice had a notion to call her Angela. She'd heard that that was what she was supposed to have been called and that both her grandmothers had vetoed the choice. So that's what she told the priest to refer to the poor wee wean as – poor wee dead Angela Cassidy who hadn't managed to take a breath of life.

***

You look back on the terrible tragic lives people lead and wonder how they survived it. I was glad that Jenny Munroe had added more of her family's story. These things fill you with a sense of shame at how we are, how I am, always moaning on and never content with my easy lot. I read on, wanting to know more about Alice Cassidy, Alice Lochdarnock as it was clear we could now call her.

***

A GOOD PLACE BY MARGARET MUNROE
PATRICK AND ELIZABETH – DEATH AND DISPERSAL

As Alice busied herself with the funeral her siblings seemed to 'stoat' about doing nothing, less than nothing if it is possible to achieve that.

What Alice didn't and couldn't know was what was to become of them all.

Of the four boys hanging about the room that day, Paddy would marry and move to Ayr with his new wife and her family; Johnny, a good musician would join the army and later travel about – a lonely soul – making music and money where and how he could. Whenever he visited the family he was full of life – a cheery but a poor man with no place to call his own. Johnny died young – another victim of tuberculosis – all alone. Alice had wept buckets for her younger, handsome brother – the talented and kindly Johnny had deserved so much better than the lot life had given him.

It was Alice's sister Sally, poor dear slow Sally, who caused most concern. She was twelve when Elizabeth died and seemed as bemused as poor Patrick Cassidy himself. Four years later Sally took off. It was another ten years before the family finally found out where poor slow Sally ended up.

When Alice found her, after attempting vainly for many a year, it seems that Sally had taken a train out of Glasgow when she was just sixteen. It appeared that she didn't know where she was going but had ended up in Berwick upon Tweed.

Sally married a local boy who was good to her. They had two bright children who cared to the end for their dear sweet mother. Sally was happy, Sally had a good life with a man who loved her. Dear sweet Sally who had always been such a worry to Elizabeth Cassidy had been the one to achieve a happy life – who would have guessed?

(When Jenny Munroe heard this story she was relieved to know that there could, amongst all the sadness and sorrow, be a happy ending for someone.)

Patrick Cassidy was taken away after a few months of care at home and was settled by the authorities on the 'Funny Farm' where Alice and her siblings would visit him regularly.

Patrick seemed happy there and by all accounts was well looked after. He cared for the horses and looked after the small chapel at 'The Farm' to which he was devoted.

Alice had asked him many times to come home with her but Patrick insisted he was fine as he was and that here in the countryside he could remember his beloved Elizabeth. He told Alice that he and Elizabeth had both harboured a dream of living in the country and he had managed that even if she was not there to share it with him.

It did not occur to Alice Cassidy-Maguire to be angry with her *sainted father for leaving her at such a young age to deal with the aftermath of her mother's death. How could she be angry with such a wonderful, lovely man – besides, her mother in law, Mrs Maguire could be angry for her and say and think what she liked. Alice loved her da' and nothing anyone could say would change that – not even vicious 'auld Ma Maguire'*

Jenny tells me she was thirty-five years old when she saw this extract first. Her mother had always made Jenny aware of what she termed the 'family tragedy' – not an unreasonable assessment, I think, in the given circumstances.

What happened to Margaret Maguire-Monroe has been carefully documented but the interesting part for me, of course, was her involvement with posh great-aunt Mary.

A GOOD PLACE BY MARGARET MUNROE
MARGARET DOESN'T GO TO LONDON

Alice had been getting the place ready all morning. Her two boys, Pat and Jimmy, had been in and out making more mess than she was able to tidy. Margaret, the eldest, now long and strong – the image of her mother – and dedicated to girly pursuits which at once made Alice smile and cringe, helped her mother tidy up for the arrival of Posh Auntie Mary.

Posh Aunt Mary had always taken a keen interest in Margaret. She was particularly keen to know how her education was going. Fortunately, Margaret was bright and Alice was able to report positively on her only daughter's academic achievements. The girl liked to be top of the class and was competitive. Alice knew this impressed Auntie Mary – a fact that Alice found annoying. It seemed to Alice that the daft old woman couldn't let things be, couldn't relax and let her hair down. She'd seen the Auntie's look when she'd encouraged her children to sing and dance – something they loved and shared in common with their mother, Alice.

The boys were talented singers, of course, but poor Margaret had the voice of a depressing bell, deep and tuneless. Consequently, Margaret found herself relegated to supporting her brothers' efforts in performance, by supplying the words to songs which neither boy could remember.

Margaret found her brother, 'young Pat' as he was referred to, a delight. He was a soulful boy always praying – which pleased both his parents and his doting paternal grandmother – Mrs Maguire, to boot.

Alice was glad that young Pat had been a baby when World War Two started. Fighting was not for the likes of 'oor Pat', who was a sensitive soul, like her own dear father who still lived up at the farm in the country. Alice would take the children to visit their grandda' whenever she could.

At least, she'd decided a long time ago now, she could see the man and know that he was at peace with himself and the world even if he was always withdrawn with a wondering look in his eyes. Patrick had never gotten over the death of Elizabeth. Nowadays he spoke little about anything and had never uttered a word about his dead wife since her funeral, which seemed so long ago now to Alice.

Margaret was fussing over the tenement apartment in the same way she fussed over her own appearance. The girl was never satisfied with the look of anything, or so it seemed to Alice, who herself was relieved when the old goat of an auntie turned up and duly left so that life in her chaotic but happy household could return to normal

Mary Cassidy was the only person who knocked on Alice's door. Everyone else entered and shouted out their name to announce their presence on arrival, as was the way in this part of town. When the knock at the door came, Alice ordered Margaret to answer. Margaret was forever bowing and scraping to the old woman, who seemed to enjoy the attention the girl gave to her. Had Alice known the word 'sycophant' she'd have used it for her Margaret. Certainly, Alice knew that such behaviour seemed polite but for her there was a limit to all that fancy stuff. 'Never mind,' Alice thought, 'best to keep the old yin happy!'

Mary Cassidy seemed to age each time Alice saw her. It was evident that the woman had once been pretty in the same way as Alice's siblings were but the auntie's looks had faded and her dark hair had become grey. Alice determined that she would definitely not allow her own hair to become dull and devoid of life in that way. Alice thought it unnecessarily ageing. Just about everybody these days dyed their hair. Except it seemed this difficult woman who was her own aunt. Alice supposed that was because Auntie Mary had allowed herself to become separated from her own people, living as she did at that 'posh house', in what Alice considered the countryside.

Mary Cassidy seemed flushed today. Alice guessed Auntie Mary was going through her 'change'. She'd heard of it and was as horrified by the thought of that experience as she was by the horror of giving birth – which Alice had found a most terrible event. She wondered how, in the light of her own mother's death, she had got through childbirth three times, already. No wonder her darling mother had died. Childbirth was a hideous experience. Alice shuddered at the thought and smiled brightly as old Auntie Mary entered the kitchenette.

"Take Auntie Mary into the sitting room, Margaret," Alice managed, "I'll bring the tea in."

Alice had carefully laid the tray with her best china tea-set. Her mother-in-law, Mrs Maguire, had given her a nice service she'd picked up cheaply at the Barras as a present for her wedding. Alice was proud of the rich red and cream set which was gilded and luxurious looking to Alice's eyes which were unused to such opulence.

The best biscuits had been placed on a tiny plate from the same richly decorated service. It had taken a lot for Alice to get her boy, Jimmy, to leave the biscuits alone. Alice supposed that Auntie Mary, who was not a big eater and very 'proper', would leave biscuits for the children along with her usual gift of money. Alice always refused the money and Auntie Mary always insisted that Alice took the usually substantial and useful offering without a fuss.

"Please take it, for the children, if not for yourself," Mary would stress with a pained look on her face.

It had to be admitted that these regular offerings helped she and Brian to get through life, though Alice was a good manager with money and seemed to be able to stretch her husband's meagre income a long way.

Alice supplemented Brian's pay with 'bingo' wins and the odd bit of luck she had on the horses every now and then. Alice Cassidy Maguire had a taste for gambling – she just adored the thrill of it – gambling being her one indulgence – apart that is from cream cakes.

As she entered the living room Auntie Mary was talking with the two boys. She rarely smiled at the boys, seeming to reserve all her energy and attention for Margaret who clung to the old woman's every word and seemed impressed by the prim auld great-auntie.

Alice worried about Margaret's tendency to be so easily impressed by posh people. For her part, Alice was not in the slightest bit bothered by Auntie Mary but, somehow, Alice felt quite daunted when those types, the Auntie Marys, were in her company.

The girl and two women drank tea and chattered inanely, Auntie Mary asking question after question about Margaret's achievements at school and Alice's daily 'doings' as the auld woman called them.

The time was fast approaching three o'clock when Mary usually left. Today she was showing none of the usual signs that she was ready for departure. Alice felt irritated. She'd wanted to pop into Genie's across the landing for a gossip but it looked like the auntie was set to stay a wee while longer. Alice dreaded running out of conversation and began to hum.

"You've always had a lovely voice, Alice," Mary commented. "Do you sing, Margaret?" Annie smiled and Margaret blushed.

"She cannae sing, can you hen?" Alice commented with a knowing smile.

"I'm no' good like oor Patrick and James at singing," Margaret confessed with a blush.

"Well, I hear you're the one for your school work," Mary smiled.

"I like school," Margaret replied, glowing in the positive attention.

"You must be very pleased with Margaret's progress, Alice?"

"Well, it's good and that. But she's a lassie. Whit's the point in a lassie staying on at school! She'll jist get married and have weans." Alice replied feeling uncomfortable now as the auld auntie looked at her over her spectacles.

"Maybe Margaret would like to have a job first?" Mary enquired. "Would you, Margaret? I know a lot of young girls these days like the idea of having a job or even a profession."

"Yes, Auntie Mary." Margaret replied quietly.

"That's very good." beamed Mary. Perhaps you'd like to freshen up that pot of tea, Margaret. I'd like to talk to your mother for a wee minute."

Margaret was surprised. She'd never heard the auntie ask this before and the curious child wondered what was going on. Margaret left the room and positioned her ear to the crack in the door, determined to hear exactly what was being said between her mother and Great Auntie Mary.

Alice, herself, began to feel even less comfortable and watched the older woman flush again, feeling sorry for her.

"Do you want me to open a window, Auntie Mary?" asked Alice thoughtfully.

"Not at all, Alice. But I would like a wee word with you." Mary stumbled over the words, which was unusual for her. Alice began to worry about what poor lonely Auntie Mary was going to say. The older woman had made the conversation seem momentous – "Was she sick? Was she dying?" Alice wondered.

"This is very difficult, Alice," Mary carried on.

"Well, just say it," Alice blurted, feeling inquisitive and embarrassed now.

"I'm going to be moving to England. I've given up my job at the house."

"What have ye done that for?" Alice asked puzzled. It had always seemed to Alice that Lochdarnock House was the most important thing in the world to the old Auntie. She remembered conversation after conversation being littered by tales of the Lochdarnock estates, about posh parties and dances and dinners that were held at the house.

Margaret had, Alice noticed, hung on to these tales of grandeur recounted by the auld auntie and enjoyed the fantasy world her Great Auntie Mary had described. Aye, the old auntie had wittered on about Lochdarnock House for years with total affection and now after all that time she was ready to up and leave. Just like that, with no rhyme or reason. That seemed very strange to Alice.

"Things changed at the house with the death of Lady Isabelle and the marriage of Lord Alistair to Fiona Ewart. My position isn't the same as it was and it is time for me to go – to move forward, I'll go down south," explained Mary.

"So, ye've got a job in England?" Alice enquired.

"I have a job in Brighton. The house is obviously not as impressive as Lochdarnock but the wages and life I could have should be very suitable," Mary replied tentatively, almost tearfully.

"Well, that's good for you," said Alice cheerfully. "I'm glad you've got the chance of a good job and that."

"Thank you, Alice. I shall miss you very much," the older woman blurted, clearly holding back tears.

"You'll come back and visit. If you need somewhere to stay, Mrs Maguire has room. I'm sure she'd be glad to have ye any time yer up here."

"Yes, I'm sure I shall come back and stay. The thing is, Alice, I have something to ask you – something very important."

Alice nodded not wanting the poor old thing to burst into tears. She'd never seen Auntie Mary cry in all these years, since her own mother's funeral. Even when Patrick had been carted off to the funny farm. Alice felt uncomfortable and wished the old woman would finish with this conversation, take her tea and leave.

"Alice, the gentleman I will be working for is a widower. He's a daughter of Margaret's age. He is a very respectable gentleman, a doctor." Mary coughed quietly. "His little girl has been very lonely since the death of her mother and I wondered… I wonder if you might allow me to take Margaret with me to be the girl's companion."

Alice's body registered feelings of shock which quickly turned to anger. How dare this woman come to her house and attempt to drag her only daughter away from her? What did the old witch think she was?

"Auntie Mary!" Alice managed to squeal.

"Please don't be upset, Alice. You must give the matter some thought. Margaret would have the opportunity for an excellent private education, she would be mixing in circles which would allow her to have a pleasant life, to find a man well able to take care of her for the rest of her life."

Alice was speechless now, she imagined her face to be purple. Rage overtook her after a few seconds.

"You will take my daughter away from me over my dead body," Alice thundered.

Margaret who was listening at the door, disappeared into the kitchen and hurriedly made the tea, determined to put in her bid to be allowed to go with Auntie Mary to England, to a future of sophistication and glamour. Imagine – England – parties, balls and all that stuff they showed at the cinema – all that stuff Auntie Mary had told her about. She would have the money to buy beautiful dresses, flowers, jewellery – things that were unattainable to the likes of her, here in the Gorbals.

Margaret hurriedly took the tray into the living room and passed Auntie Mary on the way out as she left.

The old woman kissed the top of the girl's head and whispered, "Goodbye, my pet. I hope… I hope you'll stay well." With that Posh Great Auntie Mary walked out of Margaret's life forever.

Alice grabbed the tray from Margaret. "Get yersel' a biscuit, hen. Boys!" Alice stormed into the kitchenette and screamed out of the window, looking down at the backs where the boys played happily, "Get up here and get yer tea."

Margaret knew she daren't discuss the matter with her mother and sat feeling crestfallen and confused on the lumpy settee, regretting the comfort she had just been denied but one day… one day she,

Margaret, would go to England and have lovely clothes and beautiful jewellery. One day, she – Margaret Maguire – would travel the entire world in style.

Jenny or someone who knew the story well had added a codicil to the end of this chapter – I suppose to keep the record straight:

Margaret Maguire went on to marry Frank Munroe who took her to live in England. She travelled widely, experienced the glamour of cruises – all on a carefully managed budget.

Margaret's chosen 'career' as she liked to call it was marred by Alice – who she forgave for not allowing her to train as a medical secretary – in case she got to 'know too much'.

That, Margaret reasoned, was a small price to pay for having a mother so devoted that she wanted to keep her child safely by her side forever.

Margaret went on to have a career as a secretary, and worked her way to a management position, always regretting that she did not achieve her ambitions as she might have done had she had the right chances.

This lost opportunity was clearly a disappointment to Margaret, who always told the tale of how posh Auntie Mary had wanted to take her to England when she was twelve and give her the good life. It was clear to anyone who heard the tale, that a little of Margaret always thought 'If only'.

31

What I hadn't bargained for in all of this was that the Big American would take himself back to the States, just as it seemed we three were getting somewhere with the research.

Unknown to me and Jenny, he'd made contact with the only remaining Ewart he could find and put himself to the trouble of going to interview the woman.

Of course, he filled me and Jenny in on the matter when he returned to Scotland after his adventure, later that month.

It seemed that the three of us were going off at different tangents but, in retrospect, this was not a bad thing. His account of the matter was a wee bit scanty and I had to question him at length about the experience – he probably thinks I'm just another nagging biddy, I've to admit to being pedantic and obsessive even in taking down his testimony.

The experience he had doesn't sound all that pleasant to me, I've to admit.

GIL AND ELOISE EWART-SANDERS MEET

Gil approached the door with caution and a certain amount of dread. He'd been in Boston before and had come across its socialites.

He hadn't much liked any he'd met in the past and knew that Eloise Ewart-Sanders was unlikely to be different. A maid, yes, a maid answered the door – 2017 and the woman was suitably dressed in an old-fashioned black and white uniform, a cliché. Gil was surprised and felt that this 'affectation' was a step too far, even for people as wealthy as Eloise Ewart-Sanders.

"For Godsake," he told me, "we're in the twenty-first century."

The maid was Mexican and slight with a determined look in her eye which hid a certain fear all new immigrants must feel in modern day America, or that was Gil's best guess.

"Miss Eloise asked me to put you in the drawing room."

Gil felt favoured – he thought he might have been asked to use the tradesmen's entrance round the back.

Gil sat in an over-upholstered chair, blue in colour – a pale blue on which he spotted a dog's hair. The pooch must have a black coat, he decided, and being not at all an admirer of the small type of dog he imagined the hair to belong to Gil felt unimpressed. (I suppose a big man like him would look stupid with a wee pooch on the end of a leash?)

He picked up a photograph which was situated in an expensive silver frame and promptly dropped it on the floor. With that a tall woman, rather straight-backed entered the room carrying the tiny, angry looking cur which growled at Gil. Gil guiltily picked up the frame and gently placed it on the table. Eloise Ewart-Sanders gave a thin smile.

"No need to worry about Consuela, she's perfectly harmless. Can I offer you tea Mr Delaney?" Eloise asked – the smile failing to leave her rather oversized mouth. Gil noted that the rest of the woman's face did not move along with her mouth.

'Botox.' he guessed.

Gil politely declined the offer of tea and sat back in his chair, more to distance himself from the small black terrier which seemed put out by his presence than to relax himself into the meeting, he noted.

"So you're here to ask me questions about Great Granny. Am I

175

to be excited, Mr Delaney? Is there a book involved by any chance?"
Eloise Ewart-Sanders looked amused.

"Just some stuff I'd like to clarify about the Beech-Ewart family."
Gil cleared his throat, wondering why he still felt so intimidated by
these people. Christ he'd been in their company often enough over the
years to relax with them by now, surely?

"Stuff?" Eloise lit a cigarette, expertly placing the filter of the long
white tube in her mouth and drawing on it slowly whilst seemingly
squinting her eyes against the smoke which had started to stream from
the cigarette's tip. The Botox made her odd look even rather more odd,
than before.

"Kenneth Ewart. I'm researching his business activities and his
personal life."

Gil paused after blurting out what seemed a confession.

"And why, may I ask?" Eloise asked evenly.

"Why, why Kenneth Ewart? OK, my family had a connection to
the shipyard the Ewart's once owned in Scotland. I guess you could say
I'm keen to set the record straight," Gil replied.

"Let me tell you right off, Mr Delaney, Kenneth Ewart was every
inch the bastard you have discovered him to be – already – judging by
your demeanour. He gave poor Grandma Harriet a pretty awful life,
and my poor father too. By the time Mother met the old lady (Harriet)
she was terribly religious, if Christian Science can be regarded as a
bona fide religion," Eloise breathed and puffed at Gil.

"I don't know much about it. The religion, that is," Gil confessed.

"I'll give you some of her old pamphlets. I have them somewhere
in a drawer." The handsome Eloise looked as bored with the subject as
she sounded.

"Pretty much a mumbo-jumbo cult from the beginning of the last
century but I don't recall Grandma being a typical Mary Baker-Eddy
devotee. She was robust. That's right. You could say the old lady was
robust. She had to be, I guess, considering what Kenneth Ewart was
like. I'll let you have her diary but I must insist on it being returned.
Now Mr Delaney, I'm hosting a dinner party tonight so if you don't

have any further questions," Eloise voice trailed off as she stared hard at the tall man sitting before her.

"Perhaps you might like to join us – my husband and some of his business associates?" she added.

"I'm sorry I have a prior engagement in New York this evening but thank you so much for the invitation." Gil felt like a small curled-up insect being inspected under a monumental microscope and Eloise Ewart-Sanders gaze did not waver in spite of his rejection of her offer.

"Perhaps another time," she stated whilst she rose to her feet, stubbed out the remainder of her cigarette and walked towards the door. Gil wondered if she expected him to follow her. He never was quite sure of the rules these people had, exactly what social code they lived by. He rose from the plump chair and followed her slowly. Eloise turned towards him.

"Consuela will show you out," Eloise said whilst walking toward the front door.

Gill wanted to say that he thought the dog was Consuela but he guessed that the dog had been called that name before the maid arrived.

As Eloise reached the long hallway which led eventually to the front door, she picked up a tattered book from a console table, then she reached into its drawer and dislodged a handful of leaflets, handing the small treasures to Gil without a word.

The two shook hands and the tiny maid appeared miraculously before them to usher Gil down the corridor towards the front door of the house in silence.

As they reached the door he turned to the maid.

"Thank you, Consuela," Gil blurted.

The girl looked non-plussed. Despite her appearance something about her reminded Gil of the accounts of poor Bridget Riley (or what he imagined Bridget might be like) so he smiled at her warmly again.

"OK," Consuela managed as she opened the front door and then added hesitantly,

"Thank you, sir."

Gil didn't know why he did it but he shook the girl's hand, which surprised him as much as the maid and the two stood for a moment regarding one another with something approaching curiosity.

"OK," said Consuela again as Gil turned to walk away down the path to his car, only this time he moved very quietly.

'Not much changes after all.' thought Gil as he continued to walk down the excessively long driveway towards his car.

"I must check out Christian Science," Gil clutched Harriet Beech's diary and various other papers to his chest, feeling keen to find out exactly what the view of the niece of an English Duke was on the matter at hand – the niece of an English duke who was unfortunate enough to be married to Kenneth Ewart.

The drive back to New York was thankfully quick. Gil wondered whether he should call Jenny to let her know he had hold of another piece of the puzzle but decided she was probably too busy or even that Jenny may be even not available.

"God, what is the time in Scotland?" he asked out loud.

The radio which was blaring inside the car failed to respond and he felt too tired to think the time difference through.

John Lennon began to sing and Gil felt sad thinking about the tragedy of Harriet Beech's life cut short by the religion which had promised to sustain her.

"Just as well you packed a lot in, buddy," he said to John Lennon as he listened to the song and its words and then Gil smiled.

32

I have to admit I was beginning to reel from all the information which seemed to be coming in thick and fast both from Jenny and the big Yank, glad, of course, that they were now including me in all matters Lochdarnock/Ewart and other – as I was them.

The speed of our progress was phenomenal but still we seemed to be getting nowhere definite in deciding where 'Jenny Munroe came from' Lochdarnock wise, which was, after all, what this quest was all about.

After the Delaney boy had updated me by phone on his trip to Boston I had a good night's sleep before I delved into more of the stuff and before I wrote up what I could remember of his report on his meeting with Eloise.

Pretty soon after I started reading all the new material the phone went. It was Gil – again.

"Jen's just found even more of the stuff you wrote on Danny Cassidy. You old goat!"

"Did she now?" I enquired, wondering which bit of the stuff the Yank was talking about.

"I'm pursuing matters down south – I'm not back in London until tomorrow night," Delaney replied. "I'll be up in Glasgow the day after tomorrow. Tell me the truth, Bill, are you well enough for visitors?"

I assured the man that I was up for anything and dying to get on with things.

"Try not to use words like 'dying', buddy. There are a lot of sensitive people around you and I'm pretty much knee-deep in trouble as it is with your women," Gil laughed.

"Women? I was hoping I only had the one," I replied.

"I was including Jenny who has informed me that you have now been taken on as a 'father figure' by her," Gil assured me.

"A father figure? Well there you go. Get to my age and all women want is a daddy and I'm no' bloody sugar," I said as gruffly as I could, though secretly feeling quite pleased by the revelation Gil had just made.

"Jen thinks you're very sweet and lovely," Gil added.

"Does she now? What is it she thinks of you, I wonder?" I replied, being mischievous.

"When you work it out let me know," Gil blurted.

The big Yank signed off on the phone and went about his business.

I knew that he'd have gleaned all he could from the National Archive on that Ewart man by the time he got back.

I have to confess I was surprised when he brought up the subject of Hove, of all places, and wondered why he was off further South.

He said Hove not Brighton, if I remember rightly and my English geography not being up to snuff meant that I was thoroughly confused. Though I couldn't at all imagine what was there which would have relevance to the Ewarts or other.

Five minutes after he finished the call with me, the computer pinged. The boy was still belting stuff through the ether or cyberspace as it seems to be known today. I picked it up and was immediately excited. What is it about wars I find so fascinating and yet so bloody terrible?

33

MY THOUGHTS AND LIFE – OR SOMETHING OF IT – GIL DELANEY I – 1942

America is at war – again. It's been a bloody long wait for my adopted country to get into this mess but it is right that we have at last, at least that is what I think. Roosevelt wanted to do this long ago and would have done except the public was averse to getting into what it considered to be a European war – it was always more than that to me.

I keep trying to empty my head 'ma poor heid' of the nonsense I witnessed in the last one – Christ what a terrible time it was and I've taken to praying again – hoping that with this one – my boys are not of an age to serve thank God – I don't have to go through the terrible times of the First War.

'Great' they call it, that war – though God alone knows why the word 'Great' applies. Massive, aye, as so many poor souls were involved but an epithet has to fit in more than one sense, I believe. What I saw in that mess seems to me anything but 'Great'. But Wars have to be fought so history seems to suggest and there is something right about this one – and at least we'll be fighting for something important.

I suppose it's this declaration that makes me want to write about those terrible days we suffered back then.

I know it's not the 'done' thing but writing it down makes me feel better about it. I suppose in my own stupid way I'm trying to make 'sense of it all' the last one – and this that is. My mind takes me back to Amiens, though why any sane body would choose to take himself back to those days is anyone's guess.

Because I am (was) a big, strong fella I was chosen to go into the US Marine Corp. I had never believed in armies or the sort of thing which led ordinary men with no choice but to kill each other at the behest of their political masters but I have to admit that the country's entry into the affair (WW1) came not a minute too soon for Old Europe, which was taking a hell of a beating back then near the beginning of this century – according to our politicians here at any rate. I had been in this country only a couple of years when I got called up. I received basic training which was tough – a real physical slog after the relatively easy life I had been living out here.

Me and my regiment were spirited away by boat to Europe to fight in the great mess. I remember thinking, 'We're in the Marines so we're the toughest of the tough' God help the rest. None of us boys was a natural sailor for a start and the amount of vomit I waded in on the crossing to Europe was nobody's business.

The good thing about the Marines was that they were all 'men'. They swore and spat and might have seemed rough and common to some but I could totally rely on my 'buddies'.

I lost too many of them in Belleau Woods – far too many good, strong boys died among the trees in France.

The Allies' victory was hard won with the blood of those boys and the grief of their families. I still see Finlay Baxter sometimes, hobbling on the one leg he was left with at the end of it – that war – and he's done well for himself with his wee business but there's a look about Finlay that breaks my heart every time I see him. It's a look that says "Why the hell me?" That was the phrase he kept repeating that day he was injured.

I've never seen the man shed a tear that day or since but I can still hear his strong, clear voice asking that question, and his face bearing the words. I suppose that's the one question in life none of us can answer and I suppose that's why I'm turning to a God I don't really believe exists – once again. It was the only hope I had to stop myself from going daft.

I suppose the biggest battle I fought in, or certainly the one that stays with me, was that fight for Belleau Woods.

I've read since that the objective of the operation was to clear the railway lines at Amiens but I know this only in retrospect.

As a US Marine there was no need for a common foot soldier like me to know the whys and wherefores and, anyhow (saps that we were) we didn't ask.

Our commander was Major General Omar Bundy. I have a vague recollection of hearing this at the time but I never set eyes on the man. I've read about the battle over the years and I think I can fit myself and my fellow marines into the story somehow.

On 1st June 1918 the Germans had moved into the woods.

The US 2nd and Marines 5th were ordered to march 10 kilometres to hold the line against the Germans who wanted to cross the river Marne, which was strategically important – I forget why.

The French brigades were ordered by their officers to 'dig in' and they set about putting in yet more trenches.

We were ordered to 'hold where [you] stand'. We set about putting in shallow fighting positions which allowed us to lie on our stomachs, our weapons ready to begin firing as and when we were ordered to by whatever officer had the loudest voice, it seemed.

I remember it was a time before the Germans advanced through the grain field towards us with fixed bayonets.

We were warned to hold fire until the Germans were within a hundred yards. The command came to 'open fire'.

The advancing Germans fell like pins to their knees or stomachs – dead or wounded. Some survivors managed to retreat into the woods – deep into the dense woods.

The story goes that the French officers entreated the Marines to retreat.

Marine folklore has it that one of our officers yelled, "Retreat! Hell we just got here." I can imagine this being right. Those boys were gung-ho to say the least.

This situation was followed by continuous German assaults on the Brigade.

We held – I now know – the area north of the line from Triangle Farm.

I suppose the mind is kind because I forget all the details and am left only with vague images of those terrifying and exhilarating days.

It took us until the end of that month to complete our task which I remember only as attack and counter attack with us holding Hill 142.

I've read since that 325 men lost their lives achieving that target alone – all those men for one wee hill!

There was a second advance through a wheat field I remember.

This time I do recall an officer shouting at us by way of encouragement

"Come on, you sons of bitches, do you wanna live forever?"

More stuff of folklore but I can tell you the words were actually said.

That decision led us into heavy hand-to-hand fighting which I found strenuous at the time and vile to remember in hindsight. Nothing can prepare you for the feeling of bayoneting a fellow human being and hearing the flesh rip, looking at the face of a man who dies not swiftly enough right in front of you and because of you.

It took us until near the end of the month to complete the routing of the woods. By then 9,777 casualties on our side had been sustained and 1,811 men were killed. Those boys were buried out there in France. I will visit that country one day to remember them. I personally lost Jakie Bell, John Docherty, Lewis MacIver, and Fred Samuels. All good men – no – looking back now they were merely boys not much older than my sons are now – God help us all this time round.

I read this account aloud to myself.

I have read many original pieces about these kind of things and they all fill me with the same feelings – every time. And the question always remains – why do we do it? And we don't ever seem to learn, do we?

I found out later that (after sending me this material, which he had by then handed to Jenny) the Delaney boy took off for London, and the newspaper library in Colindale to see what he could find out about Angus Lochdarnock and the murdered girl, before his visit to Hove – I still couldn't work out Gil's reasoning or where his research trail would be leading him at this stage.

34

Jenny was no slouch either in getting source material together. She told me she thought that to have me dealing with the Lochdarnock material would be better than me brooding and annoying 'poor' Hetty with my grumpiness.

Jenny had noticed that when I'm bored I tend as she put it 'to rather take it out on your very patient wife'.

Women! They stick together – you'll have notice that, I suppose.

Jenny passed on more of her mother's recollection to me. Of course, one of Jenny's ploys was to send me information that was not in strict chronological order. She thought I did not guess. I am sure that Margaret Munroe would have had her writing neatly set out but Jenny seemed insistent that I got her family story piece-meal and she was obviously forcing me to make sense of the stuff and giving me no easy ride.

MARGARET MUNROE – *A GOOD PLACE* – ELIZABETH CASSIDY DIES – 1933

The birth was going horribly wrong. Morag Lennox – midwife and local woman (a mother of eight herself) was struggling to know how to cope. This birth should have been easy. Elizabeth Cassidy had had six children before and should have known the ropes but the thirty-eight-year-old was doing badly. The baby seemed to be in breech and Morag knew that she would have to call for Dr Stewart. Morag knew, too, that the old man would be furious about being awoken at this time of night.

The nurse ordered young Paddy Cassidy to go to the doctor and gave the boy a note that she had quickly scribbled.

Morag only hoped that the poor woman would survive until the old grouch arrived.

Morag was out of luck that night. It wasn't twenty minutes after Paddy Cassidy had taken to his heels and run through the streets like the wind before Elizabeth had given up and died along with her poor little girl – later to be named Angela.

Morag had done this bad birthing business with women time and time again, closing the woman's eyes on the world as gently as she could, making tea for the grieving husband and shattered children. The midwife thanked God the sister-in-law was there.

Mary Cassidy had been glad that it was a Sunday on which Elizabeth had gone into labour. She knew that the note she'd sent to the house would be received by Mrs MacDonald with sympathy – the old woman had handed over much of the running of the house to Mary now. Increasingly since the death of Lady Isabelle, Mary had taken on Margaret MacDonald's duties which were made difficult for the older woman by her chronic arthritis and failing eyesight.

Mary was glad to help run the house.

Fiona Ewart-Lochdarnock had made the lives of the servants a nightmare, these last few years, laying off several good people she imagined to be 'against' her.

Mary's own job was saved by Lord Lochdarnock who told Lady Fiona that Mary was to be 'valued'.

This order had only increased Fiona's determination to rid the household of the maid.

Mary's life under the rule of the new mistress was a misery at the best of times but as Fiona and Lord Alistair were away in London for the week Mary was afforded time and scope to take action, or what miserable action she could.

Mary sat with her distraught and clearly suffering friend, Elizabeth, holding the woman's hand which was strangely hot given the time of year. Mary did not want to encourage Elizabeth to exert herself.

"Strange thought," Mary said out loud.

"Whit?" demanded the young Alice Cassidy whose tears were unstoppable as she watched her poor mother's breathing become increasingly shallow.

"I'm sorry, Alice. I was thinking aloud." Mary pulled the girl close to her and held Alice tightly. Alice continued to cry until the tardy Dr Stewart arrived, announcing rather too loudly to Nurse Lennox, "You left it very late again, Nurse Lennox."

It was clear to everyone in the room that poor Elizabeth had 'passed'. The corpse was still.

Morag Lennox knew she had indeed left it too late but the consequence of being too early for her at the hands of that old 'B' Stewart had affected her judgement. The nurse decided that the next time – oh, yes the next time! Morag knew indeed that there would be a next time.

It was Alice who reacted to the news.

"Whit d'ye mean she left it too late?" Alice demanded.

"Just sit down, young woman," Dr Stewart ordered. "You've had a shock. Nurse Lennox will give you tea. Calm yourself and be of use to your father."

Alice burst into tears again. Mary told her gently to sit a while. Mary followed Dr Stewart into the hallway.

"Doctor?" Mary demanded. "Why did Nurse Lennox leave it too late?"

"I'm not minded to get into a discussion with you at this time on a Sunday night."

"Well, I'm minded to have the truth off of you," Mary said. She heard a growl in her voice which reminded her of her own mother – Annie Cassidy.

"These women carry on having baby after baby. They are bound to end up in trouble with a birth eventually. Nurse Lennox acted perfectly appropriately," Dr Stewart's voice was angry and hoarse.

Mary thought she smelt drink on his breath.

"You know what I think?" Mary started.

"I'm not in the least interested what you think Mrs…?"

"Miss Cassidy," Mary corrected him in her best posh servant's voice. "I think Nurse Lennox was afraid to call you out. I think you put the fear of God into the midwives so you can have your wee drink. That's what I think."

"I am not minded to listen to a woman like you. You'd be better taking care of these children and minding your own business," the doctor replied.

With that he slammed out of the door. Alice stood at the other end of the hall admiring her aunt.

"At least you tried, Auntie Mary," said Alice, crying again.

"I'm sorry you had to hear that, Alice. I'm that sorry about your mother. She was a very good woman and the best friend to me," Mary managed.

The Quinns, Elizabeth's brothers and sisters, arrived within the half hour. Patrick Cassidy sat silently by the fire; tears tripping him. He wanted to speak to no one.

"My daddy." Alice wailed. "Look at my poor daddy."

"He'll be better tomorrow. I'll send word up to the house and stay the night here," Mary managed.

"I don't want you getting into trouble," said Alice, pulling herself together. I can manage. My auntie Agnes and uncle Norrie are here now. It'll be OK. It really will, Auntie Mary."

Mary Cassidy felt proud of the beautiful, tall, competent and loving girl who was indeed every inch a Cassidy.

Mary put all thought out of her mind and set off for Lochdarnock

House feeling cold and sad and worried about Elizabeth and Patrick's children – she so wanted to help and felt utterly powerless and useless – yet again.

Mrs MacDonald was kind when Mary arrived. She shoved a cup of strong, hot tea into Mary's hands.

"Take this, Mary. You've had a terrible shock." Margaret MacDonald rubbed Mary's shoulder and peered through her strong lenses into Mary's face, which was ageing now.

Mrs MacDonald thought of the fresh-faced child who'd entered the house long ago and felt sad that the beautiful creature was here alone with no one but an old housekeeper to give her comfort now. Margaret MacDonald increasingly hated the way Fiona Ewart treated poor Mary Cassidy.

"It'll be quick to a funeral," Mrs MacDonald declared, trying to put the conversation on a practical footing as usual. "You Catholics are quick to bury your beloveds. I think we could learn a thing or two from you. All that waiting is what causes so much upset. Yes, it is best to get the thing out of the way quick."

"Aye, it is, replied Mary, remembering the length of time it had taken to arrange memorials for the now departed Lochdarnocks and just how fast it had all been when each of her own parents had gone – within a year of one another. Mary smiled at the thought the pair might be together again now. Martin Cassidy up there trying to ensure that Annie Cassidy wasn't telling God what to do!

"What – a smile?" Margaret MacDonald laughed. "Already."

"I was thinking about my mother ruling Heaven."

"God might have something to say about that."

"Aye, well God has his work cut out wi' my mother," Mary said quietly.

"I imagine he does." Mrs MacDonald replied as she switched off the electric light in the servants' sitting room and the two women made their way to the maids' sleeping wing.

35

I had been wondering whether I should let Jenny and Gil have the next piece of writing I had with me. The information I had given Jenny was emotional stuff but even she, I knew, had a limit. By the time I got round to 'pinging' the next bit of my material off to her I wondered if the girl would actually crack at long last and show some emotion.

May be something in me needed Jenny, in the light of my recent wee scare, to take this Lochdarnock stuff personally.

Ach, it seemed to be the story of the Cassidys rather than the Lochdarnocks that affected her most. Obvious that it would be I suppose – that was the family she had known. The Lochdarnocks were merely strangers to her. Perhaps that liaison with the Cassidys and Lochdarnocks that we knew about might loosen things up a bit.

I'd written the extract years before which summed up the matter.

I was sad, yes that's the only word I have to describe my feelings, when I found the papers referring to Daniel Cassidy (19th March 1894–22nd April 1926). So young.

My God, the boy had got through the war – had found companionship with James Lochdarnock and his place in life up at the lodge at Braeside. It all seemed so bloody cruel.

Daniel Cassidy's death certificate read 'Bronchitic Complications'. Poor boy had never been right after the gas attack in the trenches and James Lochdarnock's writings pointed to the fact that poor wee Danny Cassidy – young man that he was – had been a martyr to his chest since 1917.

It was on the date of Danny Cassidy's death that James Lochdarnock's diaries came to an abrupt end. I suppose the man had nothing important to write about after that event with the love of his life departed.

His political writings stopped then too. I imagined James struggling on forever like a Miss Haversham with clocks stopped all around him and the curtains drawn and Lillian and Patricia creeping about the place afraid to offend the Patrician boy but the indications are otherwise.

My God, tragedy follows tragedy for the Lochdarnocks right enough. Two weeks after Danny Cassidy was interred in the grounds of the lodge – his grave can be seen to this day (I must point that out to Jenny and the Delaney boy) – Isabelle Lochdarnock breathed her last.

Her battle over, Fiona Ewart soon set to work on matters and was the new Lady Lochdarnock within a year and a month of Isabelle's death – but that's another story.

Danny Cassidy's funeral was mentioned in a letter from Bob MacKenzie to Mrs MacDonald that I stumbled upon.

The Lochdarnocks seemed to encourage the whole household to put their thoughts to paper. Handy for me. I remember the night I found this stuff and smuggled it out of Lochdarnock House so that I could study it at my leisure.

Hetty and I were living in a wee villa (as she insisted on calling it) by then and I had a garden shed that I'd managed to get electricity into with the help of my pal, Peter Swan. Peter was an electrician and could do wonders with a bit of cable and some tape. Hetty was put out by the birth of my wee office out in our tiny garden which was no more than a backyard really.

"That ugly looking thing," she said referring to my recycled haven, "in my wee garden. I wanted flowers."

"We'll get yee a pot plant," Peter Swan said, trying in his abrupt way to placate a very put out Hetty. I knew his ploy would fail. Peter was not a charmer or much to look at – but handy – my God, the man was handy. Sadly that alone was not going to endear him to Hetty.

The wife sniffed the way she does when she's annoyed with a stranger and I knew I was in for it later that evening after Peter had made his way home, but still it would be worth an ear bashing to have my own wee place to hide away in.

I noticed Hetty encouraged Heather and William to interrupt me as often as they could over the next couple of weeks. The good thing about my weans was that with a wee bit of encouragement (and the odd silver thrupnee bit) they would give me peace, no bother.

So it was one dark and cold winter night that I unfolded my stash of purloined papers. I suppose all historians put their own spin on matters and here's my 'take' on the events.

My – but that year was a mighty fine year for the Lochdarnock 'curse'. I found the following extract which tells of events better than I ever could:

***

JAMES LOCHDARNOCK'S DIARY

The household here at Braeside has been quiet and the dogs sullen and slumped in the kitchen not eating or moving for hours now. I find this unnerving. Daniel has been ill on so many occasions but this time is worse. He is, of course, enduring this present illness with his usual stoicism and fortitude, neither of which, unfortunately, is catching. I wish such qualities were. I dearly wish I could be braver than he for once.

Patricia and Lillian nurse him when I sleep but his rasping breath disturbs my attempt at rest even though I am fit to drop.

And yet, when I see him each morning he still smiles and we are able to hold hands and talk – if haltingly. Last night he asked me to hold him and as I held him close to me all I felt was the thinness, the boniness of his wracked body and I wanted (and still want) to breathe for him. He eats little but is at least able to drink.

Doctor Ferguson is pleased with this, seeing his ability to tolerate liquids as a positive sign. I wish I weren't afflicted by this disturbance to my thought which predicts catastrophe. I have been wrong before and I am sure in my logical mind that I will be proven to be wrong again but I wonder how much more, just how much more, Daniel's frail and emaciated body can withstand.

Ferguson assures me that he is not consumptive and claims that he has treated more than one man for the after effects of wartime gassing. I re-read Owen's account of the gas attack and his description of 'froth corrupted lungs' sings as yet in my ears. That calamitous war has been over the best part of a decade and still that event punishes us all.

I wonder if he will sleep less fitfully tonight. Ferguson has given me a powder to help me rest but I am loath to take the medicine in case Daniel might need me. Lillian says I must do as the doctor orders and she and Patricia are most insistent that I rest – but how can I? How can I leave Daniel in these moments knowing that no matter what the circumstances he would never leave me to my own limited resources and terrible fate?

Daniel talks of God. Not in the usual way he is guilty of, in that sneering and dismissive manner he has devised over the years – his (as he calls it) sophisticated veneer of logic and disbelief which masks his deep suspicion of the existence of an afterlife.

No. I do believe that Danny wishes that his God, the God he was brought up to revere, is in his heaven and waiting for brave Cpl. Cassidy to come to his side, to take his rightful place. I cannot help but despise such an entity which would deprive me of my love, my life but I know that such cruelty exists in the world and I fear it. I fear a life without Daniel. I will simply not have the strength to endure such an existence.

The powder I have taken insists that I sleep now – at last.

***

Sad stuff. Bob MacKenzie's letter to Mrs MacDonald gives a sketchy account of what it must have been like up at Braeside during this period but I wrote my version of what happened to the Chauffeur on his arrival there based on his letter to Mrs MacD.

***

Bob (Robert) MacKenzie drove the Bentley slowly from Glasgow. His mission was to 'deliver essentials' to the lodge at Braeside. From Bob's point of view it seemed to him that the lucky ones up there (James Lochdarnock and Danny Cassidy) had it pretty good and that all the essentials they might need were to hand in the lodge itself.

The roads had improved over the years and no mistaking. The journey had been a nightmare only fifteen years before causing the then new Bentley to work harder than its considerable horsepower might allow.

MacKenzie was equipped for fishing and looked forward to the few days of fresh air and quiet that Braeside afforded every now and then.

Anyhow, MacKenzie liked Danny Cassidy – the wee man was a right good laugh and James Lochdarnock was easy enough to get on with. Yes, those boys had it good up there – Patricia and Lillian to do the cooking – fresh venison, salmon, rabbit and hare. A fair feast awaited Bob MacKenzie and he was looking forward to a good dinner.

Bob took one hand off the wheel and slid it underneath his belt which slotted through his stiff and expensive trousers with the certainty that this action would not be as easy a job to achieve on his return journey.

The miles of familiar but still enchanting countryside passed by – the Bentley sped by lochs and glens and waterfalls.

MacKenzie noted the deer on the way up – they were out in their droves, standing majestic against heavy clouded skies, defiantly merging with the hillsides still brown at this time of year, in a mystical symbiosis of image. The views could become mesmeric up here where the air was fresh and clean and the water in all its forms – lochs, streams, waterfalls and rivers – ran freely – tumbling over ancient rocks which stood amongst the trees just coming to life along with the surrounding grassland now that Spring was ready to burst.

MacKenzie's hat sat on the passenger seat beside him and his tie was uncharacteristically undone. The man felt at his leisure.

The majestic car sped by Loch Rogie; with its mirror-like surfaces enhancing the shapes of the gnarled and enormous trees which stood, sometimes bent over, on the banks along with outcrops of rocks which appeared to have fallen down into the water and its edges from the mountains themselves.

Bob imagined it was the wind which had caused the remnants of forest to jut out of the ground like this and landslides from the ancient past which accounted for the pretty rock formations in evidence all around.

The road was not straight, not yet. He'd noticed evidence that working parties were out with their picks and shovels along the way. The powers that be were determined that the roads to the Highlands were to be made accessible. It was good for the toffs and, MacKenzie supposed, for trade. Though whether taking unemployed men from their families in cities to do the hard labour of getting the highlands sorted out for very little cost was a fair deal Bob MacKenzie doubted.

London aristocrats and rich business types from the capital down south were frequent visitors in season to these hard to reach parts. Shooting parties after birds or venison, and fishermen and their wives, now frequented the highlands. MacKenzie knew that James Lochdarnock hated this – he'd read the young man's treatise on the subject of hunting and the ruination of the Highlands which was 'given over to a class of men who disrespect the land and its inhabitants, be they human or otherwise'. It was easy for him, James Lochdarnock, who had had access to all this beauty his entire life to make such judgements. It was understandable that he wanted to share this land – his land – with no one. Well, no one apart from Daniel Cassidy, it seemed.

MacKenzie had never been much of a one for politics and he simply didn't understand the hoo-ha about keeping the toffs away, but Bob had been around long enough on this earth and with the Scots aristocracy to be unperturbed by the 'goings on' (as Mrs MacDonald put it) at Braeside. Not usually one to gossip, Mrs Mac had made it clear to Bob MacKenzie that the place up there was a hotbed of perversion.

"That Patricia and Lillian – companions?!" she had uttered. MacKenzie was sure the housekeeper was right in suspecting the nature of the relationship between the two women but these 'goings on' were none of his business and things were staying that way.

Yes, life was pretty good and Bob MacKenzie was in no mood for the revolutionaries of Europe, even those in residence at Braeside, or for the 'judges' he knew in town, to ruin his sense of peace.

The heather was not yet at its height so colour in the landscape seemed scanty. The odd yellow bloom held its sunny head high now and again and the purples and browns and greens, though attenuated, were in abundance given the right slant of light – the land was so soft and yet so strong with its mountains and ruggedness on show.

Bob stopped the Bentley to take a pee at the roadside. Not a soul, not a car was in view. The man buttoned up his fly, relieved now, and began to turn to re-enter the car but was stopped in his tracks. Looking a little to his left he saw it there in the distance. MacKenzie guessed the reality was that it was about a mile away. The man stood and stared at the beast which grazed at the opposite side of a large loch. Its antlers were the largest he'd seen and Bob guessed that it must have taken an amount of strength for the beast to lift its head upright. As the creature did just that it seemed to stare across to Bob's position and look a while. The animal was red and full bodied. Its noble face betrayed nothing more than a simple curiosity and Bob wished he could get closer to it to assure himself that what he seemed to be seeing was accurate and not simply an affectation of his mind. With that the stag turned and walked slowly away from the water's edge and MacKenzie walked just as slowly toward the car, ready now to get on with his journey.

It was the short part of the journey now with most of the miles behind him and MacKenzie was tired enough to need a nap. He presumed he would be billeted in the lodge with the two younger men, obviously in the east wing which would inevitably be cold at this time of the year having had no visitors since Christmas last. Still, Bob thought, "A good wee break and fishing in the morning, early. Those boys like to start their sport early on."

Bob passed Loch Roskin and knew then it was barely a mile to his destination. In the old days he would have had to stop the car a few miles further down the road but advances in the surfacing of the Highlands meant that the lodge was directly accessible now.

The Bentley swept passed the gatehouse and up the bumpy track that led to Braeside Lodge. The tyres were taking a beating MacKenzie knew but if the unthinkable happened it would take no time to get a couple of men from the nearby crofts to assist him in fixing up the car.

As it was MacKenzie and the Bentley reached the building without incident. He parked the car at a jaunty angle to the lodge and picking up his small bag and a box of 'necessaries' from the boot MacKenzie walked into the open door.

James Lochdarnock greeted him with a frown. "Bob. Good to see you."

MacKenzie nodded simply. He got the feeling that something here was not quite as it should be.

"I'm sure you can see to yourself. I'm needed upstairs." James Lochdarnock turned struggling up the grand mahogany staircase, one hand clutching a stair-rail and the other holding on grimly to his stick.

Patricia came from the direction of the kitchen and spoke softly.

"I'm afraid poor Danny is not so well today."

"His chest?" MacKenzie enquired. Patricia nodded and turned. MacKenzie followed the small woman to the kitchen where she served him tea.

"It's a bad business for the boy," Patricia continued. "Lillian's been down to fetch the doctor three times in the last three days. The telephone is not working again."

Patricia pushed the plate full of sandwiches towards MacKenzie who was ravenous by now and ate heartily.

"It's good to see a body eat," Patricia whispered.

"Mr James looks very concerned," Bob offered.

"Not himself at all. This time is worse than usual, I have to admit."

The two sat in silence a moment before Lillian entered the kitchen looking grave and drawn.

"Is he no better?" Patricia enquired.

Lillian simply shook her head.

"What does the doctor say?" piped up MacKenzie.

"He's seen these poor souls like this before. That gas!" Lillian began to weep.

"It's hard to watch him like that."

Patricia moved toward her friend and rubbed her shoulder. Thinking of what Mrs MacDonald had told him, Bob wondered if it wouldn't be better if he took himself off to his room now. He was saved the bother of making a decision when James Lochdarnock appeared at the door looking gaunt and even more exhausted than he had only a half hour before.

"MacKenzie, have you been fed?" Lochdarnock enquired.

"I have, sir."

"Good, good. Might I have some tea, Patricia?" Lochdarnock asked.

Patricia delivered the tea into the tall man's hands as he stood shakily before her.

"You need to sit down," Lillian insisted sharply. "There'll be tea everywhere."

James mutely sat in an armchair by the range which was pumping heat into the room. The man simply stared ahead of him.

"Is there anything I can get you, sir?" MacKenzie asked.

James Lochdarnock looked up and began to laugh.

"I think not, Bob. I think not."

The room was silent for a moment and then James Lochdarnock tried to get to his feet, hampered by both tiredness and his oddly positioned crutch which he seemed unable to manoeuvre. Bob wondered if he should assist him but decided against it.

Lillian pressed a firm hand on James' shoulder.

"I'll go. You need to rest. The doctor has told you."

"Rest!" James roared angry now and continuing to struggle into an upright position. "You expect me to rest at a time like this. Don't you people understand?"

The man struggled out of the room and seemed to stumble at the doorway. MacKenzie got to him just in time.

"Let me help you," he demanded. James Lochdarnock gave in and allowed assistance from Bob MacKenzie.

James whispered something to MacKenzie whose hearing was not what it had been. The chauffeur was embarrassed to ask James to repeat himself but did as all communication seemed urgent.

"Of course, I'll get down to the village and phone from there presently. Let me get you up the stairs first."

Bob MacKenzie was shocked by the sight of Danny Cassidy. Wee Danny Cassidy seemed to have shrivelled to nothing and lay in the bed barely the size of a child, his face pale and yellowed and his lips a blue colour. The only pink features in the young man's face were the eyes which stared out in terror at James and Bob MacKenzie as they entered the room. Danny Cassidy whispered something and then coughed. The blood and mucus spilled out of his mouth and down his chin. James Lochdarnock gently wiped the vile mixture from Danny's mouth with a handkerchief in one hand. With the other hand he stroked the peppered locks of Danny Cassidy's small head and smiled at his love with his mouth, his eyes unable to hide the inner anguish which assailed him.

MacKenzie was relieved to get to the village and make the call from the inn there.

Jillings answered the phone as was his wont and the old Butler was surprised when MacKenzie demanded to speak with Mary Cassidy.

The girl's voice seemed thin and reedy on the phone – it had a nasal tone that MacKenzie had not noticed before.

"Mary, I need to ask you to have your parents come here to Braeside. Daniel is not well. I'm sorry, Mary," MacKenzie said bluntly.

There was a silence on the line for a moment before Mary managed.

"Yes, Mr MacKenzie. I'll do that." MacKenzie was unsurprised by the speed of the conversation and guessed that Mary, a capable girl, would want to rush off to her family as soon as she could.

By the next morning James Lochdarnock was inconsolable. Dr Ferguson had visited again and had told the household, "It's merely a matter of time."

Patricia and Lillian wept in the kitchen determined to conceal their grief from James Lochdarnock. MacKenzie prepared himself to meet with Annie and Martin Cassidy who would be arriving at the train station. Rooms had been prepared for them at the lodge. James Lochdarnock had insisted that they be treated with the utmost care. MacKenzie guessed that the couple would be embarrassed by the fuss that was about to be unleashed upon them.

When he picked the parents up at the local station, Danny Cassidy's sainted parents, MacKenzie noted that they had aged considerably since the first and last time he'd seen them.

Annie Cassidy seemed in particular so much less robust now. Her dark hair now a white snowball surrounding her small face *which had once, MacKenzie thought, been beautiful. Martin, grey haired and sombre, had grown a tummy that had not been present years' ago.*

The two sat in the back of the Bentley as MacKenzie drove steadily towards the lodge, feeling sorry for what these poor people were about to face.

MacKenzie wondered how James Lochdarnock would manage the situation. Surely the laird's son would not inflict the full reality of his relationship with Danny Cassidy on the parents. MacKenzie dreaded how the elderly pair would cope with such a revelation.

MacKenzie took the simple bags the Cassidys had with them from the car and the couple followed him into the lodge. Patricia and Lillian were there to show them to their room, next to MacKenzie's in the east wing. It was the first visit they had made to the lodge. They had missed Danny but knew that he was better off in the clean country air writing his pamphlets. At least it was a life for the boy after that fiasco – that war that should never have been. Annie had strong views on it. She read the papers and she knew the poor men had all been sent into a Godless nightmare.

James Lochdarnock braced himself to meet the Cassidys. The last thing he wanted was to offend these good people – these people who had brought Daniel into the world, and given their son to him. James felt a strange mix of annoyance at the thought of sharing Daniel with them and gratitude that these people had given him more than any others ever had, his Daniel, his love.

"Mr Lochdarnock," Martin Cassidy whispered throatily, offering James his hand. The young man took his hand and gently squeezed it.

"I'm so sorry to meet you again in these circumstances," James replied.

Annie Cassidy felt the need all at once to say everything to the Lochdarnock boy.

"Mr Lochdarnock. How can we thank you for all the help you've given our Danny? Mr MacKenzie tells us the doctor's been in every day for a week now. And his job. The job you gave our Danny! Oh, God.

We wondered if he would ever work again after coming back from France so bad." The words were pouring out of her.

James stood there, tears welling in his eyes. If only they knew, he thought, if only they knew.

"I'll take you to Daniel now," James said as evenly as he could manage.

Annie Cassidy was brave at the sight of her shrunken son lying in crisp, clean white sheets which Patricia and Lillian had changed only minutes before.

"So there you are, our Danny."

"Ma'" Daniel managed. "And Da." he coughed. "It's so good to see yees."

His breathing became more difficult and he managed a cough. James leaned across the bed, handkerchief in hand to wipe away the vile mess that emerged from Danny's mouth unendingly, it seemed.

"Don't talk, please, Daniel, don't talk." James Lochdarnock could not match the Cassidys in dignity and began to cry. Annie Cassidy put an arm round him.

"Now look, Daniel. You have this fine big fella in tears with yer nonsense. Doesn't he, Martin?"

Martin Cassidy clasped his son's hand in his own.

"This son of mine did not let the German's get him so a bit of a nip in the air in Scotland is soon overcome. We'll have ye on yer feet in a week," Martin demanded.

"No Da. You'll no'," said Danny. "But it's OK. It's fine." Daniel tried to raise his head from the pillow.

"Put your head down," ordered James.

"Just like the fucking trenches again, Lieutenant," Danny joked.

James smiled. "And just like in the fucking trenches, it's an order, Corporal."

The three sat with Danny Cassidy all night and he died at 3.27 a.m.

No-one including MacKenzie could move James Lochdarnock from Daniel Cassidy's side even after his death.

Annie and Martin Cassidy were given tea and food in the kitchen. Patricia forced sustenance down their throats with tenderness and a great deal of concern.

MacKenzie asked James Lochdarnock how he wanted things done.

James reply was direct. "Any way you see fit." The young man was silent a moment. "Daniel said there was no curse on my family. He refused to believe the old wive's tale. Is that how you see it, MacKenzie?"

"I didn't think you were a one for that kind of talk, Mr James."

"Answer the question. Is Daniel dead because of me?"

Neither man had realised that Annie Cassidy was at the door.

"Mr Lochdarnock. It cannot be said that you have been anything other than a saint in my son's life," Annie said as she advanced toward James. The white-haired woman bent down at his side. "Now where would my Danny have been without you? Can you answer that? Invalided out of the Army with no job to go to after all his union troubles, that's where! And what did you do but take him on here and give him a home and dignity and let him help you with all your writing. Please, God knows that you are the last person who should feel guilty about our Danny's death. It was the will of God, that's all. Just the will of God."

James looked at the woman and wondered what to say. How could he tell her just how much Danny Cassidy had meant to him from the first moment they had met? The poor woman would be desolate if she knew of her son's true relationship with him, the future laird of Lochdarnock.

James Lochdarnock found himself saying the kind of words he'd previously scoffed at.

"I was the lucky one knowing your son. He saved my life and has since be an invaluable source of comfort to me, Mrs Cassidy. I thank you for him."

The old woman and the young man wept together quietly.

Annie Cassidy told her family that "Mr James was that fond of our Danny he was crippled by his loss." Martin Cassidy nodded in affirmation at the observation.

The funeral was a lavish affair. Daniel had insisted on being buried at Braeside. Annie was hurt. Where was she to go to see her son?

Mr James had a photographer take a picture of the grave and sent her a copy but it wasn't the same, Annie thought, as a real grave to tend. Still, she mustn't grumble. Danny was happy with his work up at Braeside. And at least it was a Catholic service. Mr James had insisted on that even though Danny's letter never mentioned that was what he wanted. Maybe he told Mr James? Yes, that must be it. Danny must have made the request. He was a nice boy, that James Lochdarnock – a good boss and a true gentleman.

Annie just wished Danny had had a babby that she could cuddle – a wee, wee Danny Cassidy to love and chide and cook for and fuss over. But it wasn't meant to be, and that was the end of it. After all – you can't argue with the decisions of the Lord and at least Danny was at peace at last and the Devil's work the Germans had done was at an end for him at least.

36

Gil Delaney, as it turned out, had checked into a swanky London hotel before his visit to Hove. He was determined to get on with the job of investigating the story about Angus Lochdarnock and the poor murdered actress/prostitute, a tale he had uncovered whilst in Scotland.

Gil spent the evening going over the material which Jenny and I had emailed to the wee group. I read through all the stuff (some of the material I'd read a hundred times and other pieces of the newer material I had lightly and loosely read just the once) in the comfort of my bed – it was Hetty who insisted on me staying there, wrapped up in my pit, once again (apparently I had been looking a 'wee bit peely-waly – again) – and I've to admit I kind of enjoyed her doddering in and out with cups of tea and the concerned expression which hadn't left her face since my discharge from hospital. Here was the poor auld biddy trying to keep me going on her own territory. May be she thought I'd die in front of her eyes. Hetty has a terror of dead bodies. Christ, has she not worked out yet that it is the living not the dead who are the problem in life?

Jenny hadn't eaten much at dinner, she was tired and worried about the old man – apparently – that's me! She told me later that she slept fitfully and got up at 5 a.m. It was still dark outside. She looked out of her bedroom window at the house and saw him again. Jenny concentrated on the white fox who seemed to sit stock still in front of Lochdarnock House. She watched, marvelling at the creature for a full five minutes. She didn't dare turn on a light for fear of alerting him to the notion that he was under human scrutiny. Looking down on him she saw that the white coat was flecked, not with red as she had expected but with strong black streaks which stood out against the snow colour of the rest of his coat. As she was about to go to the bathroom she saw the second fox, russet coloured, join the first and it too sat silently, at the side of its mate. After a moment, the red fox nuzzled into the side of its partner. The closeness looked like an embrace was passing between the creatures, the thought of which made Jenny shiver though she did not feel cold. Jenny smiled, she didn't know why this scene pleased her so much – this little animal romance in all its simplicity seemed to her a delight which was strange as Jenny Munroe confessed that she was anything but an animal lover, or for that matter a fanciful romantic of any kind – or so she protests.

Jenny cherished her secret, determined to keep the knowledge of the vulpine lovers to herself. I suppose I feel pleased that she was able to share this with me, at least.

Putting my boxes on the table, Jenny picked out a sheaf of papers which looked interesting but proved to be dull accounts of the Ewart shipping business. She put them aside for Gil – she thought perhaps he'd be interested – but who knew? I think the big Yank is somewhat more soulful than Jenny Munroe imagines.

It was then that she found a piece signed by Isabelle Lochdarnock (it was a wee bound journal) and she jealously hugged the tiny book in which the commentary was set close to her breast.

Jenny says she was relieved and content. Contact, even if indirect, had been made at last. The tiny book in Isabelle's beautiful hand with its gliding stroke over each page was read slowly and carefully – the lovely Jenny taking in each treasured word.

ISABELLE LOCHDARNOCK – DIARY – 1ST JANUARY, 1921

As with each New Year, for so many now, I begin my journal with a wish – the wish to be close once more to Angus – darling Angus – the boy I so selfishly failed. How can I begin… he simply is no more and there is now no hope that I can make amends for my neglect of him. All I can muster is excuses for my lack. I wonder if he ever did love me and why I failed so often to tell and show him how much I loved him. How could he love me when I was so clearly enamoured of James, so blind that I could not attend to my second boy? James was always so close to me, so bright and easy (apart from his tendency to temper – which I have to say came from me rather than his father which is perhaps why he had my understanding).

Alistair is and always has been a most patient man and a loyal husband – if not always in body then most dependably in spirit. I am aware of his liaison with Fiona Ewart and I do not, of course, wholly approve it but I do understand. I am unable to fully be the wife that my husband needs and it is right that he suffers as little deprivation as possible when my failures are far from being of his making.

Of course, Fiona is a pretty but not beautiful young woman and she has a certain native intelligence which has been adequately fostered by a good education. But I feel she is limited by comparison to Alistair whose intellect is undoubtedly of a superior sort to both Miss Ewart's intellect and my own for that matter.

How bored poor Alistair must be. Two women who are simply not of his equal, one son dead and the other practically estranged from us and living in the North, living a life of such little social interaction. I wonder if James is truly happy. I can only hope that he is. It is well that he has Lillian and Patricia to care for his every need and the companionship of

Cpl. Cassidy. It is strange that two young men from such different worlds are able to share a life neither was born to, the country life.

I am told that it is a healthy choice for them both – each having suffered so much in the Great War and MacKenzie reports that James walks well even though the countryside around Braeside is rough and challenging for the most able of men. MacKenzie reports too that Mr Cassidy's lung condition is much improved by the clean air enjoyed up at Braeside.

The companions are political pamphleteers. I know that Alistair is often livid when perusing their writings. He considers them extreme and in the light of events in Europe James and Cpl. Cassidy may be liable to charges of insurrection were they both still soldiers and committed to His Majesty's Services.

James expresses himself well, as does Mr Cassidy under our son's tutelage but their views are not for everyone and their ideas concern me much. The world is indeed a changing place. The war saw to that. And my world, so changed – so shrunken – that often I view it and its goings on, as Mrs MacDonald might comment, quite unable to breathe regularly.

My health becomes poorer by the month and I weaker by the day. I am aware that all of this is exacerbated by my concern over what will become of Alistair and James at my end; yet I long, I still long to be with Angus where I can be an attentive and loving mother to him now – with God's grace.

It is my grief, the doctors say, that makes my failing health the more difficult and I know that my heart – broken and torn – will fail me soon. Is it wrong for me to wish that event comes soonest?

I am able only to talk to my maid, Mary, of Angus. Others turn away and will not indulge my whim but the poor girl is so loyal that she feigns delight in the talk of my boy. With her I am able to relate tales from his childhood which others shy away from but Mary listens and combs my hair and never tires of telling me how beautiful my skin and eyes are. Mary is a sweet child – I must bore her terribly. I have been saving my sleeping draughts for this anguish I feel must be *at an end soon. My body is wracked with pain and my mind is never at peace. I cannot endure another month of this suffering let alone another year – if only Angus were here, if only James would venture home, if only Alistair would spend time reminiscing about our boy Angus along with me – Angus, the boy we were always so hard on. Alistair claims that we were that way with him because he was always a wayward child and to an extent that is true but James had a temper and we allowed him that. What was it about Angus that we could not indulge, what was it about my boy, my beautiful boy, that we felt we had to scorn?*

I will take the draughts today as Mary is away and I would rather I was found by another servant. Poor loyal Mary is so kind I must not put upon her in this way. I will apologise now to Alistair and to my beautiful son James for my weakness and only hope that they can understand the pain which pushes and presses me to this end.

My head and legs are wracked and my mind is at a standstill now. I simply want – have – to be with Angus. God forgive me.

***

Jenny Munroe claims that on reading his mother's pathetic entreaty for death, a threat she had made over the years, she became convinced that Angus Lochdarnock could not possibly be responsible for a murder.

Gil Delaney was pretty sure Scotland Yard had got it right and that Angus bolting off to War immediately the dead body of the prostitute was found was proof positive that he had something to hide.

Gil tried to piece together information on the killer and took the three descriptions given of the man last seen with Molly Chambers and sent them through to Jenny and me. I think he was concerned that Jenny might be getting her hopes up too strongly and that the girl might find that the mob she'd obviously sprung from were far from being perfect.

Gil phoned me that night. Hetty tried to put me off answering, nibbling away at my poor head and telling me, "Just rest Bill. Doctor's orders."

I managed to get rid of the biddy so the big Yank and I could have a 'meaningful conversation'. She was in a huff for hours after.

Hetty was obviously getting bored playing Edith Cavell and was morphing back into Nurse Ratchet, for God sake! I think she assumed that my incapacity would be a chance for her to wield power over me and my doings and at the same time achieve martyrdom for her. Fat chance!

"Hey Bill!" the Yank began.

"Yo," I replied determined that he would think I was fine – which I was in fact.

"I've read Jenny's stuff and Isabelle's journal entry. I suppose, ultimately, all history is about death and destruction."

"Aye, makes you feel glad to be alive, does this stuff. Did you not know you'd be dealing with death all the time when you took this research on?"

"It all seemed so removed and distant at the beginning," Gil admitted.

"So, what progress on Angus 'the murderer'?" I asked, laughing.

"The descriptions are interesting and contradictory. I've mailed them to you."

"That's fine. I can hobble through and get them off the computer."

"Don't do anything crazy, man," Gil ordered.

"The doctor is not in the slightest bit worried. We know that."

"From what I remember the order was for you to take things easy, old man." Gil laughed. "But you don't know how, do ya?"

"No," I said simply in reply, "now give me two minutes to read through the latest and I'll get back to you."

When I got to the computer I saw that there were two or three emails – one from Gil Delaney (as he had promised) and two others from Jenny Munroe. Aye, the stuff was flying in rapidly.

Bits of journals, manuscripts, police reports and the tiny newspaper clipping – all beautifully scanned and then 'pinged' to me via the 'net' – that the Delaney boy had been lucky to find on his first attempt at newspaper research – were now laid out across the big desk in my study. Hetty was doing her nut!

37

While the American and I were digging into all things Ewart and Lochdarnock, Jenny Munroe was getting on with her job at the house. She describes the time as being 'monumentally busy and concerning' in regard to the swanky new position she held at the Lochdarnock estates.

The tall and able woman was getting genuinely worried that her mind was not on the task at hand – the job she was being paid to do by the Trust which held Lochdarnock House for the benefit of the nation.

Of course, when she told me this later, I've to admit I felt a wee bit guilty. The Delaney boy and I were free to indulge ourselves in any shinanigans we chose but poor Jenny Munroe had an actual job to do and I suppose a moral obligation to concentrate on that.

It was Gil who convinced me not to be too worried about that matter as the stuff that was turning up could only 'enhance' Jenny's standing with her bosses at the house, in the long run. I supposed he was right about that.

Personally, I think that Eloise Ewart-Sanders had convinced the Delaney boy that there was a book in his research and he seemed more than keen to collaborate on that with myself and the lovely Jenny. I was doubtful about the possibility of a book deal, though the information we had uncovered might be good from the point of view of the education department of Lochdarnock House Trust.

The very diligent Ms Munroe described to me the state of affairs for her at the time, sometime later.

That same night, Jenny stared at her computer screen. Nothing seemed to be right. The initial successes she'd enjoyed at the house were, it seemed, drying up. Jenny could only blame the recession (there's always one of those around for some reason or another) so much before having to take responsibility for the slow-down. She clicked off the screen and put the computer to bed. Bending down she rubbed her toes which had spasmed once again.

'Why,' she thought, "am I withholding this information from everyone?

Jenny rubbed her left foot vigorously to no avail. She knew she had a stash of Naproxen in the drawer in the bedroom and shuffled in there with a glass of water. The image of Gil Delaney popped into her head unbidden. She closed her eyes to rid herself of the picture but it only intensified. Picking up the phone she dialled his London number. Jenny denies it but the woman works on her instincts as much as anyone I know, in spite of her insistence that she takes a forensically scientific approach to research as much as possible.

The hotel staff she got hold of that night were keen to tell Jenny that the Delaney boy had left London that afternoon. Undeterred she attempted to leave a message on his mobile. He wasn't picking that up either which was unusual for him.

"Gil, Jenny, here. I was..." with that Delaney picked up.

"Jen? How are you?" he asked.

"Tired. And you?"

"Good. I was in Boston yesterday. I managed to see a Ewart. Did you get the stuff?"

Jenny laughed out loud. "A Ewart! A common noun!"

Gil laughed at her description, here she was again – Jenny Munroe – pedantic as ever.

"You know how it is. This thing is becoming monumental. It's consuming my life," Gil complained.

"You need to build a bridge or two. That'll put your life back on track and in perspective," Jenny replied still rubbing her toes.

"You find my work amusing," Gil said somberly.

"Not at all. It's a damn sight more practical and useful than anything I do," Jenny replied.

"Lochdarnock losing its charm?"

"No, it's just a realisation. It's… oh, this place is part of the entertainment industry and it is not, therefore, quite as crucial as keeping the world ticking over by making roads and necessary stuff like that. We *need* bridges and sewers and the people who build them – we could probably, no, definitely live without a bunch of overly erudite scholars and researchers getting to grips with the goings on of former residents of aged houses and their inconsequential histories."

"You are being very hard on my new-found vocation. Who are we to decide whose histories are of consequence or not?" Gil managed.

Jenny let out a mild yell as two of her toes went west and the other three east.

"You OK?" Gil asked in alarm.

"Just sat on my foot awkwardly," Jenny blushed at her own lie.

"That hurt."

"No, I'm really fine." Jenny insisted.

"You're terribly British," said Gil, remembering his recent conversation, "'Robust'."

"What?" asked Jenny, wishing the Naproxen would get to work, soonest.

"Eloise Ewart-Sanders described Harriet Beech as robust. Fits you too."

"Well, the one thing we can be sure of is that I have nothing to do at all with the Ewarts or Beech's for that matter," Jenny managed.

"So you accept you are a Lochdarnock?" Gil asked, picking up Harriet's diary.

"I will entertain the thought that the suggestion may have some validity," she answered.

"You sound like a lawyer."

"Funny you should say that, I've been with lawyers and accountants all day," Jenny complained.

"And how was that for you?" asked Gil.

"I've known less painful tooth extractions," Jenny replied honestly.

"I have to tell you my previous wife was a lawyer," Gil joked.

"So you will know very well what I mean."

"Yeah, the marriage was as painful as dental caries." Gil laughed. "I miss you."

Jenny was surprised. So surprised she stopped noticing the pain in her foot.

"Thank you," she said for want of something better to say.

"Thank you?" Gil laughed. "You're grateful that I miss you. Well that's a move in the right direction."

"Oh, Gil. I do wish you wouldn't try to take our friendship in a different direction. I told you, I'm hopeless at all that stuff."

"So, you're no good with lawyers, accountants, romance and…"

"You're compiling a list of my shortcomings?" Jenny laughed.

"And drinking and oh, yeah and dancing," he continued.

"Now that hurts!" Jenny laughed.

"Having you treading on my toes was pretty damn painful too," Gil complained.

"The Full Monty," Jenny piped up.

Gil paused before asking, "What?"

"The film, did you see it. About a bunch of out of work men becoming strippers and they had to learn to dance. We're quite as useless as they were," Jenny regretted the allusion as soon as it was out of her mouth.

"So I have a reason to 'believe in miracles'?" Gil asked seriously.

"So you did see the movie? Go to bed," Jenny said.

"Do you have any idea what I'm up to here?" asked Gil.

"Sorry, I'm completely clueless. Get on with Harriet's diary and report back to me by email," Jenny ordered.

"Yes, mam!" Gil used a Texan drawl. Jenny imagined him saluting and enjoyed the image of the tall man standing to attention and hanging on her every word.

"I'm going," she insisted.

"Bye, Jen," Gil said, smiling to himself and looking forward to Jenny and the old man arriving not too far in the future.

Before she arrived, Jenny was to find another bit of my account of the Cassidy/Lochdarnock saga. I know, because she's told me since that she wanted to quiz me on the matter, that she was tempted to call me up but (polite as ever) she decided to wait until Hetty and the doctors had given me the all clear before she involved me any further in the intrigue.

38

Gil had emailed the next extract to me and I think to Jenny. I called him up and told him to go easy on the girl. If her ancestor was a murderer it might be a bit hard to for her to take – a shock, even for a girl like Jenny.

"So you think Angus was the father of Alice?" Gil enquired.

"I simply don't know but he's a candidate I suppose," I replied.

"Go read my email, Bill, and see what you make of the latest," Gil ordered.

I, of course, did as I was told by the Yank. The boy was speaking my language after all.

THE LONDON EVENING NEWS – 29TH JUNE, 1914

Police are hunting the killer of a young woman, an actress – Molly Chambers. Her body was found in The Regent Hotel, Bayswater. She had been seen on the night before her murder accompanied by a tall gentlemen. He is described as in his twenties or thirties and of gentlemanly dress. The fair-haired gentleman had spoken to the witness – another guest at the hotel, earlier in the evening. Anyone with information regarding this matter should contact Inspector Lennard at Scotland Yard.

The second description by a member of the hotel staff was a little, but not much, fuller. The man was apparently in his twenties, was well-spoken (a gentleman) and *suitably attired*. He wore a moustache which the witness described as 'fair rather than dark' (hardly unknown at that time) and the man appeared to the doorman to be behaving perfectly normally. Apparently the witness could not recollect any further details as "I see dozens of guests here every week, sir" – probably true enough but not helpful either to the police at the time or to Delaney or myself now. I had never seen any images of either James or Angus with a moustache though I think the laird may have had face fuzz at one time. The thing was that the age given by the witnesses would seem to rule out the old man, which was something of a relief to me, I can tell you.

39

Gil Delaney was tired of his jaunt to the South and must have been missing me and Jenny Munroe, so he made the journey back to Glasgow – unnecessarily I thought, given the power of technology to communicate quickly and accurately these days.

The girl had given herself a couple of days off to concentrate on all matters pertaining to the murder.

She had told Gordon Barton (you remember – her wee boss) that she needed some quality time as she was about to uncover an interesting and possibly game-changing revelation about the Lochdarnocks.

I didn't know whether Gordon would be that pleased to find out that Angus Lochdarnock was a murderer and his father, Lord Alistair, an accessory after the fact. I don't think I wanted to find that out myself – to be brutally honest with you.

I was feeling a lot better in myself and was, by now, as sick and tired of Hetty as she was of me.

Thank Christ, Heather took her off on a wee Mediterranean cruise which cost a bit but seemed good value to me – the value being that the two of us, Hetty and me, were rid of one another for a couple of weeks.

Heather told her husband, John, that he was to make sure I didn't get up to any 'nonsense' – as if?

The Delaney boy and the girl arrived at my place at seven o'clock – we ate a meal out of the 'pinger' and I revealed to them the verdict on James Lochdarnock's death.

Only months after poor wee Danny Cassidy snuffed it, James was walking with his dogs and it appears that he fell to his death. Whether that's the truth of the matter no-one can say but the Procurator recorded an accidental death, which at least must have been a wee bit less hard on Alistair Lochdarnock.

The laird had lost his wife only weeks before, it would seem that that suicide was covered up.

Aye, the three tragedies fell on top of one another, Danny Cassidy, Isabelle and then James. What a bloody life they all had in the end.

Talk about the Curse of the Lochdarnocks!

Funny that a love affair that started so beautifully ended the way it did for Isabelle and Alistair. And the line ended at them, with the deaths of James and Angus, or so it was thought until Jenny Munroe turned up and put paid to that wee theory.

We 'intrepid researchers' as Jenny – tongue in cheek – was calling us, worked out our game plan.

It was wrong of me to 'hold out on them' that I'd picked up a bit of information – a lead, you might say on Auntie Mary, who as I've said had disappeared out of the picture just after World War II.

I could find no information about poor Elizabeth except an entry in a wages log book that showed that she had in fact worked at the house on a casual basis on several occasions from 1912 until her untimely death in childbirth.

Jenny took the news in her stride and told me she was fully expecting that Elizabeth was Alice's natural mother, even if Patrick was not the true father. It seemed a reasonable assumption to make, I supposed.

Even with this in mind, the girl was keen to find out where Auntie Mary ended up and Gil had had a wee bit of luck tracking her through English records to Hove rather than Brighton by following my initial lead.

I'd found a draft of a letter from Lord Alistair to Mary's prospective employer, hidden amongst papers in the library. When I'd first seen it all those years ago it didn't seem especially important but I have a habit of remembering that these things exist. Hetty would tell you that it was a pity I couldn't 'mind' where I put my keys or wallet with the same kind of ease. Moan, moan, moan…

The three of us decided that we should take the trip South to look into matters further – how about that? The last thing I was expecting at my age was a dirty weekend in Brighton with a couple of relative youngsters!

Aye, but the things you should have done when you were young, eh? Anyhow, the Delaney boy had pre-empted matters and was 'on the case' ticket-wise, as he put it – that was well before Jenny and I knew what was happening.

Of course the Delaney boy had been very surprised to find out what had happened to Mary Cassidy. No-one could have guessed the reason for her seeming disappearance from the face of the Earth.

The English death records and census material had shown nothing but we had been looking in the wrong places. If changes in circumstances happen in periods between census materials being compiled the unexpected becomes more likely to happen, as any seasoned researcher will tell you.

Gil outlined in words of one syllable what had happened to wee Mary Cassidy.

The Posh Auntie, as she came to be known in the Cassidy family, had indeed left Lochdarnock House a time after the marriage of Lord Alistair and Fiona Ewart, who we can suppose hated the idea of Mary's closeness to the previous occupier of *her* new position as Lady Lochdarnock and wife of Alistair. It must have been a pretty untenable situation for poor Mary, right enough given the nature of the Ewarts.

After I'd given the long held information I had to the pair, Gil followed the trail and found that Mary did in fact go South with a Dr Joseph Field. Apparently, Dr Field had delayed his move to the English coast and Mary was with the family in Glasgow for a good year before the Field family's transfer to the South. Instead of trying to follow Mary, the clever big Yank followed Joseph Field's records, hence our visit to Hove where, according to the record, Dr Field lived out the rest of his life.

Jenny and I arrived in Hove together and met up with the Delaney boy there at the stipulated time.

The streets of the south coast town were smart and clean. You could feel the sea air as it drifted in from the coast, filling the lungs of strollers with ozone and negative ions which lifted the mood of we three explorers from the North.

Jenny, Gil and I found a wee coffee shop, still an independent place and devoid of squelching machinery which sends my tinnitus into orbit and makes my poor hearing even worse – Christ, you can't imagine how old and annoyed being hard of hearing makes you feel!

The three of us could actually hear one another speak, in this good old fashioned place, without any bother. And I liked the touch of table cloths and proper linen napkins on the neat wee tables – Christ, I am turning into Hetty!

"We have the name of Dr Field's daughter, Rebecca. The record shows that her father and his second wife lived there until the stepmother's death in the 1970s," Gil told us.

"Is there no indication of where the daughter went?" Jenny asked. "She's our best chance of picking up information about Mary."

"A Rebecca Gould lives in the house now or was living there last year – I guess you never know at that age – sorry, Bill, Jenny's looking at me like I'm Mr Insensitivity – it could be the same woman – Rebecca Gould and Rebecca Field."

I told the big Yank there was no need to apologise to folk of my age; the realists among us knew we were on borrowed time and that I, for one, was pretty glad of having that knowledge given the state of the world.

The big Yank smiled. "It may be that she moved back in the house, once the stepmother died?" Gil offered. "And even if it's not the same woman the current owner might know something of the Fields."

We talked over whether it would be too 'intrusive' to simply knock at the door and find out if Rebecca Gould (the last recorded occupant on the electoral roll) had in fact once been Rebecca Field. Jenny thought we'd be better writing to the woman rather than turning up unannounced. I was with Gil on the matter, it could do no harm to simply chap on the door and see for ourselves what the situation was.

As we said, even if Rebecca Gould was no relation to the Fields she might know what happened to the previous residents and it would save us a lot of time, effort and money searching yet more records for information to no avail.

Jenny Munroe took some persuading of the point, I can tell you. I think my protestations about 'frustrations' being bad for me made up her mind in Gil and my favour.

Gil told me later that evening that I was a 'manipulative old goat'! A very critical summation of his – really?

It was at three o'clock in the afternoon that we turned up at 7 Hamilton Place, a lovely terraced Georgian house which the records showed had once been a doctors' surgery.

The Fields, we knew, 'lived above the shop' when they first turned up in sunny Sussex. It was not uncommon then for doctors to live and work in the neighbourhood they served, unlike now when practitioners seek to be as far away as possible from their charges and any potential possibility for inadvertent contact with their public on the streets where they all live. When that sort of change happens, and social stalwarts like GPs and dentists run off the stage, 'bang' goes a community in my opinion.

Gil rang the big old fashioned bell which adorned the door of number 7 and we waited impatiently.

Jenny said, "There is obviously no-one in," after a silence of about three minutes.

"I think I can hear somebody on the stairs," I lied.

I wanted to give whoever might be in the house a chance to get to the front door. These kinds of properties, I knew, were much larger than they looked from the outside and Rebecca Gould it seems was an 'auld yin' like me and would take time to reach the door. That much was obvious to me at least.

Duly the other two admitted hearing something from inside. We were all disappointed when the door was opened by a youngish woman.

"Yes," the brunette said.

Jenny spoke first. I suppose Gil and I had gone into 'man-mode' and we were stuck for words at the crucial moment.

"We wondered, is Mrs Gould available?" Jenny asked politely.

"The old lady's not too well today," said the woman who we later found out was a carer.

Jenny explained our purpose in being there.

"Wait now," said the woman. "I'll see if she wants visitors, but I'll have to stay with you. We're not really allowed to let strangers in to see our clients."

We waited another age until Debbie, the carer, returned.

"OK, she'll see you for a minute. But don't wear her out. She can be a right nightmare when she's tired." Debbie was obviously the formidable type and Gil and I looked at one another with raised eyebrows. Jenny simply smiled at the woman.

Debbie showed us up the stairs. The place looked that kind of dirty way houses look when their owner is no longer able to keep them up properly. You could see it had once been a fashionable and lovely house and I imagined Mary Cassidy running up and down the stairs not just looking after the child, Rebecca, but helping out the doctor who would have been about her own age at that time but that was just my fantasy.

It was possible that Mary never made it south and simply vanished without a trace.

We walked up the stairs to Rebecca Gould's room as directed.

The old lady lay on her bed wearing a bed-jacket. I haven't seen a body in one of those things for many a year. Strangely, Rebecca's hair looked immaculate and I thought I saw a trace of lipstick on her mouth which was wrinkled with a pained expression. The three of us being there was obviously going to be an ordeal for the old woman and I felt for her.

"Good morning," Jenny started. "We're terribly sorry to bother you like this but we think you may be able to help us trace someone with whom we are all connected."

"Come closer, dear," the old woman whispered. "I find it hard to hear you."

Jenny walked close to the poor old thing and repeated herself. She looked worn out as did the old lady in the bed.

"Ah, yes. I was indeed Rebecca Field," she replied to Jenny's new question. "And how is it that I can help you?"

There was a faint trace of a Scottish accent, ever so faint after all her years of living in England. Her voice had become stronger somehow after she had heard Jenny's line of probing. I suppose it was a relief to her that somebody was asking her about the past, a place she could be sure to remember.

"I'm a relative of Mary Cassidy," Jenny started. "I believe she worked for your father at one time."

Rebecca began to laugh. "Mary, oh Mary!" she said, clapping her hands together. Debbie who had left the room re-entered now bearing tea for us all. I took mine.

This was exciting stuff for me. If truth be told, I wasn't expecting to find any evidence of Mary at all.

It seemed to me that we might be here a time with the old lady, who it seemed with patience on our part would tell us as much as she could. But even I was not prepared for the revelations she was about to make.

"You knew her?" Jenny continued.

"Oh, yes my dear. I knew Mary. I knew Mary." Rebecca smiled.

The old woman lay still for a moment and seemed to be collecting her thoughts as well as her strength.

"Mary Cassidy. That lovely Catholic woman, I suppose you mean," Rebecca continued laughing now.

"She was," Jenny replied.

"For a time," said Rebecca who had begun pushing away the bedcovers and getting herself upright unsteadily. Gil and I averted our eyes. Everything of the old lady's body seemed to be on show. Debbie and Jenny helped Rebecca sit upright on the edge of the bed, Debbie demanding, "What are you doing now, Becs?"

"Do leave me with these people a moment Debs," Rebecca asked kindly.

"Don't do anything stupid," Debbie warned before leaving the room.

Rebecca looked at Jenny. "Why are you people still standing? I've had the sofa and those chairs brought into the room so my visitors do not have to stand. Please sit."

I, for one, was not about to disobey the old woman and I quickly got myself comfortable in a well-upholstered chair.

"This is what smoking does to you," Rebecca gasped. "Your Mary warned me." Rebecca laughed again. "Yes, Mary always nagged away. All those years of nagging made not a damn of a difference. I must have been a nightmare to her."

I noticed the veins on the back of the skinny old woman's hands. I think the current Poet Laureate describes the features as 'ropes' which might 'strangle'.

The old lady's lips seemed blue now, the lipstick having been wiped away by her after a coughing fit. Rebecca Gould clutched the tissue to her breast ready to deal with the next coughing episode, and duly composed herself apologising.

"I should have listened to her, as you can see. I should have listened to Mary," Rebecca said, sitting upright and quite still.

"I'm glad you knew Mary," Jenny said quietly.

"Oh, *I'm* very glad I knew Mary – as was my father."

"She was a trusted member of his staff for how long?" Jenny asked.

"Member of the family!" Rebecca corrected the tall, beautiful woman swiftly and with a smile.

"It appears all her employers then came to see her in this way. It's reported that the Lochdarnocks certainly saw her as a close confidant and ally," Gil said.

"No my dear," the old lady said, looking at the handsome American. "My, you are a looker, aren't you?"

I saw Gil blush and Jenny raise her eyebrows. I was thinking the bugger still had pulling potential with the over-eighties, even if he couldn't impress Jenny Munroe, seemingly.

"Thank you," Gil said politely. "Mary?"

"Ah, yes Mary Cassidy married my father." Rebecca smiled.

"Your father's death notice shows his wife to be a Miriam Field," Gil piped up.

"Mary converted. She would have done anything for Father," Rebecca continued. "Anything. She was loyal and devoted to the end."

The three of us sat in silence for a moment. The mystery of why Mary Cassidy had disappeared from the record was solved at last.

It was the Delaney boy who was quickest on his feet. Jenny looked stunned and subdued. I thought she was going to cry. When I suggested to Gil later that was the case he agreed and said he felt bound to continue.

"Mrs Gould, I wonder if you have any documentation on Mary Cassidy, sorry – Miriam, that we could take a look at."

The old woman thought a moment before drawing breath.

"Let me think, where it could be," she said, quietly closing her eyes – attempting to remember… something.

We three sat barely breathing. The excitement between us was palpable.

"Pa must have put it in the attic."

We were silent. Each of us thinking, 'Put what in the attic?'

Debbie chose that moment to knock on the door.

"I have to go soon, Mrs G," she said.

"Yes, Debbie dear. I'm sure you do." And she was silent again.

"Your guests should let you get some rest now, love. You look tired to me," Debbie responded as she now stood in the doorway – giving us three visitors a powerful look of disapproval.

"Thank you so much Debbie. You have been a star as usual but I think I would like my guests to stay for a while. I'm sure Miss Munroe will be happy to help me back to my bed should I become too tired." Rebecca Gould was polite and sweet. I liked her an awful lot.

Jenny nodded her head at the suggestion but Debbie's lips were pursed as she left shaking her head and saying, "OK. If that's the way you want it. I'll see you later."

Debbie looked at Gil. "Don't you overtire Rebecca. Do you hear?"

Gil, sensible man, simply nodded. I suppose I was too old to rebuke and Jenny being a woman was exempt from a pre-emptive strike from the carer.

"Dear sweet Debbie. She's terribly protective. Rather like Mary in fact." There was a distant look in the old woman's eyes and I could see she was remembering Mary Cassidy talking to her as a child, warning Rebecca just how to behave, just as Mary had been taught and warned herself by Annie Cassidy.

"Now let me think. The trunk, of course, I think my husband put it in the attic all those years ago," Rebecca continued.

"Do you have an idea what's in the trunk?" I asked. I was

thinking that if it was just a lot of rubbish it might not take us further forward and be just another disappointing waste of time.

"I have no idea at all. Just stuff that Mary – Mama Miriam – treasured, I suppose. I remember I couldn't look at her things after she died. I was so terribly upset. I was angry with myself that I'd left Miriam and father to live here alone for all those years after I married. When you are young and in love, you just fly off and leave those you love to get on with it, which must have been very difficult for Mama Miriam and Pa." The old woman closed her eyes and sighed at the memory of her youthful negligence.

We sipped our tea and waited not wanting to rush her. When she opened her eyes again she looked at Gil.

"Be a dear and find the loft-ladder. A lovely tall boy like you should be able to manage to get into the attic without much trouble."

I wanted to ask what it was that the Delaney boy was looking for. I was the most impatient of the three of us by now.

Do you feel like that when the aged are talking? I just want to wind them forward and say "Hurry up. We'll all be dead soon enough" a very peculiar attitude since, after all, I am one of them.

As it was I managed to keep my mouth shut until the old woman, who seemed to be reading my mind, responded.

"You'll find a red trunk up there. It's leather and full of Miriam's 'bits and pieces' as she called them." Rebecca pointed Gil in the direction of the loft.

At last, stuff from Mary Cassidy, which may give us clues about the Lochdarnocks was on offer, maybe. Every piece of information we got, I knew, could be crucial to our efforts.

The big Yank was slow in moving – for a change. I'm guessing he didn't want to appear to be too excited in case he came across as rude and grabbing.

Jenny was very composed and talked to the old lady. She asked Rebecca if she was feeling OK.

"I'm really rather excited, if the truth be told," Rebecca replied in hushed and conspiratorial tones. "Tell me. What is it you're expecting to find up there in the attic?"

"The exciting thing is that we don't know."

Jenny went into a long explanation about Lochdarnock and the Cassidys. The old woman nodded her head at a lot of it but I'm not so sure she picked up on everything Jenny imparted.

"There will be letters from me and Pa. I know that for sure. But I don't remember her family, the Cassidys, visiting Miriam. Mary told me her mother and father were dead and her siblings had dispersed – a real bunch of Scots diaspora folk I suspect – that was the situation she described by the time she got to us that is. Though, secretly, I always believed that she did not want her family to know of her conversion to Judaism. Strange. I heard her tell Pa that she wouldn't have dreamt of becoming Jewish had either of her parents been alive."

"Do you know if she kept a diary?" I asked.

"I doubt it. Mary was the sort of person who kept much in her head. She was very strong willed – strong willed but kind. It was difficult for her as it is for all women converting to my faith. The bloodline is simply not there and, of course, the Orthodox amongst us become very put out by the 'likes' of Mary. We, my family, are liberals as you can probably tell. Friday nights are not as they once were. Sadly."

I suddenly remembered that this was Friday night and we were probably interfering with the poor woman's religious timetable.

The Delaney boy was certainly taking his time but I guessed that the attic was stuffed full of years of items that hadn't been reorganised for decades. I heard the Delaney boy sighing with the effort he was making in extracting something from the attic.

"Do go and help poor Gil," Rebecca ordered. Jenny and I were on our feet in a second. We were hopeful that the sainted

Mary Cassidy had spilled the beans on Elizabeth or whoever was the mother of Alice Cassidy and to be honest I would have been glad to have just the smallest hint of what the servants had been through at Lochdarnock before or after the dreaded Fiona Ewart had turned up at the house.

When we reach the next landing up (Rebecca's house was on three floors and was further topped by a loft) Jenny and I helped Gil with a trunk which seemed disappointingly light. It was red, right enough, but faded by time and scuffed and covered in dust. The smell off it was not pleasant. Somebody, probably Mary, had put moth balls in and around it many years before and the reek of camphor was still there. I felt sick to my stomach because of that reek.

The red trunk had a lock but we could see no key. Jenny tried the clasps and they magically flew open as though they had been manufactured only yesterday. The three of us stood on the third floor landing enthralled by the prospects our find offered.

We were like three children at a treasure hunt. Jenny dusted the trunk's outside, closing the lid on our treasure-trove in order to do the work.

"We need to take this into Rebecca. She may want to see it and ensure that we are not looting it," Ms Munroe ordered.

I let Jenny and Gil do the hard work in humping the trunk down the stairs and I carried Jenny's wee handbag. The three of us went into the old woman's room again.

As we entered Rebecca clapped her hands. "Oh, there it is!" Her face was smiling and those old eyes twinkling. "I think I'm almost as excited as the three of you," she gasped.

"It is all right if we have a look?" Jenny repeated.

"No it is not all right but completely imperative," Rebecca replied in a surprising lively fashion. "Well, get on with it, the three of you."

I thought she'd obviously got some of her bossiness from Mary or Miriam, as she called our heroine now.

On top of the pile of stuff in the trunk were indeed letters to and from Joseph and Rebecca Field. There were love letters of a mature sort between the couple and informative and pleasant correspondence with the girl Rebecca Gould had been all those years ago.

Bundled together also were birth certificates, passports, bank books and the like.

A black hat was neatly kept in an old fashioned hat box inside of which (just under the hat) were another set of papers.

Jenny let out an unaccustomed gasp as she picked up the first of these. Gil and I held back, surprised at Jenny's emotional reaction. The old lady looked on as the three of us read avidly through the bundle of letters one after another.

Jenny began to cry and I wasn't far from tears myself, I have to admit, as I scanned the information now found after all these years.

MARY CASSIDY DIARY

I've decided to keep a diary. All the ladies do it here. I see them when they visit, sitting – one minute looking at themselves in the mirror, the next writing down all their secrets and now I have one (a wonderful secret) myself so it seems right to do it – to keep this diary. I wonder if I'll get caught storing up all these secrets.

I keep thinking I might feel bad about such secrecy but I don't. Every day I get up and think, "You'll get punished for this Mary Cassidy" but it doesn't happen. May be that's the way it is when you're in love? May be it makes all the things you thought were sins into something good.

He says that nothing we do is bad because we love one another. That's what he said. He loves me. I think he does, no I'm sure of it. He treats me so nice. He said I made him a 'grown up'.

He says that he'd never been one before he started going with me and that he was really enjoying it – being in love and being a grown up. I know I've grown up too. I know I shouldn't be doing these things with him but it can't be wrong, not when you're in love – never mind what my mother would say, never mind what the Bible says – surely when you truly love someone there is an exemption from sin – or am I just giving into temptation?

Who would have thought that he would be interested in me? I remember just how it started. Not that long ago. It was in March, the day of his birthday. The family had been celebrating. He was in trouble as usual for having too much to drink. His mother didn't like it and his father was that mad! I was ordered to take him a sachet for his 'headache' with some water – quite a bit later that day.

Ever since Bridget disappeared I've been run off my feet. Mr Jillings has been sick and Mr MacKenzie'd been sent up to the lodge to get the place ready for fishing and all that country stuff that the toffs do up there.

I was looking tired. I knew that – but he was in a worse state than me and looked it. His hangover left him a strange state – blotchy and peely-wally all at once. I knocked on his door. He didn't hear the first time so I chapped louder and he grunted really loudly. "In."

I did as I was ordered and put the tray down at his bed side.

"Mary," he said. "Can you believe I am in trouble again?" He was rubbing his head – his temples, I remember. I think he was talking to himself rather than me.

I didn't know what to say but I felt happy he'd remembered my name. Well, he is the most handsome man I've seen and there's no arguing with that.

I replied that I was sorry to hear about his bother. He laughed.

"My bother?"

I felt stupid but stuck my nose in the air and made to leave the room. That was when he caught me by the hand and started to apologise.

"I'm sorry. Truly, Mary. I don't mean to tease. I'm just a stupid clumsy oaf."

I didn't disagree with him but stood next to him, trying to show nothing as Mrs MacDonald teaches us. He was still holding my hand.

"You're angry with me," he said after a long pause.

"Not at all," I replied feeling really angry now with my nose still in the air.

"I hadn't noticed how beautiful you are before."

Those were his actual words. I must have smiled because he said, "That's better."

After that he and I seemed to talk every day. It was like magic. The next week there seemed to be a time when we were alone, sometimes in the morning, sometimes in the afternoon. I tried to tell myself that this was daft. How could we be what I wanted us to be?

It took weeks for it to happen. There was weeks of us just talking. Me telling him that he was a good man and him telling me I was very bright, so intelligent, so, so much more intelligent than him. I suppose I am. But what I've found out is that he is the nicer of the two of us. Aye, I know some people won't believe that, would never believe that but when I've talked to him I'm talking to a good man. My ma' would say that he was a kidder but I know he's not. I know that I can trust what he says.

That weekend, the weekend it happened, the house was empty. They'd all gone off to the lodge, servants too. There was only me and Mrs Laidlaw at Lochdarnock and she is a martyr to her knees and had taken off to her sisters in Ayr telling me not to tell anyone and that the sea air was good for her bones. I've to admit I was a wee bit frightened in the house on my own. There was a lot to do as well. A party was to be had when they all got back from the lodge and I knew I had my work cut out for me.

When I heard the bell go and looked at the board in the kitchen, I could see I was needed in the Music Room and went up wondering who could be here. The gardener was supposed to be acting up as sort of butler in the event of visitors arriving unexpectedly but the man seemed to have taken off, probably getting drunk at the Backhouse where the workman slept as well as worked.

235

When I got to the room, he, *my man as I call him now*, was sitting there smoking a cigarette. "Might I have tea, please?" he asked.

I bobbed and said, "Of course."

He laughed. "Why on earth do they make you bob up and down like that?"

I told him I was sure I didn't know and he laughed again. "Stop doing it," he commanded.

"I'm sorry," I said.

"Why are you sorry?" he asked. "You've done nothing wrong. In fact the only sinner in this room is me." He was looking at me. Waiting for a response, I suppose.

"Barabas?" I burst out wishing I hadn't.

"Beg pardon?" he asked.

"The first sinner I could think of," I replied, dying to get away and make the man his tea.

"Well, I am certainly not Christ," he replied and made a mockery of the Lord slumped on the Cross. I must have blessed myself because he started to roar with laughter then. When he saw my expression, he apologised again. I was hurt.

"That was un-Christian of me." he said stony-faced now.

"I'll get the tea," I replied turning on my heel to get away from him but he caught my hand. This time he wouldn't let go.

"I've upset you, Mary," he said quietly. "It wasn't my intention to do that."

"Why are you back?" I asked, curious about his presence.

"Made a complete arse of myself the first day up there at Braeside and fled home on the train before I was dismissed by Pa or Ma for being the absolute embarrassment I've become to them. I've decided to give up the drink. Go all temperance and stuff," he confessed.

I wasn't sure if he was kidding or not.

"It'll do you no harm," I replied but he still wouldn't let go of my hand.

"Stay with me, Mary. You're the only person I feel at comfort with in this house."

I looked up at him. There was no sign on his face that he was lying and I felt a real pity for him.

"Right," I replied, taking a seat. He came and sat next to me. I don't know how we started kissing but it all seemed quite normal and natural. Angus Lochdarnock, my Angus, is a gentle soul.

"I shan't rush you into anything you might find unpleasant," he said.

"You wouldn't be able to," I assured him. He smiled again.

"Good. Shall we take that tea?"

I replied that we should and went off to the kitchen, not realising that he was following me like a wee lap dog.

When we got there, I showed Angus how to make tea. He didn't know how to do even that and he was amazed by all the gadgetry we had down in the kitchen.

I told him that his father had done the kitchen all out a few years ago. He said he remembered a lot of work being done but thought he was away at school for the most part of that time.

"Is it awful frightening being away from your family when you're wee?" I asked.

He said that it was but all was worse as he was treading in James' shadow and, "You know what a piece of perfection my brother is."

I said I thought his brother was very nice but that he, Angus, was nice too. Angus smiled.

"He's the handsome, clever one. I'm dim and ordinary."

I told him that if he was out to get compliments he shouldn't try getting them from a Glasgow girl and he laughed.

But the truth is Angus is the better looking of the two, well to me anyway. There's something very manly about him that his brother lacks. Where James is kind, there is a sort of formality and distance between him and the rest of the world, I think. Of course, Angus is, as his father says, impulsive and loud but I like that, there's something of the Cassidys in that behaviour that makes me feel at home.

We spent hours together just talking like that. I told him I had to get on, that there was a lot of work to be done that wouldn't do itself. He asked if he could help me. I laughed.

"You'd be a hindrance, Angus."

He smiled and asked if I minded him watching. I told him I hated being watched when I was working and that he'd to go to his room.

"Like a good boy?" he asked, with a kiddie-on petted lip.

"We've already decided you're a bad yin," I replied.

He disappeared up the stairs, taking a book.

"You know I'll be bored silly, reading this thing," he complained.

"Go," I ordered.

By the time I'd completed my chores I was shattered and covered in dirt. I made to go off downstairs to the new maid's chambers but Angus was there blocking my way.

"I need to wash and I'm shattered," I complained. He walked right up to me and took his hanky out of his pocket removing a smut of coal dust from my cheek.

"That's a little better," he said and then he kissed me. I lost my breath.

"I need to go." I said hurriedly.

"You can't," he replied. "I won't let you scuttle off in that dirty state. He led me by the hand into the kitchen, boiled a kettle and made up a basin with suds.

He watched me wash my face. When I was done he took my flannel and washed my hands. He was slow and thorough like a loving mother with a small child. When he was finished washing me, he locked the kitchen door behind us. I thought he would lead me to the maid's quarters but instead he took me upstairs to his room. I was aware of my body still being dirty and sweaty but it didn't seem to matter to him. In what seemed less than an instant I was naked, standing there in front of him, my beloved, Angus. I should have felt a brazen hussy but I didn't.

"Will you be my bride one day?" he asked.

"You're being daft," I whispered.

"I forgot that I shouldn't give you choices. You will be my bride one day," he whispered kissing me with a passion, with a gentleness I had never dared to imagine existed.

Even though it was spring the night was cold and we both dived naked under the covers. I knew nothing of love-making and was surprised by it all.

"Have you done this with a lot of girls?" I asked him as he stroked me tenderly.

"One or two."

"You're lying, Angus. You shouldn't lie to me."

"Several. Yes, I have been familiar with several girls but none as beautiful as you, Mary."

I was silent.

"You believe me?" he asked quietly.

"I do. I believe that's what you think," I replied, happy now to be here with him and curious about what might happen next.

I could feel his naked body next to mine, no longer cold. He is the first man, full grown man, I've seen naked and I was kind of shocked by the hair and the size, I've to admit.

I wondered how it would go in me.

Bridget had told me that "They put it in you". I wondered how this, this thing of his would fit. Angus did not rush. He took his time. I began to feel quite giddy and I heard myself moan as his hands washed over my body. His fingers touched a part of me which had remained untouched all my life, save for washing, and it was wonderful. My body was shuddering and I was looking at Angus who smiled and said, "This is good for you, Mary. This is so wonderful for you, my angel." My moans turned into a yell and I couldn't stop myself. Angus was relentless in causing me happiness. When I screamed my final scream he kissed my mouth.

"Bride Mary," he said. "My lovely Bride Mary."

I thought the boy must be mad but he seemed, is it, sincere? Yes, sincere. I rested a while. I think I must have slept. It was dark when *he woke me with a kiss. Lots of kisses were planted over my body. My breasts were on fire, he suckled my nipples like a feeding infant and I began to cry out again. It was then that he entered me. It hurt a little but not so much as I'd expected. He writhed on top of me and I watched his handsome face contort with pleasure.*

He was the one screaming now as he thrust into me deeper with each push. It was like an explosion, I was crying out and he was too. I felt his wetness burst into me and dribble down my thighs and I yelled again with the sheer pleasure of it. The sheer pleasure of watching his face, his smile, smelling the scent of his body close to my face and then a strange smell, one I didn't recognise. It was a smell like horse chestnut. It was him, I smelled and felt, his stickiness inside me now, warm and rich and a comfort to me.

He rolled and fell to the side of me. I snuggled into his body, content.

"Sleep," I ordered.

"I have things to say," he said.

"Not now, Angus."

"I love you, Mary."

And I knew he did.

***

Gil quietly filled the old lady in on the story and by the end of the tale being told she too was weeping.

Jenny looked drawn and very tired. I suppose that's what happens when you crack the code of who you are and where you come from but just because Mary had admitted to having 'carnal knowledge' of Angus it did not mean that the fella wasn't up to shinanigans with just one woman. The second diary extract and the letters cleared up the matter for once and all.

***

240

LETTER FROM ANGUS LOCHDARNOCK
TO MARY CASSIDY – AUGUST 1914

Dearest Mary

I am writing this letter to you after our discussion. I am so sorry that I caused you to cry. I am not leaving you by choice my love but because I have no choice. Fate is against me and I need time to show that I am innocent of that which I have been accused.

I know that you wish me to tell the authorities that you will be my witness, that we were indeed together at Braeside when that poor young woman was so cruelly murdered, but I cannot do that, I cannot compromise you, your reputation in such a way. I must protect your good name until I come up with a plan which will prove my innocence of this hideous murder beyond doubt, a plan which will prove that I was not in London at the time of the girl's death.

I have sworn to my father that I was alone that night up at Braeside. His Gillie confirms this to him and as yet there appears to be no mention of you and I must protect your honour and for now your job at the house.

It will, as my father says, do me no harm to spend time in the army. I am lucky that I will join as a Lieutenant and I expect that it will be grand fun and the do over by Christmas, as they promise.

When I have worked out the true nature of what has been done to me, exactly how I have been implicated in this matter, I will return and clear my good name. I promise you that. It will be then that we shall go to Canada and start a new and different life as I have promised you.

I have an uncle there. Uncle Henry has always had a soft spot for me as you would say and I know Uncle H. and his wife, my aunt Rowena? (I told you about her, I think – she is the most marvellous woman) will make us welcome and help us set up our little life in Canada together.

You and I need a fresh start to our lives. I cannot be in a place in which you are considered inferior to anyone, let alone someone like me. How could that be? How can it be that a person of your qualities is considered less than others who are so surely inferior to you in every respect? I simply could not bear your being seen as lesser than others. Perhaps it is only being with you which leads me to understand James' political point of view.

Can you bear the thought of being married to a dolt like me? You who is so clever and sweet.

I enclose with this letter a photograph taken of me along with Kenneth Ewart.

I want you to know that whatever you hear, Mary, I am innocent of any heinous crime. I hate and detest Kenneth Ewart. That man has ruined so many lives, I can tell you – you will notice the similarities in looks between myself and Ewart. Mary, those similarities in appearance are the only sameness which exists.

You will see that in a certain light he is not unlike my brother and myself. He is a few inches shorter than we, however, and his hair slightly darker. He wears a moustache. The police were keen to know whether I had shaved my facial hair. As you know, I do not favour the fashion and have not the hair with which to impress on lookers even now at the age of twenty-one.

I think it likely that Ewart used my name in London. It would not be beyond him to behave in this way. He has used friends before to cover up his antics. As you say, you know that he is capable of cruelties though I am shocked that he might stoop to murder.

I must not burden you with my suspicions. The murderer could have been anyone who happened upon my name. All I care for now is your safety and well-being.

Know this Mary, I love you with all my heart and cannot wait to return to make you my wife.

Lovingly yours

Angus

***

MARY CASSIDY DIARY – 21ST MARCH, 1915

I hadn't expected childbirth to be easy. But neither had anyone explained to me how painful and exhausting it might be. When they handed the baby to me I knew immediately that she was to be called Angela. The tiny, perfect pink thing looked like an angel and besides Angela was the nearest female version of Angus I could think of.

I don't dare think about how Elizabeth and Patrick might explain her looks away or her unexpected arrival.

Elizabeth tells me that she has it all planned. (She's been padding out her costumes so that the people around her think she's expecting – it's not the done thing to talk about being in the 'family way' so I think we'll get away with the surprise).

Elizabeth has been the best friend to me and has worked hard to cover up and make sure that our plan is not found out.

I didn't think a girl like Elizabeth would have it in her – she's always been so straightforward in everything and our Patrick is honest as the day is long. How she persuaded him to keep the news from my mother I don't know. Elizabeth had talked to Patrick about our family. On my ma's side there are fair-haired people and Patrick and Elizabeth will just say that the wean's a 'throw-back' to them. That'll please her.

The truth is Angela is the image of her father, soft-skinned, blonde-haired and blue-eyed. One day I will tell her the truth, when she's grown up and can decide what to do with the information.

She'll probably jump at the chance of making herself known to the Lochdarnocks so that she can have the kind of life the rest of us can only dream about.

Someone told me that all babies were born with blue eyes but that they changed within a short time. It is unimaginable to me that Angela's beautiful eyes will ever be anything other than blue. It is simply not possible that Angela will have my own dark eyes and hair. The child is a Lochdarnock – long and perfect and blonde. We may have blondes in the family but long people I know nothing about!

As the baby fell asleep in my arms I began to cry. How could I possibly give Angela away to anyone else to care for? She is mine and Angus' child.

Sleep overtook me shortly after I delivered her but I will live always with this thought – how could I let Angela go? Of course, if her father were alive there would be no question that we would uproot ourselves and move off to Canada. It is so hard to lose them both. What sort of monster does it make me to give up the child of the man I love? I am not fit to be a mother to anyone never mind that wee angel.

Angela's cry woke me early. Lillian and Patricia came in and showed me, stupid, inexperienced girl that I am, how to feed my beautiful wee baby. God knows how the two spinsters know about all this mothering stuff. I was surprised. I imagine they both have sisters who shared the experience with them.

As they left the room, I heard Lillian ask Patricia, "Do you think we should have fetched a wet nurse from the off? Poor girl, getting so close to the child and then having to give her away, well it must be terrible."

Patricia answered, "Heaven knows what should be done for the best. I could weep myself. But the poor thing at least has someone to give the child to. It will not be brought up a bastard and that I think is important."

I know that the two women must have sat in their living room in silence taking turns in coming up the stairs to assist me and wee

Angela. I think they were heart broken in their own way that I had to give up my poor wee girl in just a day or two's time.

I remember talking to them later about that day, the day I gave my girl away. They said that Mr MacKenzie knocked on the front door of the gatehouse. Invited in for tea, the chauffeur sat in silence listening to the little cries of Angela and Patricia tells me they heard me cry – stupid and silly as I thought at the time I was making a good job of keeping my upset to myself.

"She's in a bad way – the mother?" MacKenzie had asked them at last.

"She's a brave girl. It's a hard time for her but she will manage," Lillian piped up. With that Patricia left the room and they heard her race upstairs. The child was screaming now and they heard me beg wee Angela to stop. I remember feeling distraught and out of control. I was crying so hard by now that I could barely breathe.

"When will you drive her back to Glasgow?" Lillian said, handing MacKenzie a much needed cup of tea. They were both staying out of Patricia's way – allowing that good and lovely woman to do what they knew she was good at doing.

"Not for a day or two," the chauffeur answered. "I'll need to come back when I can."

"So they are completely unaware of the child's father?" Lillian asked.

"It would do them no good to know and the poor girl doesn't... ach! She can't bear the thought of them knowing. She's ashamed enough of herself as it is," MacKenzie replied.

It was true. I was filled with a sense of shame but above that feeling I was missing Angus. I was angry with him for getting himself killed. I had asked him why he was going into the army. I know it had something to do with that business in London.

Angus had told me that Kenneth Ewart murdering that girl was at the back of his decision and I begged him so often to let me tell the police that I was with him. He seemed to be, was, more concerned about my circumstances than his own innocence and freedom. Oh, Angus!

Ewart literally got away with murder and I will never forgive him and his for placing the blame of my Angus, my poor, sweet lovely Angus.

MacKenzie knew and Lillian too that Angus was the father of my wee Angela, though how that was I don't know.

Lillian asked Mr MacKenzie, "Would the Lochdarnocks not acknowledge the child if they knew?"

His reply was blunt but probably accurate.

"I'm not so sure they could take this news. Losing their boy hit them hard," MacKenzie said, sipping his tea, "Anyhow, we shouldn't gossip. It'll do none of us good, especially Mary and wee Angela."

I found out about this conversation later but I would have told them that I did not want Lord and Lady Lochdarnock knowing of my shame. I wasn't sure if anyone would believe that Angus truly loved me. I suppose I'm the only one who can be sure of that.

It was Lillian who confirmed to me the notion of the Lochdarnock family curse.

I think from my point of view the Lochdarnock family is cursed and it is as well that wee Angela is not embroiled with them. I don't want her bitten by that terrible taint – not my only baby.

"It's well seen this family is cursed," Lillian uttered under her breath to Mr MacKenzie.

"It will not help to bring up that daft nonsense, either, Lillian. I thought you at least knew better than that," MacKenzie spat out.

"I'm sorry. Up here they are convinced of the truth of the curse, especially since poor Angus Lochdarnock got killed."

"Och woman, if that were a sign of a curse, half the families in the country could claim themselves afflicted," MacKenzie said levelly.

"I suppose you're right.' The woman paused before asking, "So when do you think this terrible war will go away?"

"Wars always go away eventually – only not as fast as we want them to. And this war, is like no other war I've heard of so who can tell. It'll last as long as Lucifer allows."

"Slaughter – we're sending those boys to." Lillian told me she felt

a lump in her throat – one way or another this time for her was a torture. "Here's hoping to God that Mr James comes back OK."

"He's a tough one that," MacKenzie added. "Not a hot head risk taker like poor Angus Lochdarnock."

"You think the boy, Angus, was a risk-taker as well?" Lillian asked. I wished she hadn't told me about this conversation. Something of me does not want to know all the unfair things people say about Angus.

"I think the man knew what he was doing. A brave young man. From what I hear not a soul could have predicted what this war would have done to the young men who waste their lives on it."

"Mr MacKenzie, I thought you were every inch the patriot," Lillian said with a wry smile.

"I'm not so sure it's patriotic to send this country's fine young men to the hell they say is out there. I'm not so sure this war should have happened."

MacKenzie bent forward and coughed a little. "A crumb caught in my throat and look at me. Those young fellas are having hell thrown at them and I'm in a state about cake crumb."

"You always were too hard on yourself, Bob MacKenzie."

Patricia returned to the room with the baby, my baby, in her arms "The mother needs her rest," she said simply.

I did not rest. I simply wanted my child back so that I could hold her.

MacKenzie rose to look at the child. He hadn't seen her yet. "Her name?" Bob asked.

"Angela. She is like a wee angel, is she no'?"

MacKenzie smiled at the child. "I remember seeing two little men just like this. It seems like just yesterday. Now one is gone and the other, the other one stuck out abroad. Christ knows what will happen to him."

"You're right, Mr MacKenzie. It does seem like yesterday when those two wee men, in their blankets, arrived up here for the first time. If only we had known the outcome for those boys?" Patricia paused. "Wee Angela is awful like them both."

There was a noise at the kitchen door. The three servants turned to look. I stood there in a dressing gown that was far too big for me. Lillian tells me my eyes were red and that I stooped slightly.

"I need my baby back now." Apparently I sobbed heavily until I received my baby back.

***

"How sad," Rebecca said as she listened to Jenny read out the diary entry. "They each had so much to live for, Mary and Angus."

"Unbearable," Jenny replied.

I've to admit I was surprised. I was sure by now that the stoic Jenny found nothing from the past unbearable. Gil put his arm around her and I saw the girl cry. I was close to making an idiot of myself too and hung my head, biting my lip to make sure I didn't blubber like the women.

"I believe that there is another extract," Jenny went on. "Later that month."

"We don't have to do this now. We could ask Mrs Gould if we could copy the material. There must be a library or something quite close with a Xerox machine," Gil said quietly.

"That won't be necessary," Jenny said. "I'd like to get on with it."

The old woman sat bolt upright again. "You will take the trunk and its contents with you. It's yours," Rebecca replied.

"She was your step-mother." Jenny said simply.

"And your great-grandmother, Jenny. She was your blood and so her things are morally yours," Rebecca managed breathlessly. "It would give me great pleasure if you were to take them."

Jenny hugged the old woman. I think they were both mourning a loss – Jenny the relative she never knew and Rebecca the mother she had acquired – quite by luck – as she described it.

40

Gil and I managed to get the trunk down the stairs and onto the pavement.

We'd to wait there an age before Jenny came out. She had had a bit of bother in manoeuvring the old lady into her bed and getting her comfy for the next visit of Debbie or a clone of Debbie who would come and settle the old woman down for the night.

Apparently, Jenny and Rebecca laughed that life 'actually does come to this in the end.' The return to the dependence of the child – poor kids. The poor elderly incapables!

I've to admit it is not a prospect I'm relishing – all that outside interference with bodily functions alone makes old age a horror story to me. I pray to God, if there is one, that I just drop dead one day without knowing a thing about it.

As it was we got the messy, tattered old trunk to the guest house we were staying in and past the reception without being seen by the snotty owner who seemed to behave as though she usually expected royalty as guests. It was tough luck on her it was only us, although – as I've said – there is something very regal looking about Jenny Munroe and now we know why.

Gil decided that we should go out to dinner before tackling the rest of the material in the trunk.

I couldn't eat much and I noticed that Jenny was nibbling at her food distractedly. The Delaney boy didn't get much change out of either of us but he tucked in heartily to the large piece of hake on his plate. I've to admit the fish (I, too, had ordered this) was delicious and it was a shame I couldn't do the meal justice. Jenny had chosen a prawn concoction which seemed to quickly congeal on the plate. When quizzed she told the waiter the food was fine but her appetite was not good that night.

The Yank and I consumed a lot of wine with the meal which eased the tension for me at least. Again, Jenny sipped at her glass of white, elegantly, but was clearly distracted.

In the end the Delaney boy gave up on us both and paid the bill in double quick time.

The trunk was in Jenny's room and we rushed off there to get a look at the next instalment. They say telly programmes can keep you on a knife edge but this real life drama had the three of us on tenterhooks, for sure.

The next piece of writing was another diary extract from Mary Cassidy from a couple of weeks after Bob MacKenzie's initial visit to the lodge.

***

MARY CASSIDY – DIARY

Mr MacKenzie had made the appropriate arrangements. The car pulled up at the appointed place and Elizabeth Cassidy was waiting ready to greet my newborn baby with open arms Little Angela was only a year younger than baby Patrick, Paddy as they gladly called him, who rested in the make-shift pram my best pal, Elizabeth, pushed. He was sleeping now, not ready to meet his new wee sister. I asked Elizabeth if they would manage and she told me the extra money they would get from me would help her and Patrick. Little Angela being with them would make all their lives easier, financially. I hadn't told

Elizabeth the name of Angela's father. She only knew that he'd been lost to the war.

This war had been good to my brother- and sister-in-law. Patrick was able to be at home in Scotland. Elizabeth was glad. She knew her gentle, gentle man would not like a war and all its savagery. My lovely brother Patrick was too soft for that kind of thing and I felt that at least he would be spared all that horror people are talking about now, that the boys out there are facing. It was right that Patrick was in the yards, involved in war work that kept him far away from killing and savagery.

Elizabeth watched as I alighted from the car with my tiny babe in my arms She told me that she knew it would be a terrible struggle for me to give Angela up even to her and Patrick. Elizabeth was shocked by the look of me, she told me later. She didn't know why she should be. She herself had found the bearing of Patrick a hell but at least she got to keep her son, she said.

"Mary," Elizabeth whispered as she reached out to me.

"Leave her a minute," I begged.

"I just wanted to give you a hug," Elizabeth said, the tears streaming down her beautiful face.

"I'm sorry, Elizabeth, but I don't want to be touched. Not now. Not ever," I uttered as matter-of-factly as I could.

I braced myself and then suddenly held out little Angela.

"She's Angela. Have you got that?"

"Angela," Elizabeth repeated. "That's lovely."

I turned, leaving Angela in her new mother's arms and watched as Elizabeth took the wadding from round her body and placed it in the make-shift pram beneath wee Paddy before laying Angela next to him. I lifted up my chin, refusing to cry anymore. The tears were done.

Angela would be safe and well loved. All I could do now was save and ensure that Patrick and Elizabeth did not lose out in terms of money because of my… what was it? A mistake? No, I will not have that. Misfortune? Was it simply a 'misfortune' to lose Angus and now little Angela? I knew I had to stop thinking this way. The decision has been made – the deed was done and could not be undone – not now – not yet.

"Can we go to the house now?" I asked Mr MacKenzie evenly as I approached the motor having turned my back on Elizabeth and my child.

Bob MacKenzie manoeuvred the car expertly and headed towards Lochdarnock House – a place where I had no choice but to get on with my life.

***

Jenny passed this letter to Gil and me. We read it feeling nothing but sympathy for the girl. The next papers Jenny picked up were letters unrelated to her own predicament. I think we were all glad and relieved not to have to carry on reading of Mary's plight, although what we did then read was hardly light relief. We'd be needing a good drink tonight to get over all of this, I thought as I began to read.

LETTER FROM MRS MACDONALD – LOCHDARNOCK HOUSE TO MARY CASSIDY – BRAESIDE

Dear Mary,

Here in Glasgow it is still cold and we are looking forward to spring. I know that you are being of great help to Miss Reid and Miss Bell up there at Braeside. They tell me you are doing well and, I must say, we are looking forward to your return to Lochdarnock House in the coming weeks.

I wanted you to know that Bridget is returned to us. We were so pleased. Her state is continuing to improve. She has managed to extricate herself from a difficult involvement and I know you will show her friendship *and kindness when you return to us. It will be good to have you two friends reunited after the difficulties. Bridget has dictated a letter to you. As you know, her writing is poor. Little Bridget does not have your abilities but she has a good heart. She tells of her troubles in a great deal of detail. I believe Bridget wants you to understand. She knows God will judge her for her faults so we must not add to her troubles by pouring scorn upon the poor girl. I would ask you to destroy this letter once it is read. It can do no one good for it to be found and I know you will agree that a person's privacy is of great importance, particularly when they cleanse themselves of sins by what you Catholic girls call confession.*

What she writes is a letter of confession, I think.

Mary, continue to be of use at Braeside and I wish you the greatest luck in your trials to come. Return to us safe and well. You are in my prayers.

With kindest regards
Margaret MacDonald

As I handed over the last part of Mary's diary to Gil I picked up Margaret MacDonald's letter to Mary and watched for a moment as Jenny began to read Bridget Riley's account of her 'troubles'. For the first time since we began our research I watched as Jenny Munroe wept, feeling that may be this woman was not as strong as I had imagined. I suppose it had become all too much for even her. I've to admit that when I got through all the material I could have sobbed for Scotland.

The world, in deed, as Mrs MacDonald was obviously fond of saying, can be a very 'wicked place'.

***

253

LETTER FROM BRIDGET RILEY TO MARY CASSIDY – UNDATED

Dear Good Friend Mary,

I am back here at Lochdarnock House. I arrived looking for you about a month ago. I asked Mrs MacDonald not to tell you as you are so far away and I didn't want you worried. I am sorry I ran away, Mary. So sorry. I have no good reason to give you for my stupid behaviour.

Mrs MacDonald says I let my heart rule my head and that that gets a girl into bother. I think, may be she's right. Mary, I wish so hard that I was like you. A sensible girl – a good girl who gets on with her work and can be proud of herself, but I'm not.

Mary, I've been off. Had my head turned by a gentleman, or at least I thought that he was a gentleman. You know of him but I can't remember you meeting that man. I met him at the house, Mary. He was a guest there. He was handsome and he turned my head. I don't have any other excuse. You would not have been as stupid as me.

He promised me the good life and I believed him. Thinking of it, why did I think that he would be interested in a wee scullery maid like me? He turned my head. He told me I was lovely.

I ran away with him (or I thought that was the plan) and he put me in a room in the Cowcaddens.

I didn't know where I had been put up until I got away.

Mary he gave me a terrible life, filled with beatings, locked in a room not able to get away, tied to the iron bedstead.

The room was filthy. My poor body was not my own.

He filled me with drink. You know I never was one for that stuff but it made the life he gave me easier to bear if I just didn't think of what was going on. I think you can imagine the goings on. Maybe you can't because you are a good girl, not like me. Mary, promise me you'll always stay good and not end up like I did.

When I managed to run away – and God knows it took some doing – I headed straight for the house, straight for you. I knew you would know what to do for me. Mary, you are wise and know what to do about everything. It was the thought of getting to you that made me able to get away.

I was lucky. Frank MacCauley the garden boy found me. He told Mr MacKenzie. Mr MacKenzie and Mrs MacDonald took me in, Mrs MacDonald bathed my wounds and Mr MacKenzie talked to Lord Lochdarnock. The laird's a good man, Mary. I heard he lost Angus and I think that's made his heart that bit softer than ever. I got my job back and I'm here for as long as they'll let me stay. I miss you, Mary, and I can't wait till you come back and we can sing our songs and talk silly talk again. The thought of you keeps me going.

Your friend,
Bridget.

In a scrawl underneath a poor writing hand had elucidated in tiny letters:

It was Kenneth Ewart that did this to me.

***

"I don't imagine that when Mary started her diary that her entries would end up being like this and her correspondence would be so…" Jenny muttered starting to cry and looking down at the notes. "Isn't it odd how life seems blisteringly golden when we are young and then very quickly turns sour?"

Gil put an arm around her. "It doesn't have to stay that way.

Look at how Mary turned it round. She did end up with a family and a daughter in Rebecca and she was loved and cherished – in the end."

"She lost the best of her youth and looks before she found love. Christ, by the time she and Dr Field got together she was a worn out old maid," Jenny answered.

"Not so worn out she didn't enjoy a happy family life." I countered. In my opinion it was time Jenny Munroe 'got with the programme'.

"I suppose," Jenny replied quietly.

The next extract we encountered from Mary's diary showed just how much the young woman had suffered and how it must have been for her.

***

MARY CASSIDY – DIARY

I found myself running as fast as I could towards Shamrock Street. It had been a fortnight since I'd seen wee Angela and I was feeling desperate. A pair of bootees and a cap had been knitted by me in that time and every ounce of love I could muster had been put into their making.

I wondered whether Angela would still look like her father. I'd been told often enough that babies change rapidly, and I'd seen it for myself. I wished hard that the look of Angela was still of dear Angus. I found that I couldn't take the stairs of the tenement two at a time as I had thought I would. I was still feeling so weak that I walked more sedately. Things were still hurting and the nice doctor at Braeside had told me to take it easy.

Lady Isabelle seemed to know that all was not well with me. The excuse that had been given to send me off to Braeside did not seem to impress her. She was a little shirty with me when I got back but she soon settled down. I wished I could tell her about my baby – her grandchild after all but I was and still am afraid the news might kill her. In the end Lady Isabelle insisted that I rest after my 'illness'.

"Dear Mary, please let us both rest now," she said several times. "We have both been through so much."

I've to admit I did wonder whether Mrs MacDonald told her something of the truth but Mrs MacDonald assures me that Lady Isabelle is unaware of my secret.

I hadn't the heart to tell Angus' mother the full extent of my loss and so pretended I was all right, insisting on overdoing my work to compensate for the kindness Lady Isabelle and Lord Alistair had been good enough to show to me during my problems with 'breathing'. As it turns out that excuse was not such a lie. Since I've given up Angela I can barely breathe properly.

Lady Isabelle has been much more honest about her own condition since I've had my 'trouble'. It's as though she needs someone who can understand how it feels to be really sick.

"Did you know my family was cursed?" Lady Isabelle asked me the other day. The woman was in one of her low, melancholy states.

"I don't think I believe in curses," I lied. "I'm a Catholic. We're not really supposed to."

"I believe in little else these days," Isabelle replied and that made me think of little Angela and want to run to my baby to ensure that all was still well with her and that she, at least, was not tainted by this curse – the Curse of the Lochdarnocks.

Reaching the door of the tenement flat in Shamrock Street, I felt relieved. I could hear the baby's cry.

Rushing in, I plucked Angela from Elizabeth's arms

"So there you are," I uttered with excitement, clutching the small bundled up baby to my breast which was as yet producing milk. I checked myself and hoped that I had bound myself well enough so that it didn't show.

"What are you like, Mary!" my mother shouted. "Come here and give your ma' a hug."

I carried the baby toward my mother. The three of us, mother, me and wee Angela, were locked in a warm embrace as it should be – if only I could tell my mother, if only the knowledge and the truth would not break her heart.

"God, we'll like as smother poor little Alice if we carry on like this," my mother blurted.

I froze. Turning to look at Elizabeth I saw my sister-in-law bow her head.

"Your mother and mine, didnae like the first name I picked for her. They prefer Alice," Elizabeth explained.

"I'd have thought it was your choice," I seethed.

How could they do this? How could they even deny me the right to name my own baby? I knew it was useless arguing.

"Leave the poor lassie," my mother rebuked me. "Alice is a good family name on both sides. Sure she looks every inch a wee Alice. Don't you, darling," said my mother chucking my baby's chin.

'This is the beginning.,' I knew. 'The beginning of me losing my child, proper.'

The realisation that any power I might have in Angela, now Alice's life, has been lost, as lost as dear Angus himself. I wanted to cry (I still do) but I managed to smile at my beautiful girl.

I caught Patrick's eye. My brother seemed to send love through the air when he looked at me and then at wee Angela.

Yes, Alice – wee Alice – would be fine with these two special people as parents. They are the next best thing to me, of that there is no doubt.

But the hurt – the pain! I do not know how I will, as Lady Isabelle would say, 'endure' such a fate.

"It's a terrible thing," I said quietly. Gil and Jenny did not respond but each sat on the edge of Jenny's bed looking as shell-shocked as I felt. I didn't want to push on too fast for them. They obviously both needed time to assimilate the information which had now been thrown at us in its totality and sadness.

The three of us simply sat in silence. I looked at Jenny who had her head down. I thought the Delaney boy was about to weep. I suppose we were all thinking 'Poor wee Mary Cassidy.'

I looked down into the trunk for what seemed forever before touching things inside. Jenny was the first as usual to pick herself up. She started to rummage in the trunk again.

Beneath the letters and other 'bits and pieces' was a larger item wrapped neatly in tissue paper. I was intrigued to know what was in there.

"May I take the tissue away?" I asked Jenny. "I don't think it will spoil the contents. Unfortunately, I didn't bring gloves. Did either of you?"

The two shook their heads and I proceeded ever so lightly to undo the packaging, then decided that it was wrong for me to do this and asked Jenny to complete the task. My heart was pounding with anticipation of what I might find.

The tissue paper simply crumbled under Jenny's delicate touch. What was revealed not only shocked us but answered a question which had been posed weeks before.

The proportions of the red dress were tiny and the colour a little diminished by age – it looked almost like the garment of a child but it's style, it's colour, it's presence here answered a crucial question for us.

Angus Lochdarnock had indeed been up at Braeside with a lady in a red dress at the time of Miss Chambers' death, as was reported to the laird by a Gillie at the lodge. And, here was evidence at last, that the lady was Mary Cassidy. The letters we had, showed fully now that Alice Cassidy was the love-child of a Lochdarnock who was not a murderer but a loving, caring man who was intent on protecting his amour and his family from a needless scandal – Angus was a man who had gone off to war rather than have his family and beloved put through the hell and embarrassment of a courtcase. The final extract was a copy of a letter sent from Mary to Angus – it appears she cannot have got the letter to him and had simply decided to keep it and her secret.

Dearest Angus

I am so sorry I have been angry with you. I should not have made things more difficult than they already must be.

You must know that I want to tell those awful police people from London the truth of the matter. I still don't understand why you won't let me do that and then the matter will be dealt with and you and me could go off to Canada as you've asked me time and time again since the beginning of the month to do.

I know, Angus Lochdarnock, that even if you hadn't been with me that night that you could never do such a terrible thing as they are accusing you of. What do these people think you are? I wish you would at least let me tell your father. If I lose my job it doesn't matter.

I know you say we need assistance from him for our passage to Canada but we could find another way of getting there. I could ask my brothers and my da would be good about it.

Instead I have to watch you go off to war. Do you know how that must be for me? I haven't been off my knees praying this week.

You need to come back to me, Angus. I don't know if I will survive a week without you there for me. So you must come back.

I know your mother is heartbroken that you're leaving. She says she thinks James will be not long after you even though your father says James' politics would not allow him to do that – to go to a war – any war. I can only hope that your big brother has more sense than you. I hope his politics does stop him from throwing himself into a madness and that he can with others stop the whole business and peace can be had again.

Listen to me, ranting at you when you need me to be the strong one. I just can't, Angus. I haven't got a good thought about this war and the actions you are taking, and I wish you would stay and let me clear your good name once and for all. I don't care about the shame it might bring on me. I just don't care.

And now I can't stop you because you've done this really daft thing already – joining up for a war.

You, a soldier! Just imagine. You couldn't hurt a fly even if you tried.

You better come back to me, Angus Lochdarnock, or you'll break my heart, so you will.

I love you.

Mary

***

I cried, Gil cried, Jenny cried and so did Rebecca Field when we called on her the next day to fill in the details of her 'poor, dear Miriam's life'. I think we must all be overtired now.

"I always knew there was more to Miriam's story than that which she told," the old woman said throatily when we saw her before we left Hove. "I'm so glad she was loved by two good men and three good families."

The American took the old woman in his arms and she appeared to like this very much. Jenny sat in silence.

Jenny Munroe knew at last who she was for the first time since the portrait's unveiling. I am sure that that was good – good for Jenny that she knew she was from a good place indeed and from good people.

41

I suppose a story can end where it started – here at Lochdarnock House where Gil, Jenny and I have been 'hanging out' these last few days. But I have my doubts that this story is done with yet.

Is it part of the condition of my old age and this recent experience of Lochdarnock that fills me with unaccustomed hope? Maybe?

I wasn't supposed to be privy to the conversation but I overheard it all. I would like to say I didn't mean to but I've got quite good hearing in one ear and if I positioning myself well…

You'll have noticed that trick I've developed I'm sure. It means that I get the most information I can in every given situation. I don't like to think of myself being nosy. I suppose if you chose to be kind you'd call me interested.

The pair (Jenny and Gil) have become like children to me. Aye, that's it. Children – the greatest project a body can embark upon. Raising them up and gently letting them go.

By God, it's hard to do the last part if Hetty's doings with our William and Heather are anything to go by. I fair feel sorry for the two of them – my biological kids. Not a week goes by without her peering in, or trying to peer into their domestic, work and emotional set up.

As far as Gil and Jenny go, should I be disappointed by what I heard? I'll leave you to judge.

The room was warm so Jenny opened the small casement and peered out across the wide lawn in front of her.

"Something interesting in view?" Gil asked.

"Just need the air." Jenny didn't shut the window in spite of the room temperature dropping rapidly. Gil shivered but said nothing.

The evening light was fading quickly. They were both silent for a while.

"My plane leaves at 7.30," Gil said quietly. "I guess I should get an early night."

"Yes," I heard her reply.

"So, it's a fond farewell." Gil laughed.

"Seems so."

Silence descended for another moment. I was outside the room willing the man on, but the big American was unusually quiet. It was Jenny who spoke first this time.

"Not a pleasant business, long haul flights."

"I'm lucky. I sleep," Gil replied.

"Oh," she replied quietly. "Yes, that is good."

"You're supposed to say you'll miss me," Gil whined. His voice was serious.

"Of course."

"Best you can do?" he asked.

"Oh, Gil." Jenny started to laugh, it was a nervous high-pitched sound that came from her.

"Something funny?" he asked.

"Now Voyager."

"What?"

"Oh, Gerry, let's not ask for the moon – we have the stars!" Jenny was laughing quite loudly now.

"Bette Davis," Gil responded unnecessarily.

"You know that film?" asked Jenny.

"Damn sure. Favourite of my mom's." he said. "Don't much see that it's such a great movie, myself. But I can imagine myself as the dashing Paul Heinreid." He sighed with a disappointed air.

"I can confirm you are actually nothing like him and my eyes are far too piggy to be those of the lovely Bette," Jenny joked.

"I will miss you," said Gil. "Are you glad about that at least?"

"We're both already losers in love and I for one am not about to lose a good friend for the risk of 'romance'. Done it before and it's far too horrid a performance to repeat in old age," Jenny stated directly, her voice sounding harsh and definite.

I wanted to kill her! It was only the vision of Hetty in my mind that kept me from dashing into the room to sort out this nonsense that kept me back from making a dramatic entrance into what would become a fray. What right did I have to interfere?

"What if it was second and third time lucky for us?" he asked limply.

'Aye,' I thought. 'Stick with this tack, ye bloody big Yank.'

"But it won't be. We both know it."

"Doomed at the outset. Is that what you're saying?" asked Gil, quietly.

"The prospect of all that angst and discomfort, we're both far too bloody old and sensible to risk it!" she replied.

"You don't know what old is yet, girl," I whispered to myself as I stood ear-wigging outside the door.

"You keep using that word 'risk'. Isn't anything worth doing a 'risk'?"

"You're behaving like a spoiled child whose mummy won't let him have sweeties before bedtime," Jenny said with ice in her voice.

"Why can't you just take a chance, for once?" Gil persisted.

"The dentist wouldn't like it if I took too much sugar – ruined teeth, painful fillings…" Jenny replied.

"Has it been that bad?" asked Gil.

"Us?"

"Us? Christ, Jenny – you might have noticed there's been no 'us'."

"So all the work, all we've found out and achieved is meaningless for you? God, Gil. That's been the great and exciting part of our coming together and you want to ruin it with sex."

"I don't think intimacy would ruin it, just make it more… Christ, more solid and real."

"I think friendship is real and important for both of us." Jenny paused. "Tell you what, if neither of has found anyone in twenty years, let's agree to pushing one another's bath chairs round. How about that?" Jenny sounded tired now.

Gil was silent. The air was awkward. I felt guilty that I'd heard so much and I wanted to say to the girl, "For goodness sake, Jenny. Give the boy a chance."

Instead I stayed silent, my ear almost glued to the door.

"That's not gonna do if for me, Jen," he replied. "Isn't the real problem here the man who did let you down? We don't all do that, Jen not all men are him. I am not Phillipe Martineau."

"Gil, please don't make this any more difficult than it already is."

The big man must have grabbed the girl and kissed her because all was silent for a moment – or is that just my imagination?

"I don't think there was any need for that!" I heard Jenny squeak.

"Any need? God, Jenny, you know I'm wrong. It's not men you don't trust, it's yourself you have the issue with – it is you that you don't trust."

"Ridiculous," replied Jenny, sounding really angry.

"You wanna hit me I can tell, so that is the reason. Jenny Munroe can do anything and everything but pick the right man. Isn't that what's goin' on in your head?" Gil shouted at her. "For Christ's sake, Jenny, grow up. Take a fuckin' pill and get over the fact that you screwed up once upon a lifetime and chose a man who didn't deserve you."

I heard him head for the door and tore away from my side of

it as quickly as I could. I didn't dare get captured.

When he passed me in the corridor, he hardly looked up. I had to stop him, "You're off then?" I stupidly asked.

"In the morning." The man sank into silence.

"You'll need a good sleep," I replied for want of something better to say.

"You fancy a drink?" Gil asked.

How could I refuse?

We walked away from the estate, down the winding pathway towards the nearest pub. Ironically, the pub Danny Cassidy had left that fateful evening in 1911, changed now and a flimsy reminder of a better place once filled with better people and sawdust, and smelling of stale beer and cigarette smoke.

I took a beer, feeling embarrassed in case the big man started to weep about his lack of success with the lovely Jenny.

I sipped at my beer as soon as it arrived, not wanting to be the first to speak.

"Here's to the amazing journey we just had," said Gil raising his glass.

I raised mine in response, still not knowing how to talk to the man.

"Certainly been an interesting one," I muttered.

"Over now," he said, a little sadly I thought.

"What are you talking about, man? It's only just begun," I replied.

Gil looked at me oddly.

"No more loose ends to tie up that I can see," Gil responded.

"Och, we haven't even started yet. You young fellas, give up before you've even begun."

"Mystery solved, I'd have thought. Jenny knows who she is, now," said Gil despondently.

I took a swig of my beer, feeling courage flowing now I was half way through my half-pint.

"Come on, man. All we managed here was putting a wee piece

of a jigsaw in place. There's the sky done but the water and the grass and the castle – still totally missing."

"I don't understand," the American admitted.

"Have you not noticed that running through all of this we keep coming up with the same word in the documents, over and over again. Or have you been concentrating that hard on the Ewarts you've missed the main event here?" I was attempting to provoke the big man.

He sat quietly for a moment. He drank his beer and then got up and ordered another, obviously not feeling pressured to continue the conversation. When he finally sat down, his long legs stretched out in front of him, he said, "OK, I give up."

"What is it you're giving up on now?" I asked, thinking he might get really annoyed – hoping.

"The big secret we've yet to uncover. Christ, I thought the whole Jenny thing was put to bed and the Ewarts and Lochdarnocks. You're saying there's something more?"

"Och, that stuff we've done is small fry, Gil," I replied, enjoying my enigmatic ramblings.

"What's the biggy?" he asked finally, looking at me hard.

"There's just the wee matter of the 'curse'." I was silent then and the big American started to laugh.

"So, you, you of all people, believe in curses now?" Gil asked.

"Not at all. But I am fascinated with how the 'myth' of it has led and directed the people of the house, where the daft story comes from and that. Aye, it's been a big part of my interest for a while now and I'd like to nail down the details before I die," I replied at length.

"I'll have to come back for that one," Gil replied, looking satisfied with a smug wee look on his face.

"You will," I said "You will."

About the Story

Lochdarnock – The Kiss And The Curse – is a fantasy. It was, in fact, inspired by my mother's novel *A Good Place* which she completed before her death in 2001.

That story was based on the history of her family.

From that work I took a loose end which always haunted me.

It is a cliché, I know, but *Lochdarnock – The Kiss and The Curse* – seemed to write itself.

My mother did have a great aunt who was in service but her work was in a vastly different house than Lochdarnock (I've based descriptions of the Lochdarnock (Glasgow) property loosely on Pollok House in Glasgow). The book, however, is not a reflection on the family history of the residents of that house.

'Posh Aunt Mary' did indeed disappear from the scene post World War II only after offering to take my mother south, using the same offer made by Mary to Margaret in this book. No one alive seems aware of where the 'auld auntie' went.

For my part, I was always intrigued as to why the 'posh aunt' asked to take *my* mother, especially as there were other girls in the family who could have accompanied her – as in the book, Posh Auntie Mary was given short shrift by my mother's mother.

I still wonder where Mary ended up. My enquiries, thus far, have led me nowhere.

This book is for my mother and my forebears who were, like the Cassidys, quite simply good people, very good people, of whom I am proud to be a part.